A little shiver ran through Clare as she recognized Matt's brown velvet voice behind her.

She slowly turned around. No one could look as good as that voice promised.

He did.

He stood behind her, thumbs hitched in his belt loops, his broad shoulders encased in dark cotton, and his black boots making a statement in this bleak inner-city neighborhood. Tug a Stetson over that dark hair and he'd look like Wyatt Earp taking on the bad guys in Tombstone. A rush of contradictory feelings washed through her, warm and confused.

The man was trouble, she thought. He was a danger to her work and a threat to her peace of mind. But his dogged adherence to duty compelled her respect. His understated humor roused her liking. And that voice of his was beginning to invade her dreams....

Dear Reader,

Winter's here, so why not curl up by the fire with the new Intimate Moments novels? (Unless you live in a warm climate, in which case you can take your books to the beach!) Start off with our WHOSE CHILD? title, another winner from Paula Detmer Riggs called *A Perfect Hero*. You've heard of the secret baby plot? How about secret *babies?* As in *three* of them! You'll love it, I promise, because Ian MacDougall really *is* just about as perfect as a hero can get.

Kathleen Creighton's *One More Knight* is a warm and wonderful sequel to last year's *One Christmas Knight,* but this fine story stands entirely on its own. Join this award-winning writer for a taste of Southern hospitality—and a whole lot of Southern loving. Lee Magner's *Owen's Touch* is a suspenseful amnesia book and wears our TRY TO REMEMBER flash. This twisty plot will keep you guessing—and the irresistible romance will keep you happy. FAMILIES ARE FOREVER, and *Secondhand Dad,* by Kayla Daniels, is just more evidence of the truth of that statement. Lauren Nichols takes us WAY OUT WEST in *Accidental Hero,* all about the allure of a bad boy. And finally, welcome new author Virginia Kantra, whose debut book, *The Reforming of Matthew Dunn,* is a MEN IN BLUE title. You'll be happy to know that her second novel is already in the works.

So pour yourself a cup of something warm, pull the afghan over yourself and enjoy each and every one of these terrific books. Then come back next month, because the excitement—and the romance—will continue, right here in Silhouette Intimate Moments.

Enjoy!

Leslie Wainger

Leslie Wainger
Executive Senior Editor

Please address questions and book requests to:
Silhouette Reader Service
U.S.: 3010 Walden Ave., P.O. Box 1325, Buffalo, NY 14269
Canadian: P.O. Box 609, Fort Erie, Ont. L2A 5X3

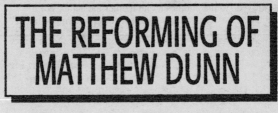

THE REFORMING OF MATTHEW DUNN

VIRGINIA KANTRA

Published by Silhouette Books

America's Publisher of Contemporary Romance

SILHOUETTE BOOKS

ISBN 0-373-07894-3

THE REFORMING OF MATTHEW DUNN

VIRGINIA KANTRA

credits her enthusiasm for strong heroes and courageous heroines to a childhood spent devouring fairy tales. For several summers she trailed her English-professor father through Europe's romantic grottoes and England's battle-scarred castles. She wrote her first stories on hotel stationery to bribe her younger cousins to go to bed.

She continued to share her love of books as a children's storyteller, and still visits local classrooms on Valentine's Day dressed as the Queen of Hearts. When her youngest child started school, Virginia fulfilled her dream of writing full-time. Her first two stories were both RWA Golden Heart finalists. She has won the Georgia Romance Writers of America's Maggie Award and the Orange County Romance Writers of America's Orange Rose.

She is married to her college sweetheart, a musician disguised as an executive. They live in Raleigh, North Carolina, with three children, two cats, a dog and various blue-tailed lizards that live under the siding of their home. Her favorite thing to make for dinner is reservations.

This book is dedicated to Michael,
for believing.

And to J., D., and M.,
for trying really, really hard not to interrupt.

* * *

Special thanks to Judith Stanton,
to Kit Stewart and to Officer Timothy J. Pittman
of the Raleigh Police Department.

Chapter 1

The cabbage had worms.

Kneeling between the pale green rows, Clare Harmon gently pressed the roots back in the earth and sighed. They couldn't afford to lose their first spring crop. She'd have to dust the plants and hope for the best.

"Isaac! Do we have any bacteria dust in the shed?"

No answer. She rocked back on her heels, wiping her hands down denim-clad thighs as she looked up for the half-dozen men and boys working the Neighborhood Garden Project this morning. They hung on the chain fence that surrounded the lot, drawn by the commotion across the street and the Channel Five news truck parked by the curb.

Clare watched as the camera crew, in jeans and polo shirts, snaked wires across the littered strip of grass. The female correspondent, her frosted bob immobile in the light March wind, checked her makeup one last time before taking up her position along the concrete walk that led to the unimposing bungalow.

Isaac, the project's team boss, snorted. "Man, who do they think's moving in over there? The mayor?"

Another gardener, who should have been unloading strawberry plants, poked him in the side. "Naw. It's Supercop, playing house in the 'hood. Don't you read the paper?"

Until Clare hired him four months ago, Isaac had been living out and sleeping rough. He grinned. "I been sleeping under the paper, man. Don't have time to read it."

That raised a laugh. Stifling her own smile, Clare climbed to her feet. "We've got twenty flats of bare-root strawberries here to get in by two o'clock," she called. "Can I see some action, please?"

Isaac swung around. "Truck ain't brung around yet."

Clare planted her hands on her hips. She'd taken Isaac on right before Christmas, when she'd found him sleeping in her shed. Since then he'd earned both her respect and the position of team boss. Isaac was one of her successes, one justification for her difficult decision to move into this neighborhood. But the satisfaction she felt didn't mean she could let up on him now.

"So, who do you figure is responsible for that?" she asked.

He scratched his head under the navy knit cap he always wore. "Guess I am." Tugging off his gloves, he headed for the driveway.

Satisfied, she nodded. "We need mulch," she told the team. "And the rototiller's broken again, so—"

A groan interrupted her. "That's right," she said cheerfully. "We'll be digging trenches. I'll get it fixed, guys. Promise. As soon as we get some money."

Which wouldn't be any time soon, she thought, striding in search of bacteria dust to infect the worms. The spring crops wouldn't bring in any income for another three weeks, and her corporate angels had financed the project only through the winter.

The first year hadn't been so bad. She'd still had Paul's insurance money then. Dazed with grief and driven by frustration, she simply hadn't worried about the project's finances. She was more practical now.

Too bad the news hounds couldn't be bothered to flush out a few donations, she thought, glancing across the street. But obviously they were baying after some more sensational story. Who cared about one run-down neighborhood in Buchanan, North Carolina? Paul had, she remembered. And now it was up to his widow to cultivate the deserted lots and abandoned properties of the southeast side. To give at-risk kids a chance to grow and bloom. And to kill the cabbage worms.

Propping open the shed door with a broken pot, she dragged out the sack of dust. Being strong didn't change the fact that she was built like a rake. And a short rake, at that. As she tugged and wrestled with the forty-pound bag, the project's battered green flatbed truck groaned around the corner, signaling Isaac's return with the strawberries.

Clare blotted the sweat from her upper lip with the back of one grimy hand. The immature plants really ought to be unloaded in the shade. She turned to direct Isaac up the drive just as some idiot in an over-size rental truck rumbled up and blocked the way.

She dropped the sack. "Hey!"

The cab door opened and a pair of scuffed black cowboy boots descended on the street. Big boots. Long legs in black jeans followed them down. A dark-haired giant with broad shoulders, a powerful chest and lean, long-boned thighs stepped out from behind the truck door.

Big man. She swallowed. He wore a black T-shirt and a killer smile. Propping a massive forearm in the open window of the truck, he directed the smile her way.

"Problem, sugar?" he drawled.

The gleam in his eyes suggested he didn't give a damn if he caused a problem or not. Cocky, Clare decided. And tough. With his black eyes and wicked grin, he was also one of the sexiest men she'd ever seen.

She set her jaw. She'd come a long way from the sheltered

young wife of a rising legal star. She was used to cocky now, and she could handle tough. She didn't want sexy.

As for calling her *sugar...!* It might just be a thoughtless Southernism, but Clare's size made her intolerant of large men who used patronizing endearments. She'd worked hard for her crew's acceptance and harder for her own self-respect. This cowboy could take his "sugar" and stick a spoon in it.

She wiped her hands on her back pockets. "You're blocking the drive."

Work stopped on the strawberry trenches.

He didn't move. He glanced up the graveled strip that separated her house from the lot before his dark, dismissive gaze returned to her face.

"I don't see your car," he said.

She jerked her chin to the street where Isaac hung out the window of the project truck, trying to catch their exchange. She couldn't back down. Her team was watching. She kept control on the lot like a lion tamer: Show no fear and, when necessary, crack the whip.

"My truck," she said. "Move it, cowboy."

Matt Dunn eyed the militant pixie before him with amusement. Nobody bossed him. Nobody dared. He needed to unload the truck somewhere, and the media buzzards across the street had blocked access to his new house. When Will, his ex-partner, had called to say he'd be late, Matt had finished loading on his own, straining the healing wound in his thigh and making the muscles in his whole left leg twist in sympathy.

He ignored the pulse throbbing against his bandage to smile at the pixie, his mood unexpectedly lightened. How often did a guy his size get dressed down by Tinkerbell?

"I need a place to park," he said, keeping his tone reasonable. Mild, even. "But I'll pull up while you get your truck in."

"And when I need to get my truck out?"

Lord, she was prickly. "Then I'll get out of your way. Deal?"

She nodded, a quick, decisive movement that tumbled her short, straight hair into her eyes. A redhead, he noted. It figured.

An excited voice rose across the street. "There he is!"

"Sergeant?"

"Detective Sergeant Dunn!"

Matt braced as cameras whirled and microphones bobbed along the curb like long-necked geese. The anchorwoman in a powder blue power suit started purposefully across the narrow street, trailing wires and support personnel behind her. Connie Cameron, Buchanan's own answer to Diane Sawyer. Damn.

Tinkerbell blinked. "What's going on?"

He should've figured he wouldn't get in without a lot of fuss. Mayor Robert Hunt would be delighted by the free publicity his hire-a-hero was generating for Buchanan's new community policing program. Hell, knowing the mayor, he'd probably arranged the coverage himself. It was just Matt's rotten luck that he was going to have to smile and make nice for Camera Connie and her crew when all he wanted to do was drag his carcass to a chair and drown the throbbing in his leg with beer.

He rubbed the back of his neck to relieve the tension building there. "'Meet the Press'?" he suggested wryly.

Her eyes flicked back to his. This time he thought he saw a gleam—of sympathy? of humor?—in the whiskey brown depths. He felt the kick of attraction and took a mental step back. He couldn't afford a distraction right now.

But her voice was cool, almost antagonistic. "Just keep them out of my cabbages."

He grinned at her. "I'll see what I can do."

The bouffant blonde in blue reached them, claiming him with rose-colored talons. "Matthew Dunn, you look wonderful! How's the leg? Do you have a minute?"

"Hello, Connie. Not really. Got to move my truck."

"Oh, no. I'm not letting you get away from me again." She squeezed his arm, smiling for the camera. "Tell me about Mayor Hunt's new community policing program, Matt. Do you really believe it can end the gang activity in our neighborhoods?"

Hell, no. He'd seen too much to believe anything could do that. But he knew better than to say so in front of Connie and her crew. He knew the lengths she would go to for a story, her ability to manufacture a sound bite. The men on the fence listened in, no doubt waiting for him to say something stupid. The little redhead had stepped back and was watching them with grave, assessing eyes.

"Studies have shown that community involvement can be effective in deterring crime," he said carefully. "Mayor Hunt believes it can work here."

"But don't those programs involve cops on the beat?" Connie persevered. "Why choose a detective to launch the program here?"

Good question. Matt himself had requested—argued—for his old place on the street the instant his sick leave was up. But Will's retirement had left him without a partner, and the department doc had nixed his return to regular duty for another three months. So, the chief had jettisoned him into strange waters without Will at his side, leaving him to flounder alone with a bum leg and a hopeless assignment.

Swallowing his frustration, he said easily, "That's really a question you'd have to ask Mayor Hunt."

"What about your credibility in the neighborhood? Do you think your high media profile after the Miller case affected the mayor's decision?"

She should know, Matt reflected bitterly. Channel Five's news van had reached the convenience store almost as soon as the black and whites. He'd never planned on being a hero. He and Will had been coming off shift when they'd stopped for coffee and walked in on a robbery gone bad. The perp had fired at the cashier and snatched a ten-year-old girl by the candy counter. While Matt negotiated with the pin-pupiled junkie for the girl's release, news crews had been interviewing her terrified mother, inflating her kidnapper's ego and desperation along with their five o'clock ratings. The coverage had been the last straw for Will's wife, anxiously watching at home.

Matt took a deep breath. "Like I said, you'd have to ask—"

A horn blared behind them. Matt looked up the street. Tinkerbell, apparently fed up with waiting, had climbed into the cab of the flatbed truck. Stretching to peer through the dusty windshield, she pointed meaningfully at the blocked driveway. He could have kissed her.

"Sorry," he told the reporter. "Gotta move my truck."

He winced getting in, and then smiled into his rearview mirror as the tiny redhead maneuvered her battered vehicle around and into the graveled strip. How could she see over the dashboard and reach the pedals at the same time? The movement of the two trucks along the narrow street displaced the camera crew and threatened the sides of the shiny white news van. Matt reversed, bumping over coiled cable. Instead of parking along the curb, he pulled in the drive, behind the flatbed.

The little driver was waiting for him when he stepped down. He grinned at her. Whether she knew it or not, she'd done him a favor.

"Thanks for the space."

She quirked a slim red eyebrow. "You looked like you needed some."

So she did know, Matt thought in appreciation. He held out his hand. "Matt Dunn."

She wiped her palm on the back of her jeans before she offered it. Her hand was small and delicate, with surprising calluses along the palm and crescents of dirt under the nails. The contrast intrigued him. The woman intrigued him.

He shook his head, bemused by the direction his thoughts had taken. Maybe things hadn't worked out with his previous girlfriends, but at least they'd all been lookers. Tinkerbell was not his type. Too thin. And yet he found his eyes tracing the shape of her breasts under the plain white T-shirt she wore.

"Clare Harmon." Coloring faintly, she retrieved her hand from his clasp and glanced behind him at the moving truck. "Welcome to the neighborhood."

He was surprised. In spite of her work-worn denim, Clare Harmon didn't look like she belonged around here. He could more easily imagine her playing tennis in one of the fancy new subdivisions just outside Buchanan, or sipping a latte in the reconstructed shopping district downtown. It was the educated Yankee accent, he decided. The orthodontically perfect teeth. The straight little nose, and the way she tipped back her head to look down it. Idly, he wondered if she maintained that bright and well-brought-up attitude in bed.

"You live around here?"

"Live and work." She nodded from the small double-story house that bordered one side of the drive to the fenced lot on the other. "I run the Neighborhood Garden Project."

A do-gooder, Matt recognized, dismayed. Somebody should have told him. Warned him. He felt like he'd just whistled at a nun. Nice girls had no place in a neighborhood like this. And he had neither the time nor the inclination to mess with some pretty little girl next door. Hadn't a string of soured relationships taught him anything? Besides, her presence across the street could complicate his new assignment. He was here to ride herd on the bad guys, not baby-sit a debutante with time on her hands.

Clare registered his withdrawal without understanding its cause. "We won't bother you," she assured him. "This is really one of our smallest lots. I've only got two crews working it, and the afternoon shift is mostly moms who take payment in kind. Fruits and vegetables in season." He was looking at her as if she'd just announced they made ritual blood sacrifices to the moon. "You have something against vegetables?"

"They're all right," he answered slowly. "In their place." She had the uneasy feeling they were communicating in code and she'd misplaced the phrase book. Maybe her very awareness of the man was messing up her signals. After three long years without her feminine radar registering so much as a blip, his masculine charge lit her screens like incoming missiles over the desert.

She told herself to ignore it. "You sound like a meat-and-potatoes man," she said lightly.

The killer smile glimmered again. "Let's say vegetables weren't a big part of meals when I was growing up. Unless you're willing to count the Mad Irish Revenge on Peas."

She hadn't expected humor from a guy who looked like a martial arts movie poster. "The *what?*"

"Boiled until gray," he explained. "My dad's suspicious of anything green on the dinner table."

Clare felt herself smiling. "How does he feel about cabbages?"

He glanced over her head. "That's what you grow here?"

She nodded, relieved to get back to business. "The cool season vegetables went in at the beginning of the month. Broccoli, spinach, cabbage…" She laughed at his grimace. "You wait. You might develop a taste for it."

Matt drew a short, sharp breath as his unruly imagination suggested tastes that had nothing to do with cool season vegetables and everything to do with the skinny little redhead in front of him. Was she coming on to him? But there was nothing flirtatious in her steady gaze, no innuendo in her smile. Obviously, after a period of enforced celibacy, his libido had decided to break out big time. With his track record, he should know better. He didn't have what it took to keep a woman happy, especially not some red-haired social reformer.

He took a step back. "Thanks for letting me pull in your drive. Let me clear off that crew across the street and I'll be out of your way."

"All right," Clare said. "Need help?"

"No." His smile blazed briefly. "No, thanks."

Frowning, she watched him walk to the back of the truck and across the narrow road. What she'd taken as a swagger was actually a limp. He stopped by the open window of the news van, exchanging a few words with the driver. She saw his teeth flash in a grin and the van roll forward. The blond correspondent detained him for a few minutes and then patted his arm, wrapping up for the camera.

He hadn't needed her intervention, Clare thought, faintly chagrinned. He didn't need her help. That was fine with her. She'd redefined herself as a woman with a mission. She didn't have time to waste on a macho man with an attitude problem. She had strawberry plants to unload.

"Isaac! You want to stack these against the wall? Benny, bring the hose around."

She pulled herself up by the rope swagged across the back and scrambled into the truck. Turning with her hands full of young plants, she glimpsed Matt's dark head and broad shoulders surrounded by camera and sound men. He seemed confident, patient and polite, with no sign of the frustration she'd thought she'd sensed in him before.

But he was definitely limping.

She thrust the molded plastic tray at Isaac. "Water these down," she instructed. "Let's get them in the shade and then see if we can give our new neighbor a hand."

Isaac's eyebrows disappeared beneath the brim of his navy knit cap. "You gonna help the cop move in?"

She understood his reservations, even if she didn't share them. She had a lot of respect for policemen. Not, Clare told herself, that she'd ever get involved with one. The police were more at risk than any other profession. More than race car drivers. More than fire fighters. Certainly more than assistant district attorneys, like her late husband Paul.

Paul had always laughed at Clare's fears for his safety. Drug dealers went after the witnesses in a trial, he'd assured her, not the prosecuting attorneys. But his promises hadn't prevented him from pursuing a lead into this troubled neighborhood one night, or blocked the gang member's bullet that blew apart their tidy life. Clare knew the cost of loving now. She wouldn't wager her happiness again.

But Detective Sergeant Matt Dunn was no threat to her carefully achieved peace of mind. He was just a neighbor who needed help. And Clare was a sucker for people in need.

"You're going to help the cop move in," she corrected. "I'm going to dust the cabbages. Okay?"

Isaac shrugged. "Whatever you say."

She positioned herself at the foot of the driveway to intercept Sergeant Dunn when he came back for his truck. She couldn't help noticing he slowed when he saw her, and the killer smile that had scrambled her receptors had flattened to a professional courtesy.

Her own smile dimmed. "My crew can give you a hand moving in," she said abruptly.

His thumb scraped his jaw as he evaluated her offer, looking over her head at Isaac lifting strawberries off the truck, at the men still digging the trenches. No bandannas, she'd warned them. No gang colors. But Isaac's pea jacket had been rescued from the Dumpster, and Benny's shirt had the sleeves ripped out. Most of them were clean—drug free—but there were layers of dirt on their clothes and skin that hadn't come from the garden.

"Not necessary," he said finally. "But thanks."

She wasn't used to being turned down. "What do you mean, 'not necessary'?"

"I don't have a lot. I'm only going to be here for a couple of months."

She put her hands on her hips. "You still have furniture, though, right? Boxes?"

"Not a lot of furniture. Personal stuff, mostly. Television, stereo, stuff like that."

Stuff that could be ripped off, he meant. She bridled at the implication that he didn't want Garden Project workers in contact with his personal possessions. It was a prejudice she combatted all the time.

"You can trust my crew."

"Yeah, they look real trustworthy," he said dryly. "Where'd you hire them? City lockup?"

"Some of them," she admitted, smiling as he scowled. "Listen, you want to be accepted in this neighborhood, you're going to have to be a little more accepting. Take the help."

He hesitated, his cop's training obviously warring with his need. With unexpected grace, he gave in.

"Fine," he said. "Thanks. The guys from the station aren't due for another hour. Besides, the chief wouldn't like it if I antagonized all my nearest neighbors the minute I moved in."

When he smiled, Clare noted, his dark, rather somber face transformed. He didn't look any less dangerous, but it was the kind of danger foolish women courted. She wiped sweaty palms on the seat of her jeans.

"Great," she said briskly. "I'll tell Isaac."

As she wheeled and went up the walk, she forced her mind to concentrate on her work schedule and not on the man she left behind. But she felt his thoughtful gaze like a touch between her shoulder blades.

She didn't look back.

"Okay, Isaac. Take the team on over."

Collecting her gear, she set to work. She was spraying cabbages, her hands on the pump and her duck shoes an inch deep in mud, when she saw Richie Johnson at the end of her row.

Her husband's legal crusade against drugs had failed kids like Richie, a handsome eleven-year-old with bark-brown skin and eyes soft and dark as peat. Beneath the macho cool of early adolescence lurked a sweet kid with a child's need for attention. Clare would dig trenches with a teaspoon before she failed him, too.

"Hey, Richie," she greeted him. "No school today?"

He twisted around his Atlanta Braves cap, measuring her from under the brim. "Early dismissal," he told her.

Could be. His grandmother Letitia complained that sometimes the middle school let its students out early. Clare would mention it to her later.

"Well, go on in the kitchen. Apples are in the bin and chips are on top of the fridge." Knowing any public display of affection would embarrass him, she contented herself with a tug on his cap. He jerked it off, shoving it in his back pocket, and they smiled at one another.

"Got any homework?"

He shook his head.

"Then after your snack go ask Isaac what you can do to help our new neighbor move in, okay?"

"Right." He thumped up the porch steps.

Smiling, Clare moved along the rows, making sure she treated the undersides of leaves and the surrounding soil. The pale March sun warmed the air and heated the red clay under her feet, releasing the scent of the new growing season. Breathing in, she felt its promise rush in her lungs and bubble along her veins like melted snow. For three long years grief had lain like a frost over her heart. But now something uncurled within her, uncertain and tender as the new cabbage leaves pushing through the freshly-tilled ground.

The screen door banged. Richie raised an apple in salute before loping across the crumbling asphalt to report in to Isaac. She waved back and hefted the sprayer again.

From the porch across the street, a radio wailed. Honky tonk country, as out of place in this urban neighborhood as the classical music she played for her plants. She heard jeers from her crew, and the cop's laughing, indistinct reply. Her gaze wandered, searching for his black-clad figure. Clare jerked her attention back to her garden. She had no interest in a man who got shot at for a living. She had no interest in men, period.

Other helpers arrived across the street, out of uniform but identifiably cops by their regulation haircuts and neatly trimmed mustaches, by the way they sized the situation up and pitched in without waiting to be told what to do. Stopping by the courthouse to pick up Paul after work, she used to see them, or men like them, waiting in the hallways to testify. Secretly, she'd always been a little intimidated by the type.

Clare inspected the young plants wilting in the scant shade of the shed, debating whether to call her team back or pull out the hose. But then Matt came out of the house with a cooler full of beer, and the two groups, cops and crew, converged on the spotty lawn. She hesitated. It wasn't a bad idea, having her project workers socialize with Supercop's friends. Isaac, she saw, looked relaxed and easy for a man who'd only known trouble with the law. Maybe she should leave them alone.

But then eleven-year-old Richie slipped through the knot around the cooler and reached for a can. It had to be a beer. Dumping the sprayer, she started across the street.

Matt Dunn turned at her approach, a wet can in his hand and that smile glimmering on his face. It went down in her stomach like sloe gin on a warm day. She felt it rise to her brain and shook her head to clear her thinking. She was not a drinking woman.

"Have a beer," he offered.

Her reply was sharper than she intended, cool and almost priggish. "Contributing to the delinquency of a minor, Sergeant?"

The smile vanished. His dark eyes traveled with almost insulting thoroughness over her slim torso. "You don't look under twenty-one."

Quick heat stung her cheeks. "Good guess. I'm not."

"So, what's the problem?"

"Richie Johnson."

"Richie?"

"Johnson."

He twisted awkwardly on his stiff leg to follow her pointed stare. Before she could speak, before she could react, he set his own drink down on the opened cooler lid and stalked up to the boy.

"Hand it over," he growled.

Richie started guiltily. "What?"

He extended a large palm. "Soft drinks are in the fridge, kid. Go get one."

The boy hunched his shoulders up to his reddened ears. "Right," he mumbled, turning away.

"I'll take this," Matt announced, and plucked the beer can out of the boy's slack grasp.

Clare watched Richie saunter toward the house, and her heart went out to him. She recognized the out-thrust lower lip, the bravado that masked his hurt and shame, and bristled in defense.

"Was that really necessary?" she asked.

Dark brows shot up. "*I* thought so," Matt stressed slightly. "It's not good for the department's image to have one of their cops seen 'contributing to the delinquency of a minor.'"

"I didn't mean taking it away," she said impatiently. "I meant embarrassing him like that." She tried to explain. "He just wanted to be accepted by the other men as one of the guys. He doesn't have a male role model living at home. He's very sensitive."

Matt rubbed his jaw. "He's how old? Eleven? Twelve?"

She nodded. "Eleven."

"Then I wouldn't worry about it," he said. "Hey, to an eleven-year-old, sensitive is remembering to put the toilet seat down. He'll be okay."

She pressed her lips together to keep from smiling at his unfeeling remark. "I certainly hope you're right."

His intent gaze focused on her face. Sizing her up, she supposed. She returned the look calmly, trying to keep her attention from straying to the intriguing curl of hair just below the hollow of his throat.

"You want it now?" he asked in his deep voice.

She felt her face flame. "What?"

"The beer. Do you want one now?"

Oh, lordy. If she'd needed any proof this man was trouble, her idiot response to his innocent offer was it.

"No. No, thank you." She ought to march herself across the street and get back to work right now. And yet some perverse impulse made her reluctant to leave.

"Well." She glanced toward the porch, expecting to see Richie emerge from the house with his soda. "I'll let you get back to your unloading. Let me know if I can help out at all, introduce you around.''

''That won't be necessary, thanks.''

She felt dismissed and didn't like it. She'd worked too hard on feeling useful. ''I've made a lot of contacts in the past few years. I think it's wonderful that the police are establishing a presence in the neighborhood, but the most important thing is to develop trust. This isn't really a bad place to live. There's some gang activity, and the usual family disturbances. Drug problems. But there are good people here, people who want to see things improve.''

He picked up his beer can, twisting it around between his large hands. ''Maybe we should get this straight, Miz Harmon. I'm a detective. I'm only here long enough to get things up and running before they assign a regular patrolman to take my place. In the meantime, I'm less interested in the folks who want to see things get better than I am in the ones who don't.'' His dark eyes met hers directly. ''No offense.''

Like being told she had nothing to offer and he had no interest in her could possibly offend. She smiled brightly. ''None at all, Sergeant. Have a *nice* day.''

She tramped back to her cabbages.

She didn't give Matt Dunn another thought.

Well, all right, Clare admitted later that night, tapping through her payroll files. He'd crossed her mind once or twice. His large, dark figure had loomed in the corners of her vision all day.

Hooking her feet around the legs of her chair, she hit Enter, frowning over the totals that appeared on her computer screen. It wasn't like her to lose her cool. Why, she'd been almost rude this afternoon. While she might not admire the sergeant's style, he'd meant well with Richie. And his easy manner with her crew had impressed her. She toyed with the idea of taking him some supper or something as a sort of goodwill gesture, but her cooking wasn't the kind that made friends and influ-

enced people. Anyway, the delivery of several large pizza
boxes across the street around five-thirty nixed that idea.

Clare told herself she was glad. Matt had made it clear he
wasn't interested in either a professional partnership or neighborly assistance. And in spite of her undeniable physical response to the man, anything else was just out of the question.

She couldn't help her nurturing streak. Going out of her
way to help came as naturally to her as rising early or flossing
her teeth. Conscientious Clare, Paul had called her with gentle
mockery. Even early in their marriage, she'd tried to make a
difference in the lives of the sheltered young teens she taught
French.

Paul's murder had driven her from that safe, middle-class
middle school to the neighborhood where he'd died. Now she
invested her time, thoughts, sweat and money in her husband's
cause, fighting to avenge his death one reclaimed kid at a time.
But her increased dedication on one level was accompanied
by a new caution, a careful emotional separation. She never
invested her heart. Never again her heart. The price was just
too high.

The cursor blinked impatiently against the glaring white
screen, waiting for Clare to feed it the numbers that would
spell out how deeply the project was in debt. She wouldn't
give it the satisfaction.

Pushing the mouse away, she wandered into the kitchen,
tugged open the refrigerator door and stared at her dinner options. Scrambled eggs or yogurt? Or maybe she should fix
herself some soup?

She frowned. This restless indecision wasn't like her.
Maybe she did feel some slight attraction to the tall, black-
haired cop with the woman-slaying smile and intriguing limp.
She could resist it. She had to resist it. She'd stay out of his
way, and he'd better keep out of hers. Just because they were
neighbors didn't mean she had to go knocking on his back
door begging for sugar.

The doorbell shrilled. Closing the refrigerator, Clare hurried
through the narrow hallway to the front of the house. She

checked her watch. Almost nine o'clock, late for visitors. Turning on the outside light, she peered cautiously through the glass inset at the side of the door.

Sergeant Matt Dunn stood on her front porch with his hand on the bell and a face like thunder.

It was a sure bet he wasn't after sugar.

Chapter 2

Her heart kicked in her chest as adrenaline spurted through her system. Natural alarm at the late night call, Clare told herself, refusing to acknowledge the purely feminine apprehension that shivered through her at the sight of the tall, dark figure looming at her door.

The golden light above the porch threw half his face in shadow, accentuating his slightly crooked nose and the dark hollows of his eyes. He looked tired as well as angry. His hair was mussed. His emerging beard bristled gold on one side where it caught the light and deepened the darkness on the other. Paul's beard had been sparse, almost boyish. She wondered how often the man on her porch needed to shave.

Annoyed with herself for noticing—his personal habits were none of her business—she tugged on the door.

"Sergeant Dunn." She smiled politely. "What can I do for you?"

"Can I come in?"

And a very pleasant evening to you, too, she thought, both irked and amused. "Do you have a warrant?"

The full mouth compressed. "Do I need one?"

The man had a chip on his shoulder the size of a prize pumpkin. "I was joking," she explained, stepping back. "Please. Come in."

The close walls amplified the heavy sound of his boots as she led him down the hall. She felt, absurdly, that he stalked her. "Can I get you something to drink? Iced tea? A soda?"

"No, thanks."

Obviously not a social call, Clare decided. She tried again to defuse the situation, ignoring both his harshness and her uncharacteristic awareness of his male presence. "How about a beer?"

He hesitated just inside the doorway, his dark eyes cataloging, judging, as they ranged the room. She tried to imagine how her home appeared to him, a stranger. Like the rest of the house, the kitchen needed fixing up. The avocado appliances were relics of the sixties. She hadn't mopped the scarred linoleum in weeks. But ferns thrived in the moist air over the sink, and herbs bloomed in pots along the windowsill. Fiestaware stacked in glass-fronted cupboards lent a bright note of whimsy to the dated fixtures and scarred wooden table.

He took a deep breath, and she thought his shoulders relaxed. "Coffee, maybe."

"I'll have to make it."

"Never mind, then."

She shook her head, embarrassed he'd misunderstood her. She never turned anyone away. "No, I meant, sit down. You'll have to wait while I make it."

He prowled forward, stiff-legged, cautious, like a wounded lion coming to tea. Pity she didn't have any raw meat in the freezer, she thought with self-defensive humor. Spooning decaf into a paper filter, she watched him from the corner of her eye, a little curious, a little wary, and more than a little attracted. He chose a seat on the far side of the table, angling it to face the door. A cop's gesture. With a stifled grunt, he stretched his right leg out in front of him.

He hurt. And she suspected he hated betraying it. Ready sympathy welled inside her. "Milk or sugar?"

"Black."

"Real men don't take cream?"

Unexpectedly, he smiled. "I used to. But all we have at the station is that powdered nondairy crud. I learned to drink it without."

She slid an orange mug across the table and sat opposite.

He sipped. "Thanks."

"What about sugar?" she prompted.

He didn't smile this time, but appreciation lit his eyes, kindling an answering warmth inside her. "You think I need sweetening up?"

"When I answered the door, I thought you might," she said candidly.

"Huh." A noncommittal sound, like a lion's chuff.

Well, at least he wasn't glaring any more.

"So, now that you have your coffee, do you want to tell me why you're on my doorstep at nine o'clock at night?"

Matt rubbed his jaw. Truth was, he'd just as soon forget his reason for being here. It felt good to sit down. He wanted a minute to savor the coffee, to stretch in the warm kitchen, to talk to the woman. He liked more than her looks, he decided. He liked her easy hospitality and her neat, quick hands. But experience had taught him he was no good at comfortable domesticity. Habits from the interview room died hard.

He leaned forward, taking advantage of his temporary rapport with the witness. "What do you know about the men working for you this morning?"

Those hands tightened on her mug. Carefully, she set it down and pushed back from the table. So much for rapport, Matt thought.

"They work for me," she said coolly. "What else should I know?"

"Some of them came from city lockup, you said. Do you know what they did time for?"

"Whatever they did, whoever they were, doesn't matter once they're hired. That's one of our rules."

With the number of repeat offenders running around out there, it was a stupid rule. He let it pass for now.

"But you do know," he said.

"Yes."

She didn't elaborate. Damn, he missed Will. His partner's specialty had been drawing out uncooperative witnesses, just as Matt's had been intimidating recalcitrant suspects. Even if he'd been willing to try that tactic now, and he wasn't, Clare Harmon didn't look easily intimidated.

"So, what've you got? Possession? Larceny? Assault?"

Her lashes swept down. Reddish lashes, bleached at the tips. He hadn't noticed before how thick they were, how effectively they curtained her eyes.

"Any of them follow the show?" he persisted.

"What show?"

Patiently, he asked again. "Any of them baseball fans?"

She looked up at that, her brown eyes bright and challenging. "Let's not dance around, Sergeant. Why don't you tell me what you know, or suspect, and I'll tell you anything I know that could help you out. Unless this is a formal investigation?"

He admired her spunk, if not her lack of cooperation. "Not yet," he growled.

"So." She held up three slim fingers and, one by one, ticked them off. "Everyone on the lot knows better than to use on the job. And I doubt they sprinkled drug paraphernalia in among your things as they moved you in. Which rules out possession. Obviously you got through the afternoon without anyone on the crew attacking you, so it's not assault. Which leaves larceny."

"You talk like a lawyer," he observed.

"I married a lawyer," she said.

He looked for a ring. "Divorced?"

"No. He died."

He'd broken the news often enough himself not to belittle

the moment by ignoring it or mouthing platitudes. "I'm sorry."

She smiled sadly. "Yes. So was I." Silence resonated between them like a clock ticking in an empty room. Twisting out of her chair, she padded over to the gray-patterned counter.

"More coffee?" she offered, keeping her back to him.

Obviously, Matt thought, she wasn't a woman who let strangers intrude on her grief. He understood that. Respected it. But he read the cost of her control in the delicate cords of her neck and the set of her slim shoulders. He felt uncomfortable sitting there drinking her coffee, interrupting her evening, battering on her feelings. One of his girlfriends—Marcia? No, it was Amy—used to tell him what an insensitive jerk he was.

"Yeah. Thanks."

She busied herself for a moment with pot and cups before sitting down again. "Tell me what's missing," she invited.

"A baseball. A Hank Aaron autographed ball, 1974."

Her eyebrows lifted. "Not the stereo?"

So, she wasn't a fan. "1974," Matt repeated. "The year he broke the record. The last season he played with the Braves. I was eight."

She exhaled slowly. "It sounds special."

"It is."

"Almost irresistible."

He was sure, then, she knew something. "Only to a crook," he said.

"Irreplaceable?" she ventured.

To him. But he didn't go around spouting off his feelings either. Not to strangers and not to civilians. "Yeah."

She sipped her coffee. Buying time, he thought. "What do you want me to do?"

"I need names. Addresses. Your guys were in and out of that house all afternoon."

"So were half a dozen police officers," she reminded him.

Matt rubbed the back of his neck. He was tired, bone tired. Muscle tired from moving and soul tired from Will's desertion and the frustration of his new assignment. He didn't need some perky little redhead making ridiculous accusations against his buddies. Not when he'd already figured his probable crook and suspected the lengths she would go to to protect him. "They didn't take anything."

"Neither did my team."

Right. She couldn't be that naive. "Maybe one of them saw something."

"I can ask," she said.

He could push. But experience had taught him that statements obtained under duress were usually recanted. Better to give her time to think and an opportunity to come forward on her own.

"I'd appreciate that," he said.

He didn't look appreciative, Clare thought. He looked grim, like he suspected her of poisoning his coffee. But maybe she was being unfair. A man his size could hardly help but appear threatening. And he was wounded, and almost certainly tired... Unwilling sympathy moved in her. She ought to be grateful he was giving her the chance to approach this problem on her own and in her own way, to deal with the unwelcome suspicion that crossed her mind the minute he mentioned the Atlanta Braves. *Richie's team.*

"It's most likely the offender still has the ball in his possession," he continued dispassionately. "It's an easy item to take, but equally easy to trace. Its value depends on its being identifiable."

"You're sure you didn't just misplace it?" she asked.

"I packed it in an open box of personal items. I know I didn't leave it behind, and nothing else is missing."

"It couldn't have rolled...?" Clare stopped at the barely governed impatience in his face. "No, I guess not," she answered her own question.

He stood with a controlled strength that almost made her forget his gimpy leg. His eyes, black and potent as the coffee he'd just finished, accelerated her heart rate like a dose of caffeine. Not with fear, Clare thought. She wasn't afraid of

his size or his badge or even the threat he presented to Richie.
She'd learned to hold her own on a daily basis with men far
more menacing than this wounded cop. Determined to succeed
where the legal system her husband served had failed, she
worked with gang members, parolees and delinquents. But
none of them emitted the subtle threat of this representative
of the law. None of them made the short hair on the back of
her neck rise, or a sweet, feminine heat drag her lower limbs
and paralyze her will.

"You'll ask around and let me know." It was a statement,
not a question.

"Yes." She realized what she'd just said and clarified it.
"I'll ask around."

"Good."

She trailed him through the narrow hall, murmured in response to his terse good-night, closed and locked the door.
Leaning her forehead against the cool glass, she listened to
the uneven grate of his boots on her walk until she was sure
he was gone. But her house still vibrated from his brief possession.

Clare gave herself a little shake. The danger Matt posed to
the project was far more significant and troubling than the
fluttering of her pulse. His questions, even his presence, on
the lot could jeopardize the fragile alliance she'd forged with
her team. She depended on their allegiance to keep the project
running. She owed them hers.

Deliberately, Clare suppressed her inconvenient reaction to
Sergeant Tall, Dark and Dangerous and focused instead on the
men who'd reported for work that morning. Not for a minute
would she suspect responsible Isaac or fearful Benny or hardworking George. And the rest were either too wary to steal
from a cop in the presence of half a dozen other cops, or too
practical to lift an object that couldn't be fenced. She honestly
believed none of them was Matt's culprit. But if he started
pulling them in for questioning, they'd be angry and resentful.
Some would certainly quit. Most of them had been in trouble
with the law before.

Not Richie, though. Not eleven-year-old Richie.

Jamming her hands in her back pockets, she paced the hall. She pictured the boy standing at the end of her row, squinting at her from under the red bill of his Atlanta Braves baseball cap, and her heart twinged in anticipation of trouble like an old farmer's rheumatism presaged a storm. She should have noticed he hadn't dropped by to see her after he left Matt's, with the casual cool that masked his need for attention. Guilt, painful and familiar, seeped through her. Had she failed to notice because she didn't want to see?

No. She cleared the orange mugs from the table and set them in the sink. She wouldn't believe Richie deliberately set out to steal. Letitia Johnson might be old and infirm and overwhelmed by the physical demands of caring for a preteen boy, but Clare was convinced she'd instilled her God-fearing ways in her only grandchild. If Richie had taken that baseball, Clare decided, his theft was a spontaneous thing, quickly done and rapidly regretted. Or he would have stopped by to see her on his way home for dinner.

Turning on the tap, she rinsed the mugs. She needed to see the boy, talk to him, convince him there was still time and opportunity to make good on his impulsive act. Otherwise, she feared, his failure to come forward would prejudice Matt's reaction when the detective eventually uncovered his offense. Even if Richie escaped trouble with the law, she dreaded the subtle damage to his spirit if the child, already at risk, learned to live with guilt.

The hands on the painted face of the kitchen clock pointed to an onion past corn, a quarter after ten, too late to call on a school night. But tomorrow, Clare promised herself, young Richie had some explaining to do.

"Why can't you take it back?" Richie complained. "You could tell him you found it."

"But that wouldn't be true," Clare said gently.

He shrugged, huddling inside his light jacket. March had turned capricious and cold overnight. The cement steps, unaffected by the pale afternoon sun, bit through the seat of Clare's jeans. She shifted uncomfortably, unwilling to let either one of them off the hook when Richie was on the point of a decision.

He fiddled with the straps of his book bag. "Maybe you could go in your house for a minute, see, and when you came out again there'd be this box on the porch? And you'd find the ball inside."

He looked at her hopefully.

Clare squashed her instant response. "Nice try."

"Aw, Clare."

Affection softened her resolution. Deliberately, she hardened her tone. "It's your responsibility, Richie."

"He's gonna be mad," he predicted gloomily.

"Probably," she agreed. Almost certainly, she thought.

"Couldn't you at least come with me?"

"Of course," she said, surprised he felt the need to ask. And then she remembered he wasn't used to the adults in his life always being there for him. "Do you know what you're going to say?"

He nodded. They'd been through this part before. "I'm sorry, and I won't never do nothing like it again, and I'll pay him back any way he says. And does he want his lawn mowed or anything like that."

"Sounds good to me," Clare said. She hoped the earnest recitation had a similar effect on Matt. Getting to her feet, she held out her hand. "Ready?"

"No," he mumbled. But he pulled himself up and slung his book bag over one shoulder.

They trudged silently between the parked cars and across the street. Richie tugged his hat over his eyes, burying his neck in his shoulders. He still topped Clare by an inch or more. An almost maternal pride surged through her, fierce and sweet. If she and Paul had had children...

"I gotta stop home a minute. It's under my bed."

"All right." She gave her permission. "Hurry."

Clare waited on the broken sidewalk, shivering partly with

cold and partly with what she was astonished to recognize as apprehension. Why should she be nervous? She'd lost count of the times she'd argued on behalf of members of her team to their parole officers or case workers. In the past three years, her assumed calm had evolved into real confidence, and her thin skin had developed armor.

Of course, Richie was special. And Matt's reaction to Richie mattered enormously in terms of getting the boy to accept responsibility for his actions without branding him a bad kid. But in spite of Matt's obvious anger the night before, she had no reason to suppose he wouldn't be sensible about this. They were two adults coming together in the best interests of a child.

She wiped damp palms down the front of her jeans. Two adults. That was it. Matt Dunn made her all too aware that he was an adult man, made her feel like an adult woman.

She didn't like the feeling. Mercifully numb for three years, her body was tingling painfully back to life, like a sleeping limb prickling with returning circulation. It was painful. It was absurd. She'd had enough heartbreak to last her a lifetime. And there was no way a man that blatantly sexy would ever look twice at a single-minded skinny bones like her, which also made it…safe. Maybe she'd reached the point where she could handle a little fantasy?

"What's so funny?" Richie asked grumpily beside her.

Smiling, she shook her head. "Nothing important." She didn't see the baseball, but his book bag still swung from one shoulder. "All set?"

"I guess."

They climbed three concrete steps to the detective's front door. She pushed the bell. "You'll do fine."

Richie shuffled his feet as they waited. She touched his shoulder reassuringly and depressed the bell again, listening. Was it broken?

She reached for the knocker just as the door jerked inward, leaving her hand hovering inches from Matt's massive chest. Shirtless chest. Sweaty chest. A dusting of dark hair, damp between deep pectoral muscles, emphasized the power of his broad torso and the glint of gold against his skin. The heat of his body practically singed her knuckles. She recoiled, her blood warming her cheeks.

With an effort, she focused on his face. He looked grim.

"We're interrupting," she guessed.

Matt yanked the towel from around his neck, humiliated at being caught shirtless and sweating from a series of reps a baby could have performed without effort. Stiffly, he stepped back, rubbing at his chest.

"It's all right," he said. "I was almost done, anyway. Come on in."

She danced in as if she made house calls on half-naked men all the time, easy, unself-conscious, slim hips swinging in the boys' jeans she favored. The curve of her breasts under her soft knit shirt hit him with the punch of arousal. Her red-gold hair lit the dingy hallway. He was tempted to crowd her against the wall and cover her slight body with his own hard, hurting one, to take her bare lips with his mouth. He resisted the urge. Even if his leg didn't spasm and dump them both on the floor, it would be like putting the moves on Peter Pan's little fairy friend.

Besides, she had a kid with her. He recognized him from the day before. Ricky? Richie, that was it. He slouched in behind her, careful not to touch the door or walls, never quite meeting Matt's eyes.

Matt's cop's instincts switched on like headlights on a car, cutting through the cloud of pain and the rising fog of sexual awareness. He gestured toward the living room.

"Sit down." He needed to. Carefully, he lowered his weight to the boxy couch, stretching his right leg in front of him.

Tinkerbell perched on the square-sided chair. The kid chose to stand. Casually, she tugged the back of his jacket until his rump rested on the arm of her chair. Her gaze ranged from the cartons stacked in a corner to the utilitarian brown furniture contributed by the department.

"Very nice."

He recognized the teasing. He was just too wrung out to respond. His right leg throbbed as if somebody had smacked it with a crowbar. "Nice enough."

Her smile flashed in apology. "No, really. It's a good house. Solid. You could do a lot with it."

"I don't have to. I'll be out of here in three months." The response sounded bald, brusque, even to him. "Some other guy'll get to fix it up."

Her clear eyes judged him, found him wanting. Too damn bad. She had no idea how hard he'd kicked against this assignment in the first place. He didn't need the neighborhood fairy godmother to tell him he was out of place here.

"So, what can I do for you?" he asked.

Her mouth firmed. Unconsciously, she straightened in her chair. "Richie has something he wants to tell you."

"Yeah?" He glanced at the kid, who stared defiantly back.

"Richie?" she prodded gently.

Matt knew what was coming. He'd resisted jumping to conclusions, as a good detective must, but he'd suspected all along. Though there was little satisfaction in being right this time. No pleasure at all in the woman's calm, concerned face or the kid's sullen compliance.

"I found—I took—" His words stumbled under the heavy silence.

Matt saw Clare's hand on Richie's back, lifting some of his burden with her touch. He appreciated what she was trying to do for the kid. Dragging his book bag from the floor, the boy yanked the zipper open and rummaged inside.

"Here's your ball," he said, offering it in the clear-topped case Matt's dad had made. "I'm sorry."

Even through the Plexiglas glare, Matt identified the jaunty *H,* the looping *A,* of the Atlanta Braves star hitter. For an instant he felt like a eight-year-old boy at the ball park. He could almost see the green-and-white diamond, the sun beating down on the bleachers and lighting his father's face as he turned from the hotdog vendor. Only for an instant, and then he was a cop again.

"Thanks," he said easily. "Where'd you get it?"

Richie's head dropped. "I... "

Clare made a sudden movement, quickly stilled. "Why ask?"

"Habit," Matt replied. "I like to know who's done larceny on my beat."

Richie looked scared. Good. Maybe he'd think twice the next time he felt an urge to pinch something.

"There was no larceny," Clare said.

He admired her championship, even if he disagreed with it. The kid needed a lesson. "Wrongful acquisition of property," Matt said.

"But you haven't established intent to steal," she argued. "The ball's been returned. You can't prove he meant to keep it."

A tiny hammer began pounding behind Matt's eyes, matching the driving pain in his leg. She'd been married to a lawyer, she'd said last night. God bless the American justice system.

"You expect me to believe Richie here never intended to permanently deprive me of my property?"

"I expect you to understand that he acted impulsively. He's sorry now."

"I said I was sorry," Richie interjected.

"Which doesn't change the fact that you helped yourself to something of mine because you were ticked off I wouldn't give you a beer."

Clare's face reddened as if he'd slapped her. Matt had a feeling she'd have preferred the slap.

"Richie?" she said into the silence.

He wouldn't look at her. Matt felt an unwilling tug of sympathy for them both.

"Well," she said at last. She wiped her palms down the front of her jeans and laced her fingers together. "Whatever your motives were, you've given Sergeant Dunn your apology. You wanted to add something?"

"Yeah." He raised his head and met Matt's eyes, surprising him. "I just want to say I won't do nothing like that again.

And if you've got something you need done, like chores, you know, I'll do it. And I'm sorry about the ball. And, like, the beer, too.''

Nice speech, thought Matt. It worked on Clare, anyway. Her smile glowed like a two-hundred-watt light bulb. He tried not to wonder how it would feel to have that approval beamed his way.

''Thanks,'' he said. ''If I think of something, I'll let you know.''

The boy nodded. ''Right.''

Clare's smile dimmed slightly. ''Richie, could you wait for me outside?''

''Yeah, sure.'' He hitched his book bag over his shoulder. ''Later, man.''

''See you,'' Matt said. Clare stirred restlessly in her chair. She was making him crazy, twitching around. She was making him nuts, period. ''What?''

She waited until they heard the front door close before she spoke. '' 'If you think of something'?'' she repeated. ''What kind of a brush-off is that?''

His head ached. His leg hurt. And this tiny woman with her big heart and sky-high principles was a pain in the butt. ''A polite one, I thought.''

''If you won't accept his apology...'' She blew out a short, exasperated breath. ''I don't think you appreciate the effort it took him to come here.''

Matt massaged the back of his neck. ''No, I accepted the apology. And I know it was hard. But that doesn't change the fact he took the ball in the first place.''

''Which in your eyes makes him a thief.''

He shrugged.

''So, what does that make me?'' she challenged. ''An accomplice?''

''Misguided,'' he said.

He had to give her credit, he thought grudgingly. She didn't huff or pout or flounce. She stood like the chief of police calling an end to an interview and fixed him with her intelligent, whiskey brown eyes.

"I'll tell Richie you've assigned him to the project to work off what he owes you. I'll supervise him, and you can take payment in vegetables."

Matt didn't like vegetables. He was pretty sure she remembered. It was a neat payback for him as well as a punishment for the kid.

"Sure, fine." He could take them. He didn't have to eat them. He figured she was hardly likely to stand over him making sure he finished his peas. And was struck by an incongruous image of her slim, pale body over him, urging him, begging him to open his mouth.

She interrupted his brief fantasy. "And I'd appreciate your coming by from time to time to see how he's doing."

She was even beginning to sound like the chief of police, Matt thought, amusement seeping through his irritation in a subversive flood. "You been talking to Dennis?"

"Who?"

"Dennis Kelton. Police chief. Mr. Walk-in-the-Neighborhood himself."

"No." She looked about to say something, apparently thought better of it.

"What?"

"I thought getting to know your neighbors was the whole point of community policing. What's wrong with walking in the neighborhood?"

Her innocent comment hit him where it hurt. Instinctively, he lashed out. "Lady, right now I couldn't walk you to the door."

She stiffened.

"Then don't," she said, and spun on her heel and marched out.

Matt started after her. And dropped back on the couch as the muscle in his thigh clenched and collapsed. Hurting, humiliated, he gritted his teeth, his hands tightening on the upholstered arms until the rough weave imprinted his palms.

Only four exercises, he thought in disbelief. Four exercises, not more than thirty-five reps each… He forced his hands open, willing his screaming muscles to relax. Okay, maybe fifty. Pushed too hard, he should have cooled down gradually, not let his quadriceps cramp and curl to aching immobility.

He'd told Tinkerbell the truth. He literally couldn't walk her to the door.

Chapter 3

His left foot on the clutch, Matt eased his right foot on to the brake, smiling grimly as the blue pickup coasted to a stop. At least his driving had improved, he thought. Why the hell didn't the hospital therapist tell the department that, instead of emphasizing all the things he still couldn't do?

"I told you what would happen if you overexercised," she'd scolded unsympathetically at his one-thirty appointment. "You're supposed to strengthen that muscle, not strain it. Who do you think you are, some kind of super hero?"

Supercop, Connie Cameron had labeled him, and the papers had picked up the moniker. Matt hated it. He wasn't any kind of hero, just a cop doing his job. Another cop, any cop, would have done the same. But he didn't try to explain that any more.

He'd rubbed the muscle, tried a smile. "Hardly. You told me twice a day."

"Twenty minutes twice a day," the therapist corrected. "And I can't get most of my patients to do fifteen."

"I want to get better." Had to get better. The inactivity of this dead-end assignment was killing him.

Her square, middle-aged face softened. "You will," she promised. "But a gunshot does a lot of tissue damage. Just be patient."

Patient. Right.

Matt let up on the clutch and slid his tired right leg from the brake to the accelerator, hitting the gas fast and hard. The Chevy lurched and died. Stalled. Again. You needed two good feet to drive a stick.

Deliberately, he relaxed his grip on the steering wheel, shifted into first, and restarted his truck. He could do patient, he thought, exhaling.

In his mind, he heard his partner, Will, chuckle. Over-and-Done Dunn, the veteran officer had dubbed him when they'd first been assigned together. Matt was no longer an eager rookie, burning to save the world and itching for action. But he missed Will's steady presence. His absence chafed Matt like a sore tooth or the wound in his leg. No hard feelings, he'd said, when Will told him in the hospital that he'd decided to take early retirement.

It was the only time Matt could remember not being straight with his partner.

He turned the pickup onto the rundown street he was forced to call home for the next three months. A half-starved cat ran for the bushes alongside an empty house. An old man, well wrapped against the chill, sat motionless on his porch. Three boys hung on the corner, watching with hostile eyes as the Chevy passed.

Matt found himself scanning the lot across from his place for a boyish figure with red hair. She wasn't there. Pulling into the drive, he told himself he was glad. He didn't need the hassles. He didn't want the woman, any woman, even one with sunlight in her hair and the earth's warmth in her smile and the devil's own determination. And then he caught his eyes in the rearview mirror taking one last, quick check across the street, and his mouth quirked up.

Liar.

Movement pulled his attention to the front of his house. His cop's instincts went on alert. Someone crouched on the other side of the concrete steps, half hidden by a screen of bare-branched bushes. Vandal or robber? Matt's lips compressed. He wasn't wearing his shoulder holster. His gun was in the house under lock and key.

Stiffly, he got out of the car, never taking his eyes from the kneeling intruder. His boots crunched on the graveled drive. For all his size, he knew how to move quietly, but it was better if his unknown visitor heard him coming. He didn't want to startle the guy into firing.

The jean-clad rump wiggled. Matt stepped away from the vehicle, arms loose, hands ready, and slammed the car door.

A dark head wearing an Atlanta Braves cap popped into view above the steps.

"Damn," said Richie Johnson. "You trying to give me a heart attack?"

Matt felt his tension ease even as he tamped down his irritation. "What are you doing here?"

The kid waved a muddy trowel. "Planting."

"Planting what?"

"Flowers, man." His tone was defensive.

Matt grinned. So, real men didn't plant flowers. He approached the porch. Soiled clumps of squiggly roots dotted the ground. A line of holes edged the bush in front of the boy. Tan sticks stuck up like grave markers from mounds by the house.

"I don't want flowers."

Richie shrugged. "Don't tell me. Tell her."

Matt didn't have to ask who *her* was. "Where is she?"

"Back of her house. She keeps digging stuff up and bringing it over for me to put in," he confided, faintly aggrieved.

Matt glanced across the street. Sure enough, here came Tinkerbell, slim arms corded with the weight of the pots she carried, small breasts outlined by her Earth First T-shirt. He noticed her nipples. In spite of the sun, the air was chilly. She ought to have on a jacket.

Squashing his involuntary pleasure at the sight of her, he

rested his weight on his whole left leg, hooked his thumbs in his back pockets, and waited for her explanation.

He was back.

Clare's heart gave a foolish little bounce, like a rabbit practicing its hop.

She didn't know Matt's schedule, hadn't known when to expect him. Isaac, who seemed to distill information from the very cracks in the street, reported that he drove to the hospital. Therapy, she supposed, and wondered again how badly he'd been hurt, and how. In spite of his stiff-legged stance, his broad, hard body looked strong and competent looming over the kneeling boy. His expression was cool.

She lifted her chin. Well, she had to, to meet his gaze. She didn't come up to his armpit. "The cabbages aren't ready."

Dark brows raised. "So?"

She set down her pots by his porch steps. "So, Richie's planting flowers for you. I had to divide my perennials anyway. You've got a really nice selection now. Hosta, daylilies, daisies. They'll be beautiful in July."

"I won't be here in July."

He sounded almost amused, as if he enjoyed baiting her. She refused to lose her temper.

"Your yard will," she said. "Your neighbors will. The neighborhood will benefit."

He nodded once. "And what about you? What do you get out of it?"

She wasn't about to divulge the demons that drove her. "Oh, I'm putting in for the Yard of the Month award," she said lightly.

His eyes gleamed. "I pegged you for Garden Club."

"First in Flowers," she retorted.

"Queen of the May."

They smiled at one another. Liking tightened between them like a rope pulled taut on both ends, drawing them together. Little details imprinted on her awareness: dark hair swirling at the neck of his shirt; faint lines fanning beside his eyes; a slight stubble just under his jaw where he'd missed with the razor. She saw the almost imperceptible rise and fall of his broad chest, and her own heart pounded painfully.

Too close, she thought, and looked away. "Richie, go get the bonemeal out of the shed, okay?"

He scrambled to his feet. "Yeah, sure."

She waited until he was out of earshot across the street before she said, "Thanks for letting him stay."

Matt shrugged. "Did I have a choice?"

"I think so, yes."

"Don't go making it something it's not," he warned. "You want to supervise the kid, that's fine. Don't go making me something I'm not."

She wondered what in his training or experience made him such a hard case. "And what aren't you, Sergeant Dunn?"

He spelled it out for her. "I'm not a role model. I'm not a baby-sitter. I'm not even a particularly nice guy. I'm a cop. The kid messes up again, I'm slapping him with a juvey delinquent action."

She refused to be intimidated. "Very tough. You kick puppies, too?"

His wicked smile splintered his face, shattering her animosity. "No. But I don't take in strays."

"Thanks very much for the warning," she said dryly. "And I'm so sorry for taking up your time. Now if you'll excuse me, I'll get these plants in the ground before their little roots wither up and die."

"What's that?"

Kneeling, she reached for a brown-and-purple clump, welcoming the distraction. "Hosta. *Sieboldiana,* or it could be *glauca.* They'll grow lovely lavender clusters."

"No." His voice was impatient. He looked over her head, across the street. "Who's that with Richie?"

She twisted around, shoving her bangs off her forehead with the back of her hand. The lot should have been deserted. The team had knocked off for the day, and Isaac was out with the truck picking up a load of composted manure. But she could see two teens hanging on the chain-link fence by her drive. Three other boys crowded around the open door of the shed where Richie stood balancing a sack of bonemeal.

She bit back an exclamation of dismay, but Matt was quick.

"Trouble?" he asked.

"Maybe not."

She got to her feet anyway, unwillingly conscious of his solid presence at her back. She would not let herself depend on the illusion of security offered by his broad shoulders and wide stance. If she ever got involved with a man again—and it was a big if—she wanted a partner, not a protector.

Across the street, Richie hunched his shoulders defensively, but he was laughing at something. No one had touched him. It wasn't time to intervene yet.

"Who are they?"

"Tyler Boothe," she answered absently. "Jerome Butler. I don't know the others."

"Vipers?"

She wondered if he'd recognized the names. Smaller Buchanan didn't have quite the same problems as nearby Raleigh or Durham, but any detective in the department was going to be up on gang turf and activity in the city's neighborhoods.

"Tyler is."

"You want me to go over?"

The offer surprised her. She'd thought he wouldn't care, or wouldn't think to defer to her judgment. But her gratification was offset by concern over his earlier words about Richie. She didn't want some hostile cop moving in on her garden, slapping kids with charges of delinquent activity, and she couldn't afford to rely on him. She would handle the situation on her own and in her own way.

"No," she said firmly.

Not, "No, thank you," Matt noted wryly. What did she think he was going to do, bust them all for disturbing the peace? He watched them posturing, unsure in their growing bodies, laying claim to the space around them with large gestures and big words. Boys.

The kid who shot him, Matt reflected, had just turned fifteen.

One of the taller boys lifted Richie's cap. He snatched for it, and the thief, laughing, flicked it to a friend.

"I'd better get over there," Clare murmured.

Matt looked down at her in disbelief. She barely came to his shoulder. What did she think she could do with that gang of hormone-proud punks across the street? But before he could say a word to dissuade her, she'd sailed into their huddle like Tinkerbell zipping over a ship full of pirates, broadcasting authority and charm like so much pixie dust. If she weren't so criminally careless of her own safety, he would have admired her bravery.

He wasn't close enough to hear what she said, but he could see its effect.

The circle of boys shifted and re-formed, Richie sliding to the periphery and Clare taking the center. Matt watched the boys' bright glances, could imagine the dumb remarks. They showed off for her, shoving and joking, until a rake balanced against the side of the shed clattered to the ground. One of them pretended to use it as a ninja stick before replacing it carefully against the wall. Matt felt his muscles tense. If they made a move, he was going to step in. He'd deal with Clare's offended feelings later.

She said something, her head tilted a little to one side, her expression earnest.

The boys laughed and shook their heads. Three of them shambled off. At the corner of the lot, their leader turned, tossing the Braves cap through the air. Richie grabbed for it, stuffed it on his head, and scooted behind the house. The rake rescuer stayed behind, lounging against the side of the shed. He was older than the others, fourteen or fifteen, with razor-shaved blond stubble and a badass attitude. Matt didn't like the way he looked at Clare. He balanced on his good leg, itching for an excuse to cross the street.

But when Richie reappeared to steer the wheelbarrow out of the shed, the punk hesitated and then pushed away from the wall. The boys exchanged a few words before disappearing together behind Clare's house. She came back across the street, red-gold hair shining in the sun, looking pleased with herself.

So, she was good with kids, Matt thought, releasing his breath. Will, who had walked a beat when turf wars in Buchanan were still being fought with fists and bottles, would have approved her handling of the situation. Matt thought she was asking for trouble.

He hooked his thumbs in his belt loops and waited for her to come to him. "So, what did you offer him?" he demanded cynically. "Money?"

She smiled, her dancing eyes inviting him to share a joke he couldn't see. "Pretty nearly. I offered him a job. Three-fifty an hour today, four-fifty in two weeks if things work out."

He reminded himself not to blow his cool. He knew she hired adult ex-cons, but he'd assumed she screened them somehow. He hadn't imagined she co-opted active gang members right off the streets.

"You can't be serious."

"It's not a lot, is it? He could make five times that much as a runner, or even as a *yo*." A *yo* was a drug dealer's lookout. She looked briefly discouraged, and then brightened. "But if he weren't at least a little interested, he wouldn't have stuck around. I think he'll take it. And anyway, I can't afford to offer more."

The protective surge he felt astonished him. Her naivety made him want to punch out a wall. "You don't know what you're doing. You don't know what a kid like that is capable of."

She tipped up her fine-boned jaw, as if daring him to take a poke at it. "You're wrong. I know precisely what a kid like that is capable of."

"I'm talking violence," he said bluntly. "Not his unexplored human potential or any of that social worker psychobabble. He probably has a rap sheet as long as your arm."

"Probably," she agreed calmly.

"You don't want him around."

"Yes. I do."

She looked so certain. Cool, immovable. He wanted to shake her. He seized the back of his neck instead.

"You're begging to get hurt. Is he a Viper?" he demanded. "Is he one of Eddie Boothe's gang?"

Something flickered behind her whiskey brown eyes. Not fear, he thought. He would have understood fear.

"One of Eddie Boothe's cousins," she said.

She wiped her palms on the back pockets of her jeans. She filled the soft denim very nicely, Matt noted, for all she was so small. A man could span her pretty buttocks with his hands.

The image aroused him, and that irritated the hell out of him. Not that it wasn't reassuring to know that more than his leg was regaining regular function; but he was used to having control of his sexual appetites. He'd learned to seek his pleasure with women who didn't mistake the physical satisfaction he could bring them for an emotional commitment. Women who wouldn't be hurt by his failure to communicate or sulk over his disinclination to try. Women who knew the score. Little Clare Harmon didn't look like she even knew the name of the game.

If he needed proof of that, he only had to look at her foolishness in hiring the kid. Eddie Boothe's cousin. *Damn.*

"What shift is he going to work? Are you going to be alone with him? Do you carry protection?"

Her brows flicked together at his rapid-fire questioning. "After school, I don't know, and no. I don't need protection."

"Sure, you don't. You're what, five feet tall—"

"Five-two."

"—and maybe a hundred pounds dripping wet, and ready to take on some punk kid from a bad background with probable priors without any thought to your own safety."

She had the gall to look almost amused. "I don't need a bodyguard, Sergeant Dunn."

"No. You need a keeper."

She put her hands back on her hips. "Are you by any chance volunteering for the role?"

The temptation to do exactly that staggered him. He didn't want any woman for keeps. Cops were notoriously bad husbands. Even the good ones, like his dad, put their wives through hell. The job took their days and their concentration. Their colleagues got their leisure hours and their confidence. Their families, Matt remembered, got whatever was left. Sooner or later, every woman he'd ever gotten involved with got fed up with his hours, his moods, his dedication to The Job. He wasn't even going to try with Tinkerbell.

"Hell, no," he growled. "Dewy-eyed do-gooders aren't exactly my type."

He saw the hit register and the reddish brown lashes sweep down, shielding her hurt. Damn. And then her chin went up another notch and she pinned him with her smile.

"No, you need a nice, bosomy blonde to comfort you through your convalescence. What do they say in the Personals? 'Open-minded'? 'Fun-loving'?" She shook her head in mock regret. "We'll just have to be friends, then. What a disappointment for me."

It was so dangerously close to what he'd actually been thinking that he had no defense. In that moment he liked her, her spirit, her humor, about as well as any woman he'd ever met. Which made it all the more imperative that he drive her away.

"You are so right, sugar," he drawled. "Guess I'd better start calling all those nurses who wrote their numbers on my cast."

He turned and stalked off. His wounded thigh ached from his hospital session, but it wasn't pain that made him awkward as he pulled up the steps. He was still uncomfortably aroused.

He was a Neanderthal jerk, Clare thought, watching him walk away. A male chauvinist of the worst possible kind. A redneck throwback to a time when a woman could be impressed by nothing more than a man's broad, hard body and wicked, dark eyes. She hoped his nurses told him to get lost.

Stooping for the empty one-gallon pots, she started back across the street.

Paul had been thin. Tall and lanky, with a diffident, gentlemanly manner that cloaked a sharp intelligence and dry wit. She had loved her husband with the single-minded certainty of a twenty-year-old girl. She would have loved him forever, if he had given her a chance. If life had given them a chance. His determination to protect her from the seamy side of his job hadn't even bothered her before the threats on his life began.

She'd been very young, Clare thought. Young and sheltered and woefully naive.

She didn't have those excuses any more. Once, Paul's efforts to shield her had made her feel cherished and secure; Matt's heavy-handed attempt at protection only made her mad.

Glancing up as she approached the porch, she saw that the house needed painting. The white paint had rubbed or splintered away in patches like the peeling bark of a paper birch. But the green spears of daffodils poked through the ground beneath the full-moon maple, and yellow and blue pansies nodded from a bucket by the front steps.

She'd come to terms with her loss, Clare thought, delicately touching their cheerful, velvet faces. Out of the barren ground of her desolation, she'd brought forth her garden. Frustrated with the legal system's failure either to convict Paul's killer or to avenge his death, she'd taken justice into her own hands. A life for a life, wasn't that the ancient code? Only the lives she sought in return for her lawyer husband's belonged to the children she struggled to reclaim from the streets. She wanted them to have the chances denied children of her own. A chance to live. A chance to grow.

She snapped off the dead heads of the spent pansies. How dare Matt Dunn challenge her choices and her consolation?

Dewy-eyed do-gooder, he'd called her.

Clenching her fist on the draggled blooms, she tossed them

on the compost pile. Not so dewy-eyed. No longer naive. Eddie Boothe had snuffed out her naivety when he'd ordered his hit man to put a bullet in her husband.

Behind the house, Eddie's cousin whooped and Richie hollered as the wheelbarrow clattered over flagstone. Clare lifted her head, filling her lungs with cool, hawthorne-scented air, breathing in calm. They were probably pushing each other down the walk. She hoped they'd spare her border plantings. She should send Richie back to finish setting out the perennials around Matt's stoop. Tyler could help her clear last autumn's leaves from under the forsythia hedge.

And Matt Dunn and his opinions could go to hell.

Chapter 4

"Reverend Ray?" Clare tapped on the open office door before sticking her head into the tiny, book-lined room. "Are you busy?"

Sunlight streamed through the vertical blinds of the converted storefront, turning the drifting dust motes gold as pollen. Children's artwork brightened the cinder block walls. The Reverend Raymond C. Carter, pastor of Grace African Methodist Episcopal Church, came around his desk with a welcoming smile and his hand extended. A barrel-chested man in his forties, he wore black-and-white clericals and an air of warm authority.

"Clare! Glad you came by. Sit down, sit down."

The three available chairs jammed into that cramped space overflowed with papers, books and flyers. Chuckling, the minister took off his reading glasses and polished them on his jacket, as if that would help him find her a seat. "If you can locate a chair under all this mess."

Clare smiled affectionately, relaxing in the peaceful warmth of the room. "I think I can."

She moved some books to the top of a filing cabinet. He shifted some papers to the floor. They both sat down.

"Richie said you wanted to see me."

He steepled his fingers over the closely printed pages on his desk. "Mm, I did. We're having a reception in the hall after services on Sunday, and I wondered—"

"—if I'd bring my Jell-O mold?" Clare's lack of cooking skill was a long-standing joke between them.

He smiled in acknowledgment. "Actually, I hoped you could design the flyers on that machine of yours."

Grace Church couldn't afford a computer. Reverend Ray typed his sermons and correspondence on an old Selectric.

"Of course," Clare said promptly. "Do you have the information written down?"

"Mostly." He pulled a legal pad from a drawer. "I still need a phone number, though. Got an appointment coming in—you might want to meet him—at one o'clock."

She was too grateful for the preacher's support to mind a little inconvenience. "It doesn't matter. I can send Richie over later to pick it up."

"That's right. Letitia said he's doing some work for you these days?"

"Yes. *After* school," she hastened to add.

"Boy get himself in trouble?" Reverend Ray asked bluntly.

Clare hesitated. While she appreciated the minister's concern, they'd both had to learn to trust her judgment where the project's kids were concerned. Richie had already returned Matt's ball and was making good on his theft. What purpose would be served by betraying his confidence now?

"He could have," she temporized. "I think we took care of it."

He nodded thoughtfully. "All right, Clare. You let me know if I can help." He took off his glasses, rubbed his nose, and put them on again. "What about Tyler Boothe? He doing a little community service, too?"

Clare smiled ruefully. He might trust her judgment, but the

Reverend Ray still kept a watchful eye on all his flock. "Tyler's more a case of preventive intervention."

"Well, he's a child who needs it. You want to watch him."

"I can watch him better if he's where I can see him."

"All the same… Do you really want to give a job to Eddie Boothe's cousin?"

"I especially want to give a job to Eddie Boothe's cousin," she said with grim satisfaction.

"A vendetta, Clare?" The reverend shook his head. "You know they never proved there was a connection between Eddie Boothe and your husband's passing on."

"You think it was just a coincidence Paul got shot on Vipers' territory a week before the trial?"

Reverend Ray shifted the papers on his desk. "All the same, Boothe is serving time now."

"For possession, not for dealing. His sentence is up soon. Every child I give a chance is one less child for him to influence when he gets out."

"Well, don't let this child put you or your project at risk."

She lifted her eyebrows. "You sound like our new neighbor."

"Sergeant Dunn?"

"You've run into him—or had a run-in with him—too? Honestly, I don't know why a man like that was ever chosen for a program like this."

The reverend looked at her over the tops of his glasses. "A man like what? I liked him."

"I did, too." Too much. But she wasn't going to confess that. "I just don't think he understands what's involved in becoming a part of this community. It's not enough to just move into the neighborhood."

"There was a time when the same thing was said about you."

He had her there. And the remembered sting of her initial ignorance goaded her reply. "Well, yes. But I tried. I cared. Matt Dunn doesn't seem the slightest bit interested in the most basic forms of community outreach."

"Clare…"

"I'm serious. He didn't want introductions, he wasn't willing to work with Richie, and he was downright rude about Tyler."

"It's not like you to condemn somebody without knowing all the facts. Don't you think you might have misjudged the man?"

Outside in the hall, a door opened and closed. It could be the youngest Carter daughter, running in from preschool, or the minister's wife, summoning him to lunch. In spite of the distraction, Clare couldn't disregard the reverend's gentle accusation.

Because quite possibly he was right.

Something about the tall, strong cop got to her. His dark, knowing eyes invited confidences. His broad shoulders begged to be leaned on. His proximity was reviving old dreams, painful dreams that included a loving partnership and a family. Impossible dreams. Especially with a cop.

Maybe her own vulnerability had made her severe, even unfair. How could she see the good in everyone else and be blind to it in Matt?

"Well, all right, maybe. I mean, he's been injured, obviously. And I can understand he's directing most of his energy right now to regaining his health. He came right out and told me he's eager to return to his regular duty."

The minister cleared his throat, signaling an interruption. Intent on justifying her harsh words, she rolled right over him.

"But just because I can sympathize with his frustration doesn't mean I think he should have been assigned to community policing. This neighborhood shouldn't be shortchanged because the police department doesn't know what else to do with one of their hamstrung detectives."

Reverend Ray, looking acutely uncomfortable, rubbed the bridge of his nose. The back of Clare's neck prickled. Before she could turn around in her chair, a deep voice drawled behind her.

"Nice of you to make allowances for my infirmities, sugar."

Oh, lordy. Her hands flexed nervously on her thighs before she flattened them and turned around.

Matt leaned in the doorway, muscled arms crossed in front of his powerful chest. In spite of the relaxed pose, he was furious. She could tell. His black eyes practically glowed, and his jaw was tight with temper. Once again an odd, quick thrill ran through her at the sight of him. Not fear, she recognized. Pheromones. And maybe something else?

"Sergeant Dunn!"

"Matt," he corrected. "If you're going to talk about me behind my back, we might as well be on a first-name basis."

Ruefully, she smiled. "I guess I really put my foot in it this time, didn't I?"

He lifted a dark brow. "In what?"

Cute, cowboy, she thought. "In my mouth."

He looked down at her, his glance lingering longest on her lips. He didn't say anything. She bet there were bad guys who found his strong, silent routine intimidating. She imagined there were women who found it exciting.

She drew a short breath. "Anyway, I'm sorry you overheard that."

He shrugged. "I've heard worse, believe me."

He strolled forward, making the already crowded room contract around him. Smiling easily at the minister, he extended his hand. His palm nearly engulfed the other man's. "Reverend."

The desk chair scraped the floor as Reverend Ray stood. "I appreciate your coming by, Sergeant."

"He's not...?"

"Sergeant Dunn is my one o'clock appointment," the minister confirmed gently.

She'd survived embarrassment before, Clare reminded herself firmly. When she was new to the project and made mistakes on the lot. She knew better than to compound her humiliation by blithering.

"Well." She tried to think of something constructive to say. Failing that, she stood. "I'll leave you to get on with your meeting, then."

Angling out of her chair to avoid brushing against Matt's broad torso, she almost fell over his legs and between his thighs. Her stomach contracted. His strong hand gripped her forearm and dragged her up. She inhaled sharply. Lord, but he smelled good. He must have come straight from his shower. The smell of soap and a suggestion of aftershave overlaid the basic scent of healthy male. A tiny nick near the corner of his mouth called attention to his full bottom lip. She had a sudden impulse to kiss it and make it better.

She jerked away. The hand on her arm tightened briefly before Matt politely released her and stepped back.

"Don't go, Clare," Reverend Ray said.

She couldn't possibly stay.

Matt hitched his thumbs in his belt loops and shrugged. "Yeah, don't let me chase you away. Finish your discussion. I can wait outside."

She couldn't possibly leave, either. Matt was being remarkably restrained about her lapse. *Hamstrung detective.* Clare winced. She had to make amends somehow. She had to pull herself together.

"What a good idea," she approved brightly. "You go lurk in the hall, and I'll say nice things about you in a really loud voice, and then you can come in and we'll start over."

Laughter leapt in his eyes. Satisfaction filled her. He kept a straight face, though.

"I'm six foot three, sugar, and a police officer. I don't lurk."

Reverend Ray smiled. "Never went undercover, Sergeant Dunn?"

"Naw. They told me I wasn't inconspicuous enough."

"Imagine," Clare murmured.

He sent a grin her way that would have toppled her in the hall in high school. It still had the power to wobble her knees.

"That's the trouble with small-town brass. No imagination. I could've disguised myself as a telephone pole."

Judiciously, she nodded, enjoying his teasing. "Or put a flashlight on your head and patrolled as a street lamp."

"Now there's a bright idea."

The reverend tutted at the pun. Clare groaned. A corner of Matt's mouth turned down in an expression of contrition that only made him look more pleased with himself, like a fox caught with feathers in its mouth. She felt another sharp tug of liking.

"I really should go," she said.

"But Sergeant Dunn has that information you need," the minister objected.

"What information?"

"She needs my phone number?" Matt asked.

"No, I do not need your phone number." She looked over as the reverend cleared his throat. "Do I?"

"Mm-hm. For those flyers. The reception is for the sergeant, Clare, to introduce him to the neighborhood. He came by last week explaining he wanted a chance to meet everybody and asked if I'd help get the word out to my congregation."

She felt light-headed, as if Matt's big body had absorbed all the oxygen in the room. He'd sought out Reverend Ray to introduce him around? No wonder he'd declined her help.

"I was going to use the firehouse," Matt interjected, "but the reverend here tells me it's off the bus line."

"Yes," she said absently. She'd misjudged him, all right. She felt like a low and slimy slug.

The minister lowered himself back in his chair, oblivious to the emotional undercurrents in the room. Or maybe, Clare thought, he was giving her time to recover. "And I told him to use the hall here. We've got the space, we've got the people, and we've got Alma."

"Alma?" Matt repeated.

"My wife," Reverend Ray said, simply and with pride. "She likes to organize things."

Matt shifted restlessly. "Look, I don't want you going to a

lot of trouble. I thought we'd keep this informal, something people can drop in on. I'd like to meet as many area residents as I can in a relaxed setting. Ideally, I'd invite everybody to the house—''

He didn't call it *his* house, Clare noted. It wasn't home.

"—but there isn't enough room, and strangers might feel awkward stopping by this first time.''

The minister nodded. "I'm announcing it as a church social. Outsiders welcome, of course. The food will draw a lot of people.''

"That's another thing. You need to let me handle expenses for refreshments, Reverend.''

"No, no. Alma won't hear of it. She's making fried chicken.''

"I can't let you do that. I would've sprung for the food if the meeting was at my place.''

Clare decided to step in before he offended the pastor's pride by rejecting his congregation's kindness. She had to make amends somehow for her earlier quick judgment. It wasn't Matt's fault he affected her like the sun's heat after a frost. "It's like the team giving you a hand moving in, Matt. The ladies in the church are willing to throw you a dinner.'' She hoped he got the message.

He rubbed his jaw. "Okay. Fine. Thanks. I'll pay for the beer, though.''

Reverend Ray pursed his lips. "I'm afraid not.''

Dark brows snapped together. "Why the he—heck not? Oh.'' He shook his head over his own obtuseness. "No alcohol, right? For the iced tea. I'll pay for the iced tea. Soft drinks. Maybe lemonade for the kids?''

"Everybody likes lemonade,'' Clare assured him.

I don't, Matt almost said but stopped himself in time. He didn't want to lose his tentative rapport with the reverend. And after her response to his confessed dislike of vegetables, he was damned if he'd hand little Miss Clare another opportunity to bedevil him. The last thing he needed was to open his front door and find Richie standing on the porch with an ice-cold pitcher of the sweet yellow stuff.

"And we mustn't forget Clare's Jell-O mold," the reverend said heartily.

"Jell-O mold?"

Reverend Ray chuckled. "A little joke. Clare can't cook."

Fascinated, Matt watched as betraying color stained her cheeks. He wouldn't have guessed she was sensitive about a lack of domestic skills. In her focus on her project, she'd seemed so formidable, so clear-sighted, so assured.... Less Tinkerbell than Joan of Arc in blue jeans. Her unexpected vulnerability tickled him.

Just to test her, to tease her, he asked, "Can't cook? Not at all?"

And was rewarded when she snapped, "I can boil water, wash salad and stir-fry vegetables. Want to come over for dinner some time?"

He wanted to stay away from her. He'd planned on staying away from her. He didn't want the aggravation, he couldn't afford the complication of a woman's demands and disappointments in his life right now. So naturally, her impulsive challenge provoked an equally instinctive response.

"All right," he answered smoothly. "Tomorrow okay with you? I'll bring the steaks."

Her pretty mouth opened like a gaping bass. She closed it. To his intense masculine satisfaction, he thought he saw her swallow.

"Fine," she said coolly. "Seven o'clock."

She turned from him. "I really do have to run, Reverend Ray. Do you want to get back to me on those flyers?"

"No, you take this." The minister pushed a lined yellow sheet across the desk. "And Sergeant Dunn can give you his phone number."

She lifted her eyebrows in silent question.

"My pager number," Matt explained. "Whether people come to this dinner at the hall or not, I want them to be able to reach me."

"So, you're going to post it in the neighborhood. That's a wonderful idea."

Her smile was warm with approval. He felt it ignite in his gut and burn lower down. To banish it, he said, "Standard procedure. Or it will be, once this program's up and running."

He scrawled the number at the bottom of the page. She folded the sheet without reading it, sliding it into her hip pocket. Reflexively, his hand curled. Just looking at her made him want.

He could stay with the preacher. He liked the man and needed to talk with him. Or...

"I'll walk with you," he said. It was only a couple of blocks. He could make two blocks.

She gave his own words back to him. "It's not necessary. Besides, aren't you meeting with Reverend Ray now?"

The older man spread his hands in a little gesture of letting go. His face was bland; his voice, amused. "Y'all run along. We're done. I just wanted the sergeant's number. And I think I've got it now."

Matt cocked his head, acknowledging the gentle gibe. "Thanks for your time, Reverend."

He went into the hall as Clare said her goodbyes, and out the front door. By the time she joined him, he'd negotiated the shallow steps and was propping up the redbrick side of the church, cataloging the action on the street. The elderly woman with her steel-on-wheels carrier creaking along the sidewalk was grocery shopping. Two girls with babies on their hips and toddlers hanging on their hands meandered past the laundromat. A boy flashed by on a bicycle.

Matt studied the knot of men blocking the sidewalk in front of the convenience store. They glanced over, nodded, spat. Corner regulars passing the time, he wondered, or pushers fixing a deal? A beat cop would know. He felt crippled, not just by his injury, but by his lack of familiarity with the neighborhood. The who's-doing-what-where, as his dad used to say. You had to know that. You had to recognize trouble, anticipate it.

He should never have been pegged for this job. Except the mayor had wanted a high profile for his new program, and after the convenience store stickup Matt had the highest profile on the force.

An older guy in a button-down shirt with his name embroidered on the pocket came out of the store and lit a cigarette. The owner, Matt guessed. He exchanged greetings with the men clustered around his doorway, calling some by name. So they were regulars. Matt settled against his post.

Clare bounced down the church office steps in worn athletic shoes. Her smile was a flicker of courtesy, friendly, but guarded. That suited him fine, Matt told himself, ignoring the way every muscle in his body tightened at her approach. The lady had *serious involvement* written all over her, and he was strictly the just-for-laughs type. He didn't want a widow with baggage, and she didn't need a cop whose closest thing to a personal relationship since his partner's retirement were twice-weekly sessions with a physical therapist.

"Let's go," she said, and started briskly down the crumbling sidewalk.

He pushed off the wall and lumbered after her like a three-legged Great Dane in pursuit of a Chihuahua. She was six yards ahead of him before she realized he wasn't keeping up and figured out why. Without saying a word, she adjusted her stride.

Tactful, Matt thought, and tried like hell not to resent his need for her tact.

They kept pace, more or less, down the block of storefronts with apartments over the street, past the service station where some kid with a can of black spray paint and no supervision had scrawled the Vipers' mark over and over: an upside down V, trailing a devil's tail and a pitchfork. The sidewalks narrowed. Skimpy yards and bare-branched trees squeezed in between the shabby houses and lines of parked cars. Matt stumbled over a break in the concrete where tree roots had raised the sidewalk. Instantly, Clare's slim arm was there to brace him.

He caught himself before he fell into her. He wanted to reject her help, but her nearness socked him like a punch in the gut. Up close, he could read the concern on her clear-skinned face, smell her soap and the shampoo that she used.

Baby scented. Under his hand, her skin was baby soft. Her arm was fine-boned but strong, lightly tanned and gently marked by her labor in the sun. What had his mother called those little freckles? Angel kisses, he remembered. He ran his thumb over the smooth skin, as if to rub them away, and felt her shiver.

Support was one thing with her, he realized. She was used to offering support. It was the man-woman tension between them that made her pull away.

"You should have taken the bus," she said crossly.

"If I wanted to drive, I've got my truck. Besides, you said I should walk in the neighborhood."

She flushed. "Not if it's going to interfere with your getting better."

"It won't. I'm supposed to walk." Not this far, though. Not yet.

They started down the sidewalk again, her steps small and careful, his slow and stiff.

She cleared her throat. "How did it happen?"

So, she hadn't read about it in the paper, hadn't heard it on the news. He was glad. The media accounts were bull. He hadn't been a hero, just unlucky.

"I got careless."

Her clear brown eyes saw right through his evasion. "I thought you got shot."

He shrugged.

"How long ago?" she persisted.

Two miserable months. The wound had actually closed when the damn thing got infected. He'd spent three additional weeks in the hospital, making repeated trips to OR to get the wound incised and drained and inserted with antibiotics, while he squeezed a PCA pump, trying to control his pain with metered doses of morphine. Trying to joke with his dad while his mother cried in her chair by the window and Will hovered in the hallway looking guilty.

He almost told her about it. The temptation to tell her scared him.

"Couple of months." He glanced up the street. Another block, he thought. He could make one more block.

"Is that why you didn't walk me to your door the other day?"

She sounded indignant. He grinned. "Yeah."

"Macho jerk," she said, without heat.

He liked her scolding better than her discreet silence or her sympathetic questioning.

"So, do you mind telling me what prompted this stroll?" she asked.

She was so damn pretty, he thought. Not really beautiful, not well turned out or well endowed like the women he usually dated. She lifted her head as they passed under the gnarled canopy of some old tree, giving him an unobstructed view of her face. The pale spring sun, striking through the branches, dappled her small, even features, gilding her hair and glistening on her bare lips.

He couldn't tell her he just wanted to be with her. She wouldn't understand. He didn't understand it himself.

"I'm a glutton for punishment?" he suggested.

"Obviously," she retorted, with a pointed look at his leg. "But why now, specifically?"

He gave her the truth. Not the whole truth, but enough to honor her perception. "I wanted to check on your new hire. That kid, Tyler."

"You don't need to."

"He didn't stick around?"

"*He* did. I thought you weren't planning to."

"And I thought you asked me to come by occasionally."

"To keep an eye on Richie, I said. Not keep tabs on me."

"Get used to it," he advised.

They were nearing the project lot. She swung to face him, her hands planted on her hips.

"Look," she said. "I don't know who you're used to riding herd on, cowboy, but…"

Her attention slipped past him to her lot. Her voice died. Her mouth trembled before she bit down on the lower lip, hard.

Matt turned, already feeling the hunch that signaled trouble, the adrenaline rush of action. He followed her stare over furrowed rows of pale green leaves and piled straw to the muddy pool spreading by the gray-sided shed.

He didn't know enough about gardens to be sure how the plot should look, but he'd seen enough vandalism to know it shouldn't look like this.

The spigot attached to the shed had been turned on full. The nozzle to the hose had been opened and left running. The first bursts of water from the writhing hose had blasted more than a dozen plants right out of the ground. They lay in draggled, muddy clumps, roots exposed and leaves limp. Anchored in its own growing pool, the hose still fed a destructive stream of water over the sodden rows, uprooting some plants, drowning more.

For a short moment, Clare stood frozen over the destruction like Lot's wife looking back on Gomorrah. He was familiar enough with victims' reactions that the expression on her face shouldn't have torn him up inside. But it did.

Cursing, he stumped forward to twist the faucet shut.

As if his voice had released her to action, Clare hurried forward, seizing a short-handled spade balanced against the wall to scoop up globs of thick red mud.

"What are you doing?"

"Ditch," she panted. "Drain off the water."

It made sense. He gave her credit for quick thinking even as he sloshed into the shed—the unlocked shed, he noted disapprovingly—and selected a man-size shovel. A pickax would be even better, but he didn't trust his balance on his gimpy leg. He worked behind her, focusing on action to take his mind off her pain, deepening the channel while she directed the path of the stream. Released, the water coursed between their feet to spill harmlessly over her driveway. Behind them, the carefully set out plants slumped in uneven lines, swamped by water, weighted by mud or shriveled by the sun.

The simple act of vandalism had done a lot of damage in a relatively short time.

"Clever of somebody," Matt remarked.

Clare's head jerked up. She had control of herself again, he saw. Her face was pale, but calm. "It was an accident."

He scraped mud off his boots with the tip of his shovel. His right leg throbbed. "Yeah, right."

"It had to have been. Someone just forgot to turn off the hose."

Who was she trying to convince? Him or herself?

"Uh-huh. What about the graffiti?"

"What? Where?"

He pointed to the shed, the side facing her house. Screened by the bushes that separated her yard from the lot, somebody had taken the time to spray the signature *V* of the Vipers.

She said a word he'd never have guessed she knew.

The incongruity of that coarse word on her soft pink mouth made him want to laugh. He squelched it and grunted his agreement. "You want me to look into it for you?"

"No."

"Clare…" He expelled a short, sharp breath of exasperation. "I'm a detective. That's what I do, look into things. It's no trouble."

"Yes, it is. It's trouble for the kids, trouble to the project. Matt, I have to trust the people I hire. I can't ask them to trust me otherwise."

Her danger worried him. Her priorities made him crazy. But he couldn't force her to accept his help. He was a cop, she was just a woman who lived on his beat. They had no personal relationship.

"Fine," he snapped. "You've got my number. Use it if you change your mind."

"I won't change my mind."

It was that damn Joan of Arc thing again, he thought. In

spite of the destruction around her, she seemed perfectly calm, clear and resolute, like she was tackling some medieval fortress with only her courage and her God to sustain her. He wasn't used to that kind of courage from a civilian.

He admired her. Feared for her. And hoped like hell some enemy archer wasn't waiting to shoot her off the wall.

"Let's both hope you don't have to," he said.

Chapter 5

"I thought you didn't want kids defacing the walls."

A little shiver ran through Clare as she recognized Matt's brown velvet voice behind her. Of course, the words were confrontational. The man himself, solid, strong and hostile, was a danger to her rapport with her crew and a threat to her peace of mind. But his dogged adherence to duty compelled her respect. His understated humor roused her liking. And his voice was invading her dreams.

Dropping her brushes in a cleanup bucket milky with diluted gray latex, she slowly turned around. No one could look as good as that voice promised.

He did.

He stood behind her, thumbs hitched in his belt loops, his broad shoulders encased in dark cotton and his black boots making a statement among the empty gallon plant pots and discarded paint rags. Tug a Stetson over that dark hair, she thought, and he'd look like Marshal Earp taking on the bad guys in Tombstone. A rush of contradictory feelings washed through her, warm and confused.

Defensively, she wiped wet hands down the front of her jeans. "Making a habit of sneaking up on people, Sergeant?"

Coffee dark eyes gleamed. "Let's just say I'm making it part of the new job to check up on you."

That's what she was afraid of. She'd been grateful for Matt's quick support yesterday when the lot was flooded. And in theory, she approved of a police presence in the neighborhood. But when that presence was 220 pounds of hard, handsome cop, she panicked. She wasn't certain she could trust him with her kids. What had the legal system ever done for them? And she was darn sure she couldn't trust this edgy attraction she felt.

She'd already had the experience of being the subordinate partner in a relationship. Wouldn't intimacy with a cop be just as bad as marriage to a lawyer? Worse. There was that notorious esprit de corps to consider, as well as the macho code of silence.

Besides, if she did get involved with a man again, Clare resolved, it wouldn't be one who got shot at for a living. Physically and mentally, she took a step back.

"Don't worry about me," she said. "I can manage."

"Uh-huh." Amazing how much skepticism he could pack in two nonverbal syllables. He jerked his chin toward the side of the shed, where Richie and Tyler laughed and shoved and scribbled on the wall. "Didn't you just paint over that this morning?"

She pretended surprise. "Why, yes, Sergeant, now that you point it out, I believe I did. What were you doing, watching from your window?"

She thought he actually colored under his tan. She wished she didn't find that slight embarrassment so appealing. "I work out in the living room. I get a pretty good view of the street."

The memory of him answering his door, shirt off and skin sheened with sweat, sprang into her brain. "Yes. Well." She cleared her throat. "Why didn't you come over? The project can always use another pair of hands."

"You made it pretty clear you didn't want me hanging around." He nodded toward the boys. "Besides, I could never clean up after a bunch of vandals and then stand around and watch them muck up my hard work."

"They are not mucking up." She hoped. "They're designing a mural."

"No kidding." He squinted, but the boys' pencil scratchings barely showed against the fresh gray paint. "They any good?"

"I don't have a clue," she answered honestly.

That surprised a smile from him. "Yeah, well, it's a good idea."

His praise made her breathless. Silly, she scolded herself. "I just told them I wanted them to cover where the spray paint showed through. They decided to do the mural."

He had no clue, apparently, how he affected her. "You should get them some really bright colors," he said. "Do it up right."

"I'll put it on my list," she promised dryly. "Right after 'pay the water bill.'"

She thought for a minute he hadn't heard. He continued to stare over her head. She turned to follow his gaze to where Tyler stretched to draw on the siding above Richie. Scrunched beneath him, Richie traced a row of circles. Clare couldn't tell if he was drawing apples or potatoes. Or even pumpkins.

"My partner—" Matt stopped. "Ex-partner, now. His family owns a paint store over on Harnett. They keep discards in the back, stuff people order and then decide they don't want. It's no good to him. He'd probably let you have it for free."

She jerked her attention away from his dark, melancholy eyes—why did the reference to his partner make him sad?—and focused instead on what he was saying. "That sounds wonderful. Would he do that? Let the kids pick out colors and everything?"

"He would if I took them." The full mouth compressed. "He figures he owes me."

Her first instinct was to refuse. She didn't need his help or interference. She didn't want him on her lot, challenging the barriers she'd built to protect herself. And then she was disgusted by her own selfish preoccupation. For heaven's sake, the man was offering her free paint. More than that, he was offering his time to her kids. If only he wouldn't play Officer Tough Guy with them...

She studied his face, the combative jaw, the crooked nose, the shrewd, surprisingly warm eyes. She was willing to take that chance on him, Clare decided. Would her boys do the same?

"You're thinking too hard," he said. "Yes or no?"

She flushed, as if he could read her misgivings in her face. "Yes. Thanks. I'll talk to them. When would you want to go?"

He shrugged. "Now is good."

His quick follow-through pleased her. She was used to bureaucratic runarounds and Paul's deliberate ways. "Now is great."

Maybe once he was safely out of sight with the boys, her heartbeat could return to normal.

Calling the boys over, she explained Matt's offer. Richie's quick enthusiasm faded under Tyler's cynical regard, but both agreed to go. Clare was relieved to see that Matt took their lukewarm response in stride.

He tossed Richie his keys. "Get in the truck. I'll be right there."

As the boys ambled across the street, Clare smiled her approval. "I appreciate your giving him the keys like that. It's important for Richie to feel that he's earning your trust."

"He takes my truck for a joyride and I'll shoot out the tires," Matt said. Her startled response must have shown, because he grinned at her then. "Joke," he explained.

"Of course," Clare said. Under that tough exterior, he was really kind.

"I'd shoot the kids," he said, deadpan. "Too expensive to replace the tires."

This time, after a heart's beat pause, she laughed with him.

It had been a long time since a man had teased her with a smile in his eyes.

"So." He rubbed his jaw. "I'll see you about seven."

She blinked, distracted by the slow movement of his knuckles over his chin. "What?"

"Dinner. You invited me. Remember?"

"Maybe I thought you'd forget."

He looked at her from under straight, dark brows, and her breath caught.

"I never forget an offer," he said.

Through the rear window of Matt's truck, Clare could see the red bill of Richie's baseball cap as he turned to stare. Tyler, leaning against the open door, nudged him and whispered. Her hot cheeks got even hotter. Having just assured them they'd be perfectly all right in Matt's company, she could hardly balk at spending an evening with him.

"Seven o'clock," she confirmed.

And wondered, as she watched him walk away, just what she had agreed to.

Just dinner, Matt reminded himself, waiting on the front stoop for Clare to answer the door. He'd brought steaks and a bottle of red. Not a drinking woman, she'd said, turning down his beer, but this was a first-class bottle of merlot. Idly, he wondered if she'd warm a little under the influence of the wine. It would be nice to see what that mouth of hers could manage besides sass.

Not that he had anything more in mind. A cop couldn't afford personal involvements. Matt had seen what divided loyalties cost his father. He'd experienced firsthand the toll The Job took on an officer's wife and family. Maybe once upon a time, he'd thought it would be nice to do the white house and picket fence thing. But that was before Marcia—or was it Amy?—had told him what a cold, preoccupied son of a bitch he was, and long before Will's wife had put the pressure on Will to quit.

These days, Matt was happy if he could keep things emotionally simple and physically satisfying. He told himself he liked them that way. He knew enough about repeat offenders to accept that there was no way of reforming a cop married to The Job. Still, he tried to play according to his own personal rule book. No ties, was one of his rules, but no bruises, either.

The last thing he needed at the start of an unwelcome new assignment was to tangle with a woman with honest eyes and a vulnerable mouth. A woman whose emotions ran as deep as her sense of honor. A woman—admit it, Dunn—a woman like Clare.

But he'd sure like a taste of that mouth.

She opened the door then and smiled at him, and all the red blood cells in his body started leaping around, flexing muscles and calling attention to themselves. He'd been around the block often enough to recognize and appreciate her effort to dress up. Nothing fancy or overdone, just a suggestion of color on her cheekbones and a slick of shine on her lips. She wore white jeans and a hot yellow shirt in a silky material that brought out highlights in her whiskey brown eyes and sherry gold hair.

Down, boy, he thought.

"Come in," she invited.

Classical music drifted in from the living room, unidentified aromas wafted from the kitchen. Matt entered her house suspecting he was playing out of his league.

Shifting his weight, he offered her the paper bag with the bottle.

The sack crinkled as she accepted it.

"Hope it goes," he said, knowing it would. He'd asked at the store.

"I'm sure it will be fine," she said politely. "Come on in the kitchen. I'll get glasses."

He followed her down the narrow hallway, conscious of the push-pull of attraction, wondering if Clare was equally aware and what she planned to do about it. Hell, he wished he could be sure of what he planned to do.

"I brought the steaks."

Place mats and flowers graced the battered kitchen table. A colander of greens rested in the cracked ceramic sink, and pots steamed gently on the old electric range. Handing off the meat, Matt eased into the chair facing the door with a sense almost of homecoming. Which, when he thought about it, was odd, because Clare's kitchen looked nothing like his mother's modern, immaculate galley, and Clare had even less in common with Mary Dunn.

His mother was a tall, dark, gentle woman, whose loving ways and cheerful patter had been a perfect foil for her tough, taciturn husband. Matt was eleven or twelve before he recognized the toll that being Patrick Dunn's wife took on her, on her mouth that could never be silent, on her hands that could never be still, as if she alone had to fill the house's hollow quiet.

Clare, on the other hand, was sharp and shining as a knife. She talked like a drill instructor and moved like a thoroughbred.

Tonight, though, there was a restless energy to her movements. She paced to the cupboard to get glasses, to a drawer for a corkscrew, back to the counter for the wine. She made three separate trips to line them up on the table in front of him, and then darted back across the kitchen to stir something on the stove and flip on the broiler. Matt pried the foil from the neck of the bottle, watching her. It didn't take nine years on the force to see that beneath her bright, hostessy manner she was nervous. But was it the same edgy awareness that deviled him or something else?

Was she in trouble?

He poured the dark wine into the delicate, wide-bowled glasses she'd provided. Wedding gifts, he bet, as out of place in this rough neighborhood as Clare herself. He pushed a stem toward her and waited to see if she'd take the bait.

"Thanks." She scooped up the glass and stepped back out of reach.

He bit back a grin.

She sipped, her tongue darting over her bottom lip to catch a drop of wine. His body reacted predictably.

"Mm. This is nice."

"Yeah." He didn't mean the wine, though that was okay, too.

She must have caught him staring at her mouth, because her chin went up. "So. How did things go at the paint store?"

"They went all right."

"It was good of you to take the boys."

He felt as if he'd received a commendation. He didn't want that feeling, not from her. He didn't deserve it. "No trouble. Will likes kids."

"Will? That's your partner?"

"Ex-partner." If he said it often enough, maybe he'd learn to accept it.

She studied him silently over the top of her wineglass, as if deciding whether to press and where. "Recently an ex?"

"Yeah."

"How recently? Before the shooting?"

Her husband had been a lawyer. "No. After. What's with the cross-examination?"

"Sorry." She took a sip of wine. "So, why did he quit?"

"Family reasons," Matt said. With a feeling of sickness in his gut, he remembered Will's near-fatal hesitation the day of the shoot out. Forget it, he'd told his partner. It could have happened to anybody. But the guilt and the gratitude and his wife's reaction had eaten away at Will.

"Big family?" the lawyer's widow wanted to know.

"Yeah. Five," he said, forestalling her next question. "All girls."

Her gaze turned teasing. "You don't like girls?"

He liked *her*. Too much. "Let's just say I'm not exactly daddy material."

"Then I appreciate your spending time with Richie and Tyler even more."

He shrugged. "Will did all the work. He helped them pick out colors, gave them some stencils for lettering. I just drove."

"Doesn't that make you an accomplice?"

"Only in the commission of a crime. So as long as they use the paint for lawful purposes, I'm free and clear."

Those whiskey-colored eyes met his with an amusement more intimate than a kiss. Free and clear? If he didn't watch himself, he'd be cuffed, booked and fingerprinted.

But Clare was the first to look away. "They're really quite excited about the mural."

"Maybe," he conceded, struggling for distance. "And maybe you can cover up the graffiti on your shed. But what are you going to do to prevent them from taking after the garden again?"

Provoked, she set her glass down so sharply he half expected the stem to snap. "First of all, if the garden was vandalized, Richie and Tyler aren't the ones responsible. Secondly, vandalism is a crime of opportunity. I shouldn't have left the lot unsupervised."

"So, what are you going to do? Hire a guard?"

"No. I spoke to Reverend Ray. I'm going to turn part of the lot over to the church's daycare co-op."

He couldn't have heard her correctly. "Excuse me?"

"I'm giving the kids little garden plots. The mothers will be on site to keep an eye on things."

He didn't want to argue with her. Whatever his personal feelings on the subject, her position was in line with the reasoning behind his current assignment. But concern for her wouldn't let him keep his mouth shut.

"Yeah, that might work. *If* a lack of supervision is the only reason behind the attack on your lot."

She raised a slim eyebrow, in control again. "What other reason could there be?"

"You're assuming you're a random target," he told her. "But if you're serious about providing an alternative to the gangs around here, if you're hiring away from the Vipers, you could be ticking somebody off."

"Good," she said.

Her quiet satisfaction jolted him. "These aren't just taggers,

Clare, kids painting buildings. These are dangerous men. Businessmen.''

''I know what they are,'' she said.

She wasn't scared. Why wasn't she scared? He was beginning to be scared for her, and he hated the feeling. ''Well, don't you think that should make you a little bit cautious?''

Those sun-tipped lashes came down over her eyes. She turned to put the steaks under the broiler. ''What it makes me is determined.''

He couldn't figure her out. He wasn't even sure why he tried, except that in his line of work he was used to fitting motive to behavior.

''How do you want your steak done?'' she asked from over by the stove.

So, she didn't want to talk to him. He shouldn't care. He wasn't interrogating an evasive witness, he reminded himself. He was having dinner with a woman. A beautiful, stubborn woman. And they'd talked long enough.

''Rare, please.'' He pushed back from the table, feigning relaxation. ''Can I help with anything?''

''No, thank you.'' Vigorously, she shook the colander, spattering droplets over the sink and the counter and the yellow blouse. The material darkened to transparency where the water touched.

Silk, he thought, and his mouth dried.

''Yeah, I reckoned you'd say that,'' he drawled.

He caught the sparkle in her eyes before she primmed up her pretty mouth. Lifting the lid from the largest pot, she handed him a spoon. ''Here. You can dish up.''

''Sure.'' He joined her in front of the stove, crowding her just a little to gauge her reaction. Maneuvering neatly around him, she fetched up again by the sink.

Beautiful, stubborn and evasive, he amended, and wondered why that particular combination made him grin. He ladled rice and vegetables into a blue serving dish. ''Smells good. What is it?''

''Pilaf. And I made a salad.''

His mother would have served baked potatoes and chunks of iceberg with the steaks. Clare emptied the colander into a large wooden bowl, mingling unidentifiable red stuff with unrecognizable green stuff. Oh, yeah, he thought. Way out of his league.

She pulled matching salad servers from a pottery cache pot and whipped the whole thing over to the table. "The dressing's bottled, I'm afraid."

"That's fine," he said truthfully.

She looked at him through those ridiculous lashes of hers before turning to retrieve the steaks from under the broiler. Did she really think he would mind? She cared what he thought? Her unexpected uncertainty, so at odds with her usual cool control, twisted something inside him.

What he was doing here, putting the moves on Saint Joan? She got to him, he admitted. Maybe he wanted to ruffle her a little in return, test the uneasy attraction between them. Nothing more. He couldn't afford anything more. He was already opening up to her more than was wise. But he was beginning to think he couldn't be satisfied with anything less, either.

They served up, sat down. Whatever jokes the reverend had made at Clare's expense, the steaks were cooked to perfection. Matt poked surreptitiously at the unfamiliar-looking salad, but it was fine. It was good. He told her so.

"The rice is sticky."

He shrugged. "If you say so. I like your salad."

"Anybody can rinse lettuce."

He inspected the leaf impaled on his fork, wondering at the quiet self-deprecation beneath her bright exterior. "Is that what this is?"

That made her smile. "All right, Belgian endive. Anybody can rinse endive."

"Yeah, but not everybody eats it. Especially not at this end of town."

"I grow it."

"Why?"

She met his eyes directly. "What do you want to know, Sergeant? Why, endive? Or, why, here?"

He wanted to know everything. "Tell me both."

"Endive sells," she said bluntly. "I've spent the last three years cultivating not just the land, but buyers for our produce. We can't compete in the grocery market, but we can make a profit selling locally to restaurants and small specialty stores. And they want specialty produce."

Her business focus impressed him. He'd figured her as a good-works type. "And what do you do with your profits?"

"Expand," she replied promptly. "Hire more kids who need an alternative to gangs. Reclaim more unused and misused space in the city." She leaned forward across the table, her dinner momentarily forgotten. "Children should look out their windows at flowers and vegetables, not broken concrete and crack vials."

Her passionate explanation convinced him of her sincerity, if not of her arguments. "Nice dream," he remarked.

"It's not a dream," she insisted. "It's my job."

Her dedication pricked him, reminding him of a time when he hadn't felt so burned out, so used up and cynical. A time when he'd believed the public he served actually gave a rat's ass about his presence on the streets. "Yeah? Who hired you?"

"I draw a salary from the project." That slight, self-derogatory smile flickered again. "Which enables me to live in this luxury."

He looked around the run-down kitchen with its outdated appliances. "I can see that."

Her fork made a crater in her pile of rice. "So, what made you decide to become a policeman?"

Spilling his dreams didn't fit in with his ideal of an uncomplicated, enjoyable, physical relationship. He temporized, gave her an honest but standard response.

"Someone's got to do it. There's always work for a cop."

She raised her eyebrows. "That's it? Job security?"

Her quick challenge made him smile. "Great retirement benefits."

"If you live to collect them. Was your father a policeman?"

"Thirty-one years. Twenty-five on the beat and six behind a desk, after they chained his butt to it. Got a gold watch and everything."

She ignored his attempted banter. "Uncles? Brothers?"

"Not my uncles. Little brother's MP, big brother's SBI."

The Military Police and the State Bureau of Investigation. She raised her eyebrows. "What about your mother?"

He eyed her warily. "What about her?"

"What does she do? How does she feel about having a family in law enforcement?"

Matt dug into his steak, uncomfortable with the turn the conversation had taken. "She dealt with it," he said finally. "That's what cops' wives do. They deal with it, or they walk."

Clare heard the warning plainly. She knew the statistics on the divorce rate among cops. The stress of the job put their relationships as well as their lives at risk. There was no room in her reconstructed life for that kind of difficulty and danger.

And yet the burden in Matt's deep voice weighted her heart. Under his rough-hewn facade ran a vein of pure gold, courage and humor and compassion. She wondered if he let anyone in his life dig deep enough to uncover it.

"Were you ever married?"

He set down his knife and fork. "You are one pushy woman, you know that?"

She grinned. "Thanks. I wasn't always."

Matt heard some clue to deeper feelings in her voice. Like any good detective, he followed it up.

"You were a good little girl?"

"Oh, yes." Her smile mocked herself now. "The best. Did as I was told. Spoke when I was spoken to. Made decent grades and went to a good college and married a professional man."

"What happened?"

"He got shot. I was devastated. Mother and Daddy wanted me to come home to the Main Line. That's an area just outside of Philadelphia," she explained.

He watched her carefully, seeing the conflict on her cameo-pure face. "Nice area?"

"The nicest."

"And?"

"And while I was packing, it occurred to me that doing the expected thing all my life hadn't made me happy. It hadn't kept Paul safe. And it wasn't enough anymore."

"So, you moved here instead."

She nodded. "Paul was prosecuting a big drug case when he died. The man they'd arrested got off with a simple possession. I figured if the legal system couldn't deal with the problem, I'd quit my teaching job and tackle it myself, one kid at a time." She met his gaze, her brown eyes rueful. "Pretty arrogant, right?"

His heart squeezed in his chest. "Pretty crazy."

Clare lifted one slim shoulder, unwilling to debate the point. "Maybe... How's the unpacking going?"

His eyes met hers, dark, aware. Hurriedly, she offered him the serving dish of rice. One corner of his mouth turned up teasingly.

"Fine, thanks," he said politely. "My stereo's hooked up."

"Really?" She swallowed. "What kind of music do you listen to?"

The killer smile made its return, doing funny things to the rhythm of her breath. He jerked his head toward the hall, where the strains of a trumpet playing Haydn shivered on the air.

"Not the same as you, sugar, that's for sure."

Clare bit her lip. "Do you want me to put on something else?"

"No," he said simply. "I like it."

They talked about music, smothering their mutual awareness under a blanket of polite conversation. Even as Clare responded to the attention in Matt's face and the timbre of his laugh, she felt awkward. Sure, she worked with men. But she hadn't been on a date in nine years. She hadn't cooked dinner for a man in three. And she had never, even in her wildest adolescent fantasies, entertained a man as rough, tough and in-your-face sexy as Matt Dunn.

Gradually, though, she began to enjoy herself, at once stimulated and soothed by the masculine appreciation in Matt's dark eyes, the quiet way he listened. There was something different, something seductive, in this casual exploration of tastes and ideas, in the slow growth of liking and the gradual buildup of tension. Sexual tension. Clare watched Matt's large, well-shaped hand with its dusting of dark hair curl around his wineglass and felt as flushed and light-headed as if she'd stood too suddenly after planting in the sun.

He was an investigator, she reminded herself. He was good at inviting disclosures. He probably had people—women—falling all over themselves to tell him things.

Matt registered the widening of her pupils and the slight increase of her breath, signals of a woman's interest, invitations of desire. Her hand strayed unconsciously to touch her hair and neck, and his body responded with a force that surprised him.

His gaze followed the movement of her fingers, slipping from the faintly pugnacious curve of her jaw to the fine bones below her throat. Between the front panels of her shirt, her chest was smooth and delicately freckled as an egg. He wanted to nuzzle the silky fabric aside, nipping at her fingers, to taste her baby-textured skin.

He rubbed the back of his neck. "Let me help you clear."

Her smile was tremulous as she stood, reaching for their empty plates. "Thanks."

Inevitably, their hands touched as they collected the remains of the meal. Carefully, they orbited the kitchen, circling one another like two stars drawn by gravity into dangerous proximity. The air was warm and close, still fragrant with the herbs she'd used, humid with steam.

Matt carried the last of the dirty dishes to the sink and found his arms half full of woman when Clare turned to take them from him.

Her mouth was soft, her eyes wide and curious.

"Oh, hell," he muttered. "Might as well get this over with."

Carefully, he took back the serving bowl and set it on the counter behind her. Her eyes followed the movement before returning to his face. The tilt of her chin was a challenge. Under that watchful gaze, he debated pulling her close, settling for his palms on her shoulders. Silk glided coolly under his palms. She was small and slight, and yet he could feel the muscle in her upper arms. Her hands came up as if she might explore, might push at his chest, and then dropped uncertainly, skimming his sides, to rest on his leather belt. At her light touch, he felt fire.

He banked it. Just a taste, he told himself. A test.

He lowered his head. She stood on tiptoe to meet him. He kissed her once, twice, soft, considering kisses as he learned the shape of her lips and the textures of her mouth. Full and surprisingly lush, they tempted him to deepen the contact and tighten his grip on her shoulders. She pressed into him, opening wider, and sucked him into a firestorm of feeling.

He expected sweet. He expected cool. Lusty and hot, she drew on his tongue in a way that was an erotic revelation. Their mouths mated. She made a little sound in the back of her throat that froze every hair on his body in delight. Every thought of tasting, every impulse toward caution or restraint, fled his mind. Dropping his hands to the subtle curves of her bottom, he pulled her close and feasted on her soft hot mouth, tasting red wine and desire.

Through his mind's haze and his body's need, he felt her short nails curling into his waist. The pinch aroused him even further. Harder, he thought. Tighter. And then became aware that she wasn't using her hands to grind him closer, but to hold him away.

Hell. Reluctantly, his hands loosened. She broke contact with his seeking mouth and twisted her head, not into the shelter of his chest, but against her own shoulder. He saw the quick rise and fall of her breath and felt the heavy pounding of his heart.

Get this over with? It wasn't over. He'd started something he didn't have a clue how to finish.

She didn't act coy or play dumb or try to put all the responsibility for what had happened onto him. He recognized and appreciated that, even as his body screamed in frustration.

"Well." Meeting his eyes, she took another shaky breath. "You think those stories about frustrated widows are true after all?"

Under the bravado, he thought he heard a need for reassurance. He shrugged slightly. "I don't know. You do this kind of thing often?"

She pressed her lips together. "No. Never."

"Then I guess they're not."

She nodded, her gaze dropping again.

After another pause, he asked, "You want to tell me what you think is going on here?"

Her shoulders moved in feminine parody of his. "I don't know. I'm not interested in—"

In you, he thought she was about to say, but she discarded the lie.

"—in a relationship. I've given up on true love and happily ever after."

Matt squashed the faint sting of rejection, the unreasonable yearning for something he couldn't have and told himself he wasn't looking for. "Okay by me," he said. "How do you feel about a quick, cheap thrill?"

She smiled even as she shook her head. "I don't think that's a good idea for me right now."

"So, where do we go from here?" he asked.

"We don't," she said, and turned away.

Matt rubbed the back of his neck. She was right. He wasn't about to change his ways, and she was obviously set in hers. But all the same, he felt a moment's regret that the crusading widow wasn't tempted to take on the reform of Matthew Dunn.

Chapter 6

She should have stayed home, Clare thought.

The Grace Church basement was full of people eager to meet Detective Sergeant Matthew Dunn, to eat with him and shake his hand. No one would have missed her. He certainly wouldn't have noticed her absence. If it weren't for her own inconvenient loyalty to Reverend Ray, she could be home right now sorting her socks instead of quivering at the back of the church basement like a nervous deacon.

She slipped into an empty metal folding chair, careful not to look toward the front of the room where Matt chatted with the minister. She didn't want to catch his eye, afraid she would see reflected in those dark, knowing depths the memory of their kiss.

Passionate kisses had no place in her life. Once she'd wanted love and dreamed of children. Now the idea that she could lose herself again, heart and pride and purpose, to a man who could get shot at, scared her silly.

To steady herself, she breathed in the aromas of fried chicken and seven-can casserole, of corn bread and collards, that drifted through the basement, masking the faint scent of mildew and industrial cleaner. The reverend's congregation, fresh out of the eleven o'clock Sunday service, filled the rows of folding chairs. Old men in jackets, young men in ties, and girls with beautifully braided hair provided a foil for the blooming print dresses of the older women. Toddlers ran along the sides of the room and ducked under the long tables.

Clare's gaze traveled over the other neighborhood residents sitting in silent family groups or leaning alone against the cinder block walls. She recognized Mr. and Mrs. Rodriguez, who owned the laundromat, and Lester Lewis, who slept sometimes at the Baptist shelter and sometimes in the park. A good, representative turnout, she thought.

Pleating the soft folds of her denim jumper in her lap, she finally allowed herself to look toward the informal podium where Matt stood beside Reverend Ray. Looming large in his dark blue uniform, the police officer dominated the hall. This was the first time she'd seen him in anything but jeans. The crisp, tailored shirt fit closely to his broad shoulders and the long line of his waist. The creased pants hugged his hips. He looked every inch a cop. Maybe it was the shine on his shoes or his air of watchful authority. Or maybe it was the gun on his hip.

Clare gripped her hands together in her lap. He was a dangerous man in a hazardous profession. For her own peace of mind, she should avoid him like bean weevils or blight.

He bent his dark head to hear what the preacher was saying, and his slow grin loosed something warm and liquid that seeped under her breastbone and moved in a flood through her lower body.

Something she thought she'd dammed up and was done with.

Attraction, she named it, refusing to acknowledge it as anything more. Desire.

But it was more. She was drawn to the compassion she sensed beneath Matt's tough-guy exterior, the sensitivity she was sure he'd deny. She thought of his patience with Richie

and Tyler, his obvious ties to his ex-partner Will, the flat ret-
icence in his voice when she'd probed about his family. What
old hurts did he hide beneath that neatly pressed uniform and
blinding smile?

Reverend Ray wrapped up his introduction. Matt began to
speak, surprisingly forthright, compelling and clear. He might
not want to baby-sit bad guys, Clare thought, but he made a
convincing public case for the resident officer program.

"...aimed at creating a more trusting relationship between
the police and the community," he was saying in his deep,
easy voice. "While this area will still be served by precinct
patrols, you should consider me on call twenty-four hours a
day. You have my number. Use it."

Did she imagine it? Or did he, for a moment, look directly
at her?

A young mother in the row ahead elbowed her neighbor.
"I'd sure like to have him place *me* under house arrest," she
whispered.

"Mm. He can holster his gun at my place anytime."

Shameless, Clare thought. Not that the same notion hadn't
occurred to her. She wiped her palms on her skirt.

Matt continued. "And in addition to meeting with volunteers to set up a neighborhood crime watch, I'd like to work
with existing organizations to improve neighborhood pride.
Yard cleanups, removal of graffiti, that sort of thing."

Oh, yes, he was definitely looking at her. She put up her
chin and stared steadily back.

"Any questions?"

She could think of several. Like, did he really believe his
appropriate little speeches? Could he be so persuasive if he
didn't? His words revealed another side of him, a side she
could easily admire, of a man determined to do his duty
whether he found it personally agreeable or not. His attitude
seemed so at odds with his earlier weary cynicism. Was he
that good a cop or just that good an actor?

He answered a question about door locks and security lights
and another about block captains. He waited. If the lack of

response from his audience surprised or disappointed him, he didn't let on.

"Then, if that's all—" the killer smile flashed "—I won't keep you from this delicious lunch that you've prepared."

Reverend Ray stood and frowned over the tops of his glasses at the people sitting in the front rows of folding chairs. "We all want to thank you, Sergeant, for your time and your presence here among us. I'm sure many of us will want to speak with you while we share our meal."

Admonished, his congregation clapped politely. And they did come forward, Clare noted later as she filled a paper plate. A few older men shook Matt's hand, and Letitia Johnson, Richie's grandmother, patted it. A few folks, hesitant about casting blame in their pastor's hearing, sought out the cop to air old neighborhood gripes. Clare wondered how Matt would sort out the grudges from the genuine complaints.

It was none of her business what he did.

Yet she couldn't help noticing his patience with an elderly lady's grievance against her neighbor's dog, or his alert attention to an angry young man's charge of being hassled on the street. His respectful public manner was very attractive, she admitted. No wonder the reverend liked him. She did, too. That didn't mean she was running for president of the Matt Dunn Fan Club.

Bypassing a three-layered gelatin mold, she helped herself to Alma's fried chicken and a few spears of spicy dilly beans. At least tonight she wouldn't have to cook.

"Reverend Ray thinks you're a natural to head the Neighborhood Pride committee," Matt's brown velvet voice said behind her.

Her heart skipped. Her hormone level jumped. Discomfort over her unreliable, undeniable response made her tart. "Find yourself another volunteer, cowboy."

He shook his head, reaching around her to ladle potato salad on his already loaded plate. He came close; stayed close. She could smell the starch of his shirt and the clean, male scent of his skin. "Can't do that. The whole thing's your fault. You planted the idea, anyway, with that stuff you stuck around my porch.''

''Hosta and daylilies,'' she corrected him, and recognized her error when his eyes gleamed. With his cop's memory and his detective's eye for detail, he would have remembered what she planted. He was just yanking her chain.

''I'm too busy,'' she said.

He ignored her, snagging a slab of corn bread to balance on top of a mound of greens. ''I thought we'd start with that empty lot on Alston and Magnolia. The house was confiscated and razed in a drug shutdown a couple years back. I can get the city to loan us a Dumpster. I'll organize the cleanup, and you can handle the landscaping. Might be nice to put a playground in over there, a ball park or something.''

She liked the idea. She was impressed by his initiative, pleased by his thoughtful response to the needs of the children in the community. Determined to resist his attraction, she frowned anyway. ''Alston and Magnolia? I was negotiating to purchase that for garden space.''

He heaped barbecue on his sagging plate. ''Oh, yeah? Well, they might let you have it. Of course, you turn everything over to cabbages, the kids aren't going to have any place to play.''

''Better cabbages than crack dealers,'' Clare retorted.

''Well, there's one thing we can agree on.''

Before she'd grasped his intention, he'd taken her elbow and steered her gently to a couple of vacant chairs. Pulling one away from the wall, he lowered himself into it and stretched his right leg in front of him, effectively cutting off her escape.

''So, what's going on at the lot?'' he asked.

She wasn't sure if she was flattered by his concern or irritated by his technique. Maybe both, she admitted. Maybe some deeply ingrained genetic code made her respond to his overly protective Neanderthal attitude.

''I'm sure you've seen the team tilling,'' she said. ''Snow peas are going in this week.''

''What else?''

"Sugar snaps," she offered, knowing that wasn't what he wanted.

He grunted. "How's security?"

She crumbled a biscuit. She didn't want him to think it was anything she couldn't handle. In spite of his Mr. Public Service image today, she couldn't be sure the threat of danger wouldn't bring him stomping across the street, playing policeman to her kids, antagonizing her crews. "No problems."

He munched coleslaw, waiting.

Her appetite faded under his skeptical regard. "All right. We've had a few incidents of minor vandalism. Nothing terrible."

"Property damage?"

"Some," she admitted. "Split hoses, some torn bags of fertilizer, that sort of thing."

"Knife, probably. Did you report it?"

Clare sucked in an annoyed breath. He knew darn well she hadn't. "No. What would be the point? I'm not going to file an insurance claim, and the police aren't going to be able to catch whoever's responsible."

"No witnesses?"

"No. No one's seen a thing. The day care classes are there in the afternoon, and I'm right next door at night. You're across the street, and you haven't seen anything."

He tore the meat off a drumstick and studied the bone. A week ago, she might have thought he was just hungry. A week ago, his good ol' boy manner might have tricked her into relaxing her guard. She knew better now. She braced for his next question.

"Be hard for a stranger to do much under those circumstances," he observed. "Have you considered your culprit is someone who works for you?"

"Of course I've considered it. But no one I've hired is going to jeopardize his paycheck or sabotage his job by striking at the project."

He raised his brows in silent challenge.

"It just doesn't make sense," she insisted. "Besides, there's never been any trouble in the mornings when the team is at the lot.''

''You could hire a watchman.''

''If I could afford one.''

His thumb rubbed his jaw. She caught the scent of his aftershave. ''So, you got a dog instead?''

''You don't miss much, do you?'' Clare asked ruefully.

''Yeah, I've got my binoculars trained on your place day and night.''

His dry response made her smile and then blush.

''Where'd you get the mutt?'' Matt asked.

''Richie found it yesterday in the alley behind the Shop-N-Go.''

He started to grin. ''And conned you into taking it?''

''Only temporarily,'' she said defensively. ''If its owner can't be located, or a permanent home found, I'll have to call animal control.''

His big hands folded the edges of his empty plate together. ''I'd figured you'd be a sucker for a homeless dog.''

It was ridiculous to feel guilty. ''I don't have time for a dog. I don't know anything about dogs. And I don't want the responsibilities of a pet.''

''So, you'll take care of it only as long as you don't have to actually care about it, is that it?''

Stung, she glared at him. ''Would you adopt an animal you didn't know and didn't want, just because it needed a home?''

''I might. I'll take a closer look at it, anyway.'' He motioned toward the meal on her lap. ''Aren't you hungry?''

''Not any more.''

The response sounded childish, even to her.

He held out his hand for her plate. ''Might as well go now, then.''

Confused, she trailed him to the big plastic garbage can set by the doors. ''Go where?''

He tossed her lunch away. ''To look at your pup.''

''You're serious.''

He looked almost as surprised as she felt. "Yeah. I guess I am."

Richie had accompanied them from the church, eager to show off his find.

Matt shook his head. "That is the ugliest mutt I have ever seen."

The sound of his voice, too deep and unfamiliar, sent the half-grown dog scrambling to its feet in the shade of the shed. Its tail tucked tight between skinny haunches and its floppy ears pressed back, the dog's wide, anxious eyes darted from Clare to the boy. Somebody—Richie, probably, Matt thought—had put a cheap nylon collar on the dog and fashioned an impromptu leash of rope. A frayed section a few feet down testified that the pooch had its own ideas about being tied, but it made no attempt to growl at them, attack or run away.

"No damn good as a guard dog, either, I take it."

"He's still real young," Richie said in the dog's defense.

"And friendly," Clare added in an amused tone as the pup sidled forward.

Somewhere on the walk from the hall, she'd regained her usual sociable composure. Matt wasn't sure if the attitude was for his benefit or the kid's, but he thought he preferred her ruffled. It wasn't Saint Joan he'd held in his arms the other night, and he didn't want her to forget it.

"Swell." Matt started to hunker down. His torn thigh muscles warned against it. To cover his start of pain, he asked Richie, "What's its name?"

The boy looked at Clare.

"Trigger," she replied.

"Trigger?" The dog wagged its tail uncertainly. What a mutt. What a name. "Why Trigger?"

She elevated her pretty little nose and explained. "On TV. The dog who was always rescuing people."

He spared her a pitying glance. "You're thinking Rin Tin Tin. Trigger was Roy Rogers' horse."

Richie snickered. "Maybe we shoulda named him Lassie."

Matt grinned. "Or Silver."

Lightly, Clare cuffed the back of the boy's head, knocking his baseball cap down on his nose.

"Do I need this from you?" she asked no one in particular.

"Sugar," Matt said, "you have no idea what you need."

"Don't ride me, cowboy," she warned.

His throat went dry. He'd like to. Oh, but he'd like to. Not that he could say so in front of the kid.

Clare, meeting his eyes, suddenly blushed. Matt grinned and extended one hand to the dog.

The ugly dog. He frowned. Starved, too. Gently, he grasped its lower jaw. "Hey, Trigger. Hey, boy."

The thin tail stirred. A doggy tongue brushed his fingers.

God. A dog. He didn't have room for a dog in his life.

He looked up at Clare, but she was watching Richie, parallel lines of concern etched between her brows. Wasn't that what she had claimed? No room, no time. No claims, no responsibilities. He knew the song. Hell, he'd sung it himself. And yet he wanted to do something to shake that tidy little box she lived in. Hey, it was just a dog.

"I think it's some kind of shepherd-boxer mix," he said.

"Is that good?" Richie wanted to know.

"Depends." Matt's fingers worked the loose skin on the dog's neck, finding the exact spot that made it close its eyes in pleasure. "You want a dog that eats like a horse and poops like an elephant, yeah, it's great."

"Grandma says we can't keep it in the apartment. Even a small dog. They got a rule against pets."

He tendered this information in the matter-of-fact tone of a kid who wants something desperately and has learned too young that life doesn't always answer your dreams.

"Tough," Matt sympathized.

"Course, if you was to take him, I could visit," Richie offered casually. "Walk him for you, maybe."

The words reverberated in Matt's skull like an echo from childhood. *Can I come, Dad? I won't be any trouble. Maybe you could give me something to do.* And his dad, most often refusing, letting him sometimes come along. Off duty in the patrol car. To the station on a weekend. Little things, little times, important to a kid.

It wasn't going to kill him to look after one dog, Matt rationalized. After all, a dog wasn't a family. A dog didn't worry about you when you were late on the job. A dog didn't wonder and wait for a phone call to tell it whether you were coming back alive or already dead. A dog—especially a dog like this, a dog who'd been around—would take the little he had to give and be grateful for it. Food and shelter, that's all a dog wanted.

And the kid could walk him.

"Yeah, sure, why not?" He looked up again at Clare to find her clear, whiskey-colored eyes soft and glowing. They made him feel good. Too good, maybe, but he'd worry about that later.

"Guess we've got ourselves a dog."

He was flat on his back with his legs in the air, but he wasn't having any fun at all.

Grunting, Matt slowly lowered his feet to the floor, counting to distract himself from the pain.

"...two, three, four—damn it, Trigger!"

The dog sprang back as Matt's legs crashed to the floor. Wiping drool from his face, he glared at the mutt.

"Stupid animal."

Encouraged, the dog wagged its tail.

"Yeah, yeah. Time for your walk. Richie's late today, huh?"

Trigger's thin ears cocked and flopped forward. Matt knew the dog couldn't understand a damn word he said, but its eagerness made him smile.

"No fun being cooped up in the house, is it? Bet we're both used to more action. What do you say we call Kelton and put in for an early transfer?"

God. Matt laid his head down on the floor in disgust. Now he was having heart-to-hearts with a dog. This place was getting to him. That woman was getting to him. Maybe he *should* call the department, check in with the chief, talk to Johnson or Dingle or somebody, anybody, before he forgot he belonged in the detective division, not playing at crime prevention on the southeast side.

He rolled to his side and levered himself up, swiping the towel from the floor to rub over his face and chest. Trigger padded behind him into the kitchen, nails clicking on the linoleum.

Matt punched the number in from memory.

The desk sergeant answered the phone. "Operations. Officer Cowper."

The dog's water bowl was empty, Matt noticed. He filled it at the tap. "Hey, Tom. Matt Dunn. I've got to invoice some stuff to the department. Peggy in?"

As he bent to set down the bowl, Trigger panted gratefully in his ear.

"Sure, Matt. How's it—You got somebody with you? Grabbing a little R and R, you lucky dog?"

"*Dog*'s the operative word, Tom."

"That's no way to talk about one of your ladies, Matt."

Matt straightened, rubbing the back of his neck. The desk sergeant had met Marcia, he remembered. Amy, too. "Dog, Cowper. D-O-G. Three letters, four legs, one bite. Give me to Peggy."

"A real dog? You starting a K-9 corps now you're living on the mean streets?"

"You're a riot, Tom. The most excitement I've had this week was a picnic supper in the church basement."

Cowper laughed. "I hear you. For a minute there I thought you were so hard up you were calling about your little car thieves."

Matt's neck prickled as if he were going down a dark alley with no backup. "What car thieves?"

"Those kids. I thought you knew."

His apprehension grew. "If I knew, I wouldn't be asking. Give it up, Cowper. What kids?"

"Christ, Matt, I can't remember the names. Boothe, I think it was. And Johnny Something. No, it was Something Johnson. Know 'em?"

His gut tightened. Tyler and Richie. Which could mean Clare was involved. He fought the flicker of panic. You're a cop, he thought. Get the facts.

"Yeah," he said, keeping his voice casual with an effort. "Yeah, I know them. Threat or assault?"

"Nope. Nonviolent felony. Stewart made the collar."

Relief eased the knot in his gut. Nonviolent was good. Nonviolent meant she wasn't hurt, that Richie had been stupid but not necessarily insane. He'd go down there and make sure the kid was all right, and then he'd bust his butt.

"Parents notified?" he asked.

"As near as. One kid's father, and a grandma. Someone's bringing her in."

"Okay. Do me a favor, would you? Hold the Johnson kid 'til I get there."

"Sure thing, Supercop."

Matt hung up and swore. Trigger looked at him with anxious eyes.

"It's okay," he reassured the dog, trying, against all reason and experience, to believe it. "We'll get him home."

In spite of some trouble operating the clutch, he made it to the station in under twelve minutes. He went in through the police entrance, acknowledging the friendly greetings and ribald jokes on his way to the desk sergeant. God, he wished Will were with him. He needed his ex-partner's patience. On his own, Matt was jumpy as a rodeo bull, all anxious, angry energy with no real place to go.

But it felt good to be back, all the same. Cowper was forthcoming. Within fifteen minutes, Matt learned that Richie and the Boothe kid were being held in separate interview rooms with attendant adults present. Patrol Officer Stewart and the juvenile detective assigned to the case roved between them, asking questions. The junior court counselor had been notified.

Stewart came out, came over. Matt knew the patrolman. A

good uniform cop, levelheaded and thorough. Richie was lucky.

"Sergeant," Stewart said, shaking hands. "Good to see you back. I hear you have an interest in the Johnson boy."

Matt appreciated the patrol officer's attitude. "Yeah. Thanks. I don't want to step on any toes here, though. It's your case."

"Yeah, but it's your watch. I understand. And you got to live with Dragon Lady afterward, right?"

Suspicion tightened the knot at the back of Matt's neck. Stewart couldn't mean... "Dragon Lady?"

The officer jerked his head toward the narrow hallway that led to the interview rooms. "Miz Harmon. She drove Richie Johnson's grandmother in."

Chapter 7

Clare. Matt's gut roiled. Not twenty minutes ago, he'd been thanking the saints she wasn't involved in this mess. So, why couldn't she keep her pretty little nose out of it? He'd warned her not to get mixed up with the Boothe kid.

"Is she all right?"

Stewart looked surprised. "Her? Oh, absolutely. She's been real insistent that the rights of the juvenile offender be observed."

"Yeah, I'll bet." In spite of his anger, he smiled some as he exchanged a long, silent look of masculine understanding with Stewart. Saint Joan was obviously back in the saddle and riding to the rescue. "You want me to talk to her?"

"Thanks, Sarge. That'd be good."

Matt wasn't so sure. His first sight of her, primly upright on a bench in the hall, filled him with a combustible mixture of relief and longing, irritation and respect. One wrong word from her, and he'd blow up like a homemade bomb.

Her red-gold hair was bright against the dingy green walls and disheveled where she'd run her hands through it. He re-

membered the feel of it in his fingers, baby-fine, baby-soft.
She didn't belong here, he thought, propping up the grimy
station house walls on behalf of some thankless punk.

And yet by some combination of charm and determination,
she'd finagled her way to the interview room. Department reg-
ulations had stumped her just outside the door. She hadn't
managed to wangle her way inside.

Yet, Matt thought wryly, both exasperated and admiring.

"Matt!" Her eyes lit when she saw him. "I'm so glad
you're here. They won't let me in to see Richie."

Her total focus on the kid made a mockery of Matt's un-
voiced concern, his unacknowledged desire. The need to silence them both, to stifle the hot churning in his gut, made
him snap.

"Why should they? You're not his mother."

He watched her draw back, her slim shoulders squaring.
"Very astute, cowboy. Is that the kind of shrewd observation
they're teaching in police academy these days?"

God, she was a pistol, Matt thought, torn between laughing
and shaking her. Of course, he could do neither. No wonder
Stewart had accepted backup.

"Only in the detective division, sugar."

Her ready flush swept up. He wanted to brush the back of
his fingers over her cheek, to feel the smoothness and test the
warmth.

He stuck his hands in his pockets. "I talked to the arresting
officer. Pending the investigation, they'll release Richie into
his grandmother's custody. You'll be able to go home real
soon."

Instead of thanking him, she shook her head. "What about
Tyler?"

"Tyler's none of your business. You shouldn't waste your
time on a kid like that."

She stood, crossing her arms under her small breasts.
Damned if he knew another woman as attractive. Or as annoying.

"I can't believe I'm hearing this. He's a child."

He was a threat to her. But Matt couldn't make her see that. "He's a punk."

"He's my employee."

"So, fire him."

"I will not."

Matt made a grab for his patience. He could sympathize—just—with Clare's concern for Richie. But the Boothe kid—a Viper—Eddie Boothe's cousin! He didn't understand that at all.

"You can't want this kid around. We're talking no respect for property rights here. He stole a car."

"That hasn't been proven."

"There are witnesses, Clare. He's a criminal."

Unexpectedly, her smile glimmered. "Not a very successful one, apparently. I think he's going to need to find another line of work. And I can provide one."

Matt rubbed the back of his neck. He'd coped with well-intentioned interference from members of the public before. The important thing was not to lose his cool. But when he looked at Clare, reasoning and training flew out the window, and an irrational, unprofessional desire to grab her and stow her safely away seized his gut and squeezed his chest. He couldn't explain the feeling. Didn't want to examine it too closely. But there it was, and he was going to have to deal with it.

And so, he thought grimly, was she.

"You gave him his chance. He blew it."

"Then I'll give him another one. Everyone deserves a second chance."

He let his glance linger pointedly on her mouth. "I'll have to remember that."

Her eyes widened at his sexual implication. Good, he thought. At least he had her attention now.

But before she could respond—if she was going to respond—the door to the interview room opened and Richie and his grandmother came out.

Clare took a step forward, her shoulder brushing Matt's.

Warmth jolted through her at the casual contact. She ignored it.

He was no use to her at all, she thought indignantly. She pushed from memory the rush of relief she'd felt at that first sight of his tall, commanding figure, the bump of her heart when his gaze burned her mouth. Since his arrival, he'd proven himself totally unsympathetic, completely uncooperative, every inch the unbending officer of the law.

Poor Richie.

The boy slunk out of the interview room, chin to chest, eyeing Matt with the same hopeful, wary look she was sure she'd worn herself. Seeking comfort. Wanting rescue.

Clare pressed her lips together. Well, they were going to have to manage on their own, because the big, bad detective wasn't here to rescue anybody. He was here to kick some butt.

But even as she thought that, even as she reached to tug on the brim of Richie's cap and fuss with the shoulders of his jacket, Matt moved smoothly in front of her to take Letitia Johnson's arm.

"Ma'am? How are you doing?"

Clare stopped at his warm, reassuring tone.

Letitia's tired face creased in a smile. "Sergeant Dunn. That other policeman, he told me you were here."

"Yes, ma'am. Did he also tell you you can go home?"

Her troubled gaze sought her grandson's face. "For now, he said."

"Two to four weeks. Until the court date is set," Matt said calmly.

Clare admired his honesty as well as his support, but Letitia wasn't satisfied.

"And then what?" she demanded. "Sergeant Dunn, what's going to happen to my boy? I told him to stay away from that Tyler. I told him to listen to Miss Clare. They tell me he's got to stay with me and mind me, and I can't get him to mind. He—"

"You leave Richie to me," Matt interrupted her. "Let's just get the two of you home now."

Letitia nodded, resting her birdlike arm on his massive one.

"I can take her," Clare intervened.

"Fine. Richie can ride with me." Matt's black eyes met hers in pure challenge. "It'll give us a chance to talk."

She felt the heat in him. In spite of his controlled gentleness with Richie's grandmother, she guessed Matt wouldn't be kind. Beside her, Richie shrank deeper into his oversize jacket. Clare's own stomach contracted in sympathy. No, she thought. Absolutely not. No way was she trusting Matt to deal with eleven-year-old Richie until he'd had the chance to cool down. She opened her mouth to tell him so, but he was already addressing the boy, speaking over her head.

"The dog was expecting you," he said evenly. "At three."

Richie's head dropped even further. "Oh, man," he muttered.

"You let him down." Matt waited a beat. "You let both of us down."

"It wasn't my fault!" Richie burst out. "Tyler, he said the car belonged to his cousin. I didn't know. We were just gonna sit in it, he said."

"Was that before or after he wired it?"

Richie screwed his cap around in an agony of unexpressed remorse. "He said he couldn't find the keys. I thought it belonged to his cousin."

Clare's compassionate heart twisted, remembering a time when she had been similarly deluded and similarly blind. She felt again the guilt that ate at her after Paul's unexpected murder. You didn't see what you didn't want to know.

"It's all right," she said. "You don't have to explain."

"Not to me," Matt agreed readily. "Of course, Officer Stewart is going to want some answers. I'm sure the judge will be interested in your explanation when the time comes. And Trigger…how are you going to make it right with him, Richie? You can't explain it to him. He's just a dog."

"I'll walk him when we get back," Richie said eagerly. "Twice, if you want. I'll walk him tonight."

"No."

Richie blinked at the soft, implacable reply. "It's no trouble. I can do it. That policeman, he didn't say I had curfew or anything. Grandma, tell him I can do it."

"No," Matt repeated. "You can come visit the dog after school, same as before. But I'll have to take over the walking chores for a while. I need to be able to rely on you, Richie. Until I can, you'll see Trigger once a day, in the yard."

Even as sympathy for the boy stirred inside her, Clare recognized the justice of Matt's decision. He made Richie's punishment a direct consequence of his choice not to come home. Maybe it was the kind of call good cops made all the time, but still, Clare admired Matt's judgment. A child learned to value fairness in an adult.

She caught herself wondering if Matt had learned his tempered judgment from his own father and shook her head at her foolish abstraction. His parenting skills or lack of them were none of her business. All that mattered was that Richie live with the ban and learn from it.

Even Trigger wouldn't suffer from Matt's ruling. The only one inconvenienced, she suspected, would be Matt himself. Could he even walk the dog with his wounded leg?

"Is that a good idea?" she asked.

He propped against the wall, lifting one eyebrow. "Are you telling me who can walk my dog now?"

"No. It's just—"

"Not volunteering to do it yourself?"

"Hardly. But—"

"Then you'll have to leave this one to me and Richie."

"I just thought—"

He leaned closer, speaking low. Her heart skipped to her throat as his broad shoulders swooped over her, shielding their conversation from Richie and his grandmother.

"Maybe this time I don't care what you think. He acted impulsively, you said last time. He's sorry, you said. He won't do it again." She could feel his breath warm on her face, smell his soap and sweat and coffee. "Well, sugar, we all need to learn to control our impulses. Maybe you don't think much of me or my way of doing things, but taking away something the kid values is the only way I know to help him do it.''

Driven on the defensive by his unexpected criticism, Clare snapped, "Fine. Maybe the badass cop routine will work with Richie. I've got to tell you it doesn't do a thing for me."

Too late, she realized she'd been overheard. Matt's fellow officer—Stewart, was it?—stood just behind him. She bit her lip. Following the line of her gaze, Matt turned.

The patrolman cleared his throat, stepping back. "When you've got a minute, Sergeant, Lieutenant would like to see you."

Matt nodded. He waited for the officer to leave before he said quietly to Clare, "If I were trying to impress you, sugar, I might be upset by that remark. But I'm just trying to do my job."

He pushed away from the wall, away from her. "Take the kid home, if you want. I've got things to do here."

Matt turned the corner at Magnolia and Vine.

Right on time, Clare thought. In the three weeks since Richie's arrest, she'd learned Matt's schedule by heart.

She straightened from the rows of new peas, one hand to her back, one shielding her eyes from the afternoon sun. Isaac, uncharacteristically, had failed to show for work that morning, and she was thinning the rows with a skeleton crew. She watched Matt come down the street, moving stiffly because it was the end of his walk and slowly because his dog stuck its nose in every drooping bush and discarded candy wrapper along the way. In black boots and jeans and a gray police department T-shirt, he looked like a gunslinger hired to tame the town. He was still too far away for her to read his face, but she could see the effort in his stride and the tension in his shoulders. Her heart tightened at the subtle signs of pain.

A little girl with neat black braids skipped out from her beaten clay yard. At her approach, the dog wagged its tail, and Matt stopped and smiled. And his flashing grin shattered his big, bad image and made him infinitely more dangerous to her heart.

Slowly, Clare lowered her arm, still squinting into the sun. She'd told him—she'd told herself—she wasn't interested in a relationship. She wasn't compromising her hard-won independence with another take-charge law enforcement type. She was afraid to risk her heart on a man whose job put him in danger. She didn't want to get hurt again.

But she found now she was hurting anyway. It hurt to see Matt and never talk to him. It hurt to have him think badly of her.

Movement behind her snapped her attention back to the lot. Isaac slunk along the chain-link fence on the far side, shoulders hunched and navy cap pulled low against the sun. He staggered in the soft-tilled soil, regaining his balance with difficulty.

Drunk, Clare thought, her stomach sinking with a weight of sorrow and anger. If he were high, he'd lack the judgment to avoid her. She pressed her lips together. She liked Isaac—depended on him, really—but she was going to have to bust him. It was hard enough to get her crews to report to work sober and on time without the crew chief setting a bad example.

She set her shoulders, wiped her palms on her jeans, and strode across the lot. "Isaac! I want to talk to you."

Work stopped on the lot. Isaac stiffened in the thin strip of shadow cast by the shed.

Reaching his side, Clare dropped her voice, mindful of listening ears. "Do you want to tell me what the hell you think— Oh, dear Lord."

He'd been roughed up. Beaten. Beneath the rolled brim of his navy knit cap, a cut slashed his eyebrow. The eye itself was swollen almost shut. A gash at the corner of his mouth cracked and bled. He'd made some attempt to clean himself up, she could see that now. White wrapped his knuckles, and his face was clean. But nothing could disguise the rising bruises.

She gripped his forearm. Which one of them she hoped to support with her gesture, she couldn't have said. "Are you all right?"

"Yeah."

"Have you seen a doctor?"

He attempted a smile. Winced. "Don't need one."

"What happened?" He didn't answer. Frustrated, like a mother whose child has run into the street, she shook his arm. "Who did this to you?"

He dropped his head. "Don't know."

He was lying.

"Isaac..." she appealed.

He raised his eyes to return her gaze steadily. "Can't say," he corrected himself.

Clare sighed in defeat. "Oh, Isaac."

She glanced up the street. Matt, having finished his dialogue with the little girl in purple barrettes, had resumed his slow, uneven progress along the sidewalk. She felt a peculiar pang when he crossed to the other side. To avoid her, she supposed. Since their encounter at the police station three weeks ago, they'd barely spoken.

She didn't want to gamble what was left of her life on a man like Matt. But having seen his expert handling of Richie and his grandmother, she was prepared to trust him now.

Impulsively, she shouted across the street.

"Matt! Got a minute?"

Matt stiffened. He'd known all along she was there, watching him, weighing him with her clear brown eyes and finding him wanting. The hell with that. He'd known all along a woman like her had no place in her life for a man like him. He let Trigger get a good snoutful of whatever fascinated him under the bush before he turned, slowly.

Mistake. She was too close, too fast. He had no time to prepare a defense against her. She came up smelling of dirt and tender growing things, and her freckles danced across her nose, and the sun on her hair dazzled him.

"Clare," he acknowledged cautiously.

Trigger woofed an exuberant greeting, his thin tail whipping his haunches. Clare knelt, covering the awkward moment by fussing over the dog. When she looked up, her face was pink from pleasure or embarrassment.

Or stooping, Matt reminded himself, trying to rein in his overactive imagination.

"We've got a problem," she said, in that blunt, warm way of hers that alternately tickled and irritated the hell out of him. "Can you come talk to Isaac?"

She didn't want the man. She needed the cop. It was a change from the usual reaction he got from women, Matt reflected. Before he could decide how he felt about it, his training took over.

"Sure," he said easily. "What's up?"

She pushed to her feet. "He won't tell me."

"Okay. Let's see if he'll talk under the bright lights and rubber hoses."

She checked in the middle of the street.

"Joke," Matt explained.

She tilted that little nose of hers in the air, making him grin. "I knew that."

But one look at Isaac's face dispatched the smile. *Damn.* Someone had made one hell of a point with his fists.

"Isaac." The crew chief nodded warily. Matt tried the most nonthreatening approach he could think of. "You want a ride to the ER? I've got the hospital route memorized."

"Naw. Thanks. I'm okay."

"Yeah, I can see that," Matt said dryly. "But you might want to have a doctor take a look at that eye."

Isaac reached a cautious hand up to his oozing eyebrow. "And take pictures, right?"

Police procedure called for two sets of color photographs after an assault, one taken right after the crime was reported, and one three days later, when the extent of the injuries could be clearly seen.

"Might be a good idea," Matt acknowledged.

Isaac shook his head.

"You file a report?" Another shake. Matt wondered if Isaac was in trouble with the law, or in trouble with people who scared him worse than cops. Vipers? His gut clenched at the thought of the gang striking so close to Clare. "You know who did this? Or why?"

A sidelong look this time before Isaac answered, "N-noo."

There was enough hesitation in his voice this time to give Matt some hope. "Okay. You change your mind, you let me know."

Isaac nodded. "Thought I'd take that mulch over to the lot on Dennison," he told Clare.

"All right," Clare said, looking worried. "Take George with you to help unload."

She waited until he was out of earshot before she rounded on Matt. "That's it? Is that all you can do?"

He hated to disappoint her, but the sooner she accepted the reality of his job, and the limits of his abilities, the better. He would ask around, call the department, even look for witnesses. But Supercop was a myth. "Unless he's willing to admit that an offense took place or give up a motive or identity, yeah."

Those wide, considering eyes regarded him a moment longer, and then she nodded abruptly. "All right. Thank you for trying. And for showing up in juvenile court the other day. It meant a lot to Richie, your speaking up for him like that."

At her praise, he shifted uncomfortably. "As long as it meant something to the judge."

"It did. Without your supervision, I'm sure the judge would have assigned a longer probation."

Her candid, warm regard did something funny to the cold, tight places inside him. He'd been better off when she thought he was a shmuck. He shrugged. "Whatever. What about Tyler? He giving you any problems?"

In court that Monday, Clare had promised the Boothe kid continued "gainful employment," one of the conditions of his twelve-month probation. Another mistake, in Matt's opinion, but that time the judge hadn't listened to him.

"No," Clare said firmly. "And he won't."

"Must be nice to be sure."

She gave him her Joan of Arc look, and Matt bit back a grin. He didn't much want to interrogate Isaac or make small talk about Terrible Tyler and his problems, he realized. He wanted to kiss her again.

"No more vandalism?"

"Not as much," she said guardedly. "Having the day care on the lot in the afternoons is helping. And your patrols with the dog. I must watch you go by three times a day."

And then she blushed to the tips of her delicate ears, as if she'd just admitted to spying on him naked. Well, well, thought Matt, with masculine satisfaction.

She looked away. "I'm pretty sure the problems we were having were just caused by kids in need of supervision."

He would have envied her positive attitude if he hadn't been so certain it was going to get her hurt. "Not delinquents in need of the business end of a hairbrush?"

That brought her head back around. "My parents never spanked me."

He snorted. "Probably afraid you'd break. There were three big boys in our family."

"And your father hit you with a brush?" She sounded scandalized.

With an effort, he kept the amusement from his voice. "Naw. Dad used the flat of his hand, always. Mom used the brush."

"My parents—" She stopped.

Something in that bright, well-brought-up face nagged at him. Something eating her. Cop's instincts.

"Your parents..." he prompted.

"It doesn't matter."

"Probably not," he agreed. "So, why not tell me?"

"Oh..." She ran slender fingers through her hair. "My parents didn't believe in corporal punishment. Mother would just get this displeased look on her face, and Daddy would go on and on at the dinner table in this very low voice about how disappointed he was, and I'd want to die.''

She'd done the expected thing all her life, she said. And it hadn't been enough for her. He studied her straight, gallant little figure, the lines of laughter around her mouth and the sadness in her eyes, and had to jam his hands in his back pockets to keep from touching her.

"I'd rather get belted," he said.

He saw the shock pass quickly across her face and then her eyes danced.

"Yes," she said. "So would I."

Matt looked over her head at the curving red rows of clay and the green shoots pushing through the earth. He tried to fit her presence in the neighborhood with what he knew of her background, with the indefinable privilege that still clung to her posture and voice. It didn't square.

"So, how do your folks feel about their daughter digging in the dirt in southeast Buchanan?"

"They hate it," she answered promptly. "They think I'm throwing my life away on these kids."

"Aren't you?"

"No." Her voice was so low, he had to bend to hear. "This project *is* my life now. These kids are my reason for living."

The funny crack she'd opened in his chest yawned into a chasm that threatened to swallow him whole. Matt stepped back in alarm. He tried for a teasing reply, but it came out more harshly than he intended.

"If you can call what you're doing living."

Her eyes narrowed at his attempted humor. "Do you want to explain that remark or take it back?"

He almost apologized. That alone told him how far gone he was. "Well, look at you." He gestured. "You hide yourself in jeans and T-shirts. You won't date. You don't drink too much. You spend your time with a preschool class, a bunch of ex-cons, a minister and an eleven-year-old boy. Your life might as well be over."

As soon as the words were out of his mouth, he wanted to kick himself.

Clare stared down her nose at him like Saint Joan finding something nasty on the bottom of her shoe. "I'll have you know my life is fine. Full. Perfect."

"Yeah? What are you doing this Saturday night?"

"Why? Are you asking me out?"

He wanted to. He fought the ricochet of panic. He was crummy at this relationship stuff. "I could be."

"Too bad. Because I can't go."

"Why not?" he asked, figuring she deserved the chance to tell him what a jerk he was.

But she was too good for that. "I have plans, as a matter of fact."

"What? You going to do your laundry? Wash your hair?"

"I'm going out, as a matter of fact."

He started to feel an entirely different sort of panic. "With a man?"

"Isn't that usual on a date?"

"I don't know what the hell is usual for you. I thought you weren't interested in a relationship."

"Maybe I've changed my mind."

His body sat up and took notice. His heart began to pound in time with the throbbing in his thigh. Wresting his mind from the image of Clare's bright, intelligent eyes cloudy with desire, he asked cautiously, "What kind of relationship?"

She looked flustered. Looked away.

He smiled, in tenderness and bitter amusement. "Yeah, that's what I thought. You're a nice girl, sugar. You've got *girlfriend* written all over you."

The chin went up. "There's nothing wrong with wanting a relationship based on shared goals, shared feelings, and good communication."

Nothing wrong except that he'd never been able to pull it off. "What about sex?"

She shook her head impatiently. "I'm talking about a partnership."

"Sugar, the nicest thing about having a partner is you don't have to talk about *feelings*. Your partner's been there. Your partner already knows."

"You're talking about your job. Your partner was a man."

"Exactly."

She pulled herself up to her full height. She maybe reached his armpit. "Are you telling me you couldn't be partners with a woman?"

Matt wasn't sure any more what he was telling her. He liked her so much, her big ideas and soft heart and fighting spirit. He didn't want her to waste herself on a guy like him. But he didn't want her thinking he was a total male chauvinist pig, either.

"No. There are some really good female detectives in the department. Marge Martinez, Shirley Dickson—I'd be proud to call either one of them my partner. It's different when it's someone you work with."

"Did you ever date one of them?"

"Yeah," he retorted. "I tried for a while with Shirley. I figured she'd understand about the job."

Her face softened slightly. "And?"

He kneaded the back of his neck. "And she broke it off. Said we were too much alike or something."

"But other women would understand. If you'd explain to them, talk to them…"

He was no damn good at it. Every time he'd tried, and he'd tried plenty, he'd failed. Sooner or later, the Marcias and the Kimberlys tossed the whole litany of complaints at his head: he was cold, he was controlling, he was preoccupied, he was a selfish bastard. Eventually, he'd stopped expecting any woman to put up with him, to put up with the late nights and broken dates and his moods coming down from a bad case. He tried to make a joke of it.

"Sugar, the last thing I want to do off duty with an attractive woman is talk."

Without meaning to, he'd hit a nerve. Her shoulders were proudly straight, her chin militantly firm. But there was a world of hurt in those grave, clear eyes, and her soft mouth trembled before she pressed her lips together.

"Don't let *me* keep you, then," she said. "I've got to get back to work."

And she pivoted on her heel and marched down the tidy rows of tiny green plants, leaving him staring after her.

Chapter 8

Matt might be no damn good at the personal relationship stuff, but he knew how to run an investigation. He left Clare's lot determined to discover who was behind the attack on Isaac.

Most assaults stemmed from obvious motives: jealousy or gain or revenge. Questioning Isaac's neighbors quickly established that the crew chief lived alone and kept to himself so it wasn't jealousy. He didn't own enough to make robbery the most probable motive, and he clearly knew his assailant, so it wasn't a case of mistaken identity. Either Isaac had witnessed or interrupted a crime, or the motive was revenge.

It had taken one quick phone call to find a past association between Clare's crew chief and the Vipers, and the better part of an afternoon to find a witness, a box boy at the overpriced corner grocery two blocks from Clare's.

"I don't want trouble," the kid kept insisting, his eyes sliding away from Matt's. "I didn't really see anything. Just that the four guys were talking before they went into the alley, and three of them were mad."

But he identified Isaac's navy knit cap, and the gang colors of his assailants. It was enough for Matt to call Stewart.

"Appreciate it, Sergeant," the beat officer said. "But if the victim won't come forward… You want a search of the crime scene?"

"Done," Matt said briefly. He'd kept his field kit with him.

Stewart chuckled. "Once a detective, huh, Sergeant? What did you get?"

Matt checked his notes. "Scuff marks, no footprints. Blood, no hair. I'm bringing in a sample, but I'm guessing it belongs to the victim. No fibers, no buttons, no weapon. Looking at his face, I'd say this was fists, anyway."

"So, what can I do for you?"

"I need an ID. I've got a description of a black male, late twenties, medium build, with an arm tattoo. Anybody you know?"

Stewart swore. "The tattoo…hooded viper, left arm?"

Anticipation kicked through Matt's system. "Snake on the left arm. Yeah."

"Maybe Eddie Boothe," Stewart said. "Released about a month ago. He'll be looking to reestablish himself on the street. I can put you in touch with his parole officer."

"I want to bring him in," Matt said. "Noncustodial witness. I want to talk to him."

"He's got an alibi," Stewart reported in disgust, coming out of the interview room. "You sure your victim won't cooperate?"

"I'm working on it," Matt said. "How tight's the alibi?"

"Tight enough. Claims he was with his girlfriend. She corroborates. Without physical evidence…"

"Understood." He was an officer of the law, sworn to uphold it. He might want to lock this yahoo up and throw away the key, but without some evidence to tie him to the crime, Eddie Boothe would walk.

Tension coiled inside Matt as he entered the small, bleak

room. The air was stale with cigarette smoke. Used butts floated in a foam cup on the table.

Boothe lounged back, his chair tipped on its rear legs. He stared insolently at Matt. "Can I go now?"

"Not yet."

"You got no call to keep me. I ain't been charged with nothing."

"Not yet," Matt agreed. He strolled forward, keeping his hands in his pockets so he wouldn't be tempted to slug the guy. "What do you know about the Neighborhood Garden Project, Eddie?"

"Nothing."

Matt hadn't expected to hear different. "How about Isaac Mills?"

Eddie fingered the writhing gold snake that dangled from his right earlobe. In prison, Matt knew, it would have been a symbol of his status, announcing to the initiated that he was a man to avoid, a man you didn't mess with. "I know lots of people."

"Yeah? Give me some names."

Boothe was silent.

"Who do you know at the project? You've got to know somebody," Matt said, probing for a response. "Your cousin works there, doesn't he?"

That earned him a glare, but didn't produce a name. Matt needed names to protect Clare. He strolled closer to the tipped up chair. "Come on, Eddie. Prison take away your memory? Or just your nerve?"

Dark eyes gleamed with malice and something else. "I know the garden lady. Candy face Clare Harmon. Like to get to know her better, too."

Anger geysered inside Matt. His foot connected with the back of Eddie's chair. It toppled. With a yelp, Eddie pumped his arms in the air to right himself. The chair's front legs crashed to the floor.

"You want to watch yourself," Matt advised softly, dangerously. "You're putting yourself in a real bad position, Eddie."

"You got no call to threaten me."

Matt raised his eyebrows. "I'm just warning you about your posture, Eddie. It's not safe to lean back like that."

"You want to talk safety? You watch your back on my turf, Mr. Police Sergeant."

"It's my turf now," Matt said. It was true. He was becoming invested in that crummy neighborhood. "I moved in right across the street from Mrs. Harmon's lot." He stepped up, lowered his voice. "Now, let me tell you something. You touch her, you come near her, you even look in her general direction, and I'm coming after you. And I'll take off my badge before I do it. Are we clear?"

"Crystal." The voice hissed disdain, but the insolent gaze dropped.

Matt stepped back, satisfied he'd made his point. Maybe he couldn't make Clare happy, but he could try to keep her safe. "Fine. Don't let me see you around, Eddie."

Clare dug through the dry-cleaning bags at the back of her closet. The silk-and-sequined relics of her life as an attorney's wife rustled like the ghosts of Christmas Parties Past.

What had she been thinking? In less than twenty minutes, one of her late husband's ex-colleagues was coming to escort her to the mayor's annual law enforcement fund-raiser. She must have been out of her mind.

Although Gary Shepard hadn't seemed to think so, she reassured herself. Maybe he'd been surprised to hear from her after she'd turned down all his invitations two years ago, but he was already planning on going to the mayor's event. No, he assured her, he didn't have a date. It was more a business than a social occasion, wasn't it? A chance to network, to buttonhole opposing counsel or cozy up to an elusive city councilman. Clare understood, didn't she?

Clare, gripping the phone, had breathed a sigh of relief and congratulated herself again on thinking of blond, divorced

Gary. She understood perfectly. For the past three years, she'd gone alone to the mayor's function for the exact same reasons, to bend the ears of Buchanan's elite on behalf of her project.

There's nothing wrong with wanting a relationship based on shared goals, shared feelings, and good communication. She had so much more in common with Gary than with Matt. At least with Gary she wouldn't have this rolling feeling in her stomach all the time, like an acrobat attempting high aerial maneuvers without a net.

Matt's challenge popped into her mind. *What about sex?*

She rattled the hangers to drown him out, reviewing her options. The red dress was too revealing, the purple one made her look like an eggplant, and the basic black lacked punch. Darn it. She was too old to be fussing over what to wear like a ninth grader going to her first high school dance.

Matt's dark voice mocked her. *You hide yourself in jeans and T-shirts.*

Her mouth set. She pulled out the last hanger. Filmy blue plastic floated to the bedroom floor as she uncovered a long-sleeved ivory gown. Perfectly plain, its appeal laid in the drape of the bias-cut silk over what little curves she possessed.

It would do, she decided, and began to dress.

She was ready with time to spare.

Clare paced her tiny living room, unsteady in her unaccustomed heels, even shakier now that the moment had come and she was actually going out with a man for the first time since Paul's death. Dinner in the kitchen didn't count, she decided. Her palms were sweating. She resisted the impulse to wipe them on the ivory silk of her skirt.

Not with just any man, she reminded herself. With Gary, corporate lawyer extraordinaire, who'd attended Paul's funeral and helped settle his affairs. She was safe with Gary. With Gary she wouldn't feel the absurd highs and lows, the zings and tingles, that infected her in Matt's presence. With Gary she could pick up the strands of her life.

If you can call what you're doing living, Matt taunted her. *Get out of my head,* she replied.

The doorbell shrilled. Fixing a smile on her face, she went to answer it.

Gary Shepard waited on her doorstep in a custom-tailored tux, teeth and shoes gleaming. Not too tall, not too thin, he was medium blond going middling gray. He sported a neatly trimmed beard and a modest white flower in his buttonhole.

Paul had always said boutonnieres were for ushers. She shuddered to think what Matt would say.

Gary took her hand and pressed it warmly. "Clare! You look wonderful."

He handed her into her coat and his car like a perfect gentleman and made unexceptional conversation during their drive to the hotel. Boring, she thought, but safe. It was what she thought she wanted. But at some point during the long recitation of cases argued and bargains struck, Clare remembered disloyally that she'd never really enjoyed dining out with Paul's colleagues. Funny, how hard it was now to curb her impatience, to murmur the correct things in the right places. Ridiculous to wonder what she'd be talking about if she'd accepted Matt's invitation instead.

Clare pressed her lips together. Not that it had been an invitation, exactly. More like an insult.

The hotel parking lot was alive with headlights, with hurrying guests and servers shivering in long-sleeved white shirts. Gary zoomed through the valet parking lane and then shook his head as his Lexus was driven off by a fresh-faced young man with an earring.

"Watch him scratch the paint," he muttered.

Clare thought of Matt tossing Richie the keys to his truck. "Maybe he'll just change the radio station," she offered mildly.

Chuckling, Gary squeezed her hand. "Let's join the party. I want everyone to see what a beautiful woman I have with me tonight."

She smiled, though his words made her feel like an arm ornament. Like his Rolex, she realized suddenly, or that expensive car with its precious paint job.

They made their way up the red-carpeted stairs, through the smoky atrium with its ice sculpture of the county courthouse and into the well-lit ballroom. Gary stopped often to pat a shoulder or clasp a hand or exchange knowing remarks. It shouldn't have irritated her. She knew how to work a crowd herself. After all, wasn't that why she'd come?

The guest list was heavy politics married to money, with a sprinkling of blue uniforms to make the hundred-odd guests feel good about their noble purpose in paying the five-hundred-dollar-a-plate cover. Every year, Clare scraped the change out of her salary and hoped for a return on her investment in increased donations to the project. She recognized the mayor and the state's lieutenant governor. The current D.A., a no-nonsense black woman in a fashionable dashiki, hugged her and told her she'd missed seeing her around.

Clare smiled mistily. "Thanks, Lynn. You'll have to come down to the project and see—"

Gary slipped a proprietary arm behind her back. "Sorry, Clare, but there's someone here I'd really like you to meet."

His self-absorption set her teeth on edge. Covering her annoyance with another smile, she let him steer her over to Anderson, Jenkins and Vann, senior partners in Gary's firm. The four men plunged into conversation, while up on the dais a five-piece band played jazz that no one danced to, barely audible over the roar of talk and laughter.

Mr. Vann gestured with his bourbon glass. "Of course, since the daughter predeceased her by several months, the net income…"

They argued estate law. Clare tilted her head to one side to indicate deferential interest and let her mind wander. Was any donation worth this much boredom?

There. A tall man in rented evening clothes, smooth-fitting and subtly out of date. Over there, by the ham and hard rolls, behind an arrangement of palms and gardenias, wasn't that…?

The tall man turned, revealing a broad chest under a crisp white shirt front and a hard face under thick, dark hair.

Matt.

The glaze over her eyes cleared. Clare felt like a child wakened from a nap and promised a trip to the park.

"Would you excuse me?" she murmured.

Matt eased back between a skirted serving table and a bank of potted palms. This hero stuff was for the birds. He'd rather take another bullet than have one more person tell him how proud they were of their boys in blue.

A serving girl with masses of hair and a hopeful smile hovered by with a tray of champagne flutes. He shook his head.

"On duty?" she asked sympathetically.

"On display."

She dimpled, but her eyes remained blank. He'd have traded every one of those fancy glasses for a cold beer or a cup of coffee at Clare's kitchen table.

Clare. He wished she was with him. Someone to look at, someone to laugh with, someone to run interference with the busybodies and pols.

Fat chance. He didn't need a forensic scientist to tell him how badly he'd bungled in that direction. Again. She'd needed reassurance, and he'd goaded her instead, driven by some instinct to get to her the way she got to him. Where was she tonight? Was she safe? She had a date, she'd said. He wished that information made him feel better.

Matt closed his eyes, glad he wasn't working security and could shut out the room for a while. He opened them just as quickly, warned by a scent, a rustle, a sudden rise in the temperature around him.

Clare stood before him, her neat little body wrapped in a column of something white that shimmered ivory, her shadowed eyes sultry and her mouth the color of ripe fruit. She looked polished. Perfect. Erotic as sin.

"Surprise," she said.

He eased back, took another look, and felt desire ignite like a burning ball in his gut. "I could say the same."

"You clean up nice, cowboy."

He ran a finger around his suddenly too tight collar. "Captain's orders. You look good."

Her lashes swept down. She'd darkened them, he realized, both attracted and disconcerted by her made-up facade. He wanted to rub at her cheek with his thumb, find the Clare he thought he knew.

"So." She turned to face the room. The movement brought the skirt of her dress in whispering contact with his trousers. The scent of her hair drifted to him. Who would have guessed he'd find baby shampoo sexy? "This is your idea of living?"

He laughed at himself, relieved at the easy way she forgave him, delighted with her. "Not really. Is this where you had to be on Saturday night?"

"'Fraid so."

"Where's your date?" he asked before he could stop himself.

She gestured. "Over there. Talking to Handles-some, Jerkface and Vain."

He grinned, relaxing. "You're shocking me."

"Why do I have trouble believing that? What are you doing hiding out by the potted palms?"

"Same as you," he said, recognizing it as true. "Taking a breather."

Her eyebrows raised. "Public relations is not your forte?"

"Public relations I can handle. I just didn't figure on getting thrown to the social sharks like a bucket of chum."

"You poor thing," she drawled. But her hand touched his jacket sleeve in a gesture of support that warmed his heart and heated his blood.

"It gets worse," he said hoarsely. "I'm supposed to 'say a few words' after dinner."

"How about, 'Give money. Go home.'?"

Settling his hands in his pockets, he smiled down at her. "Sounds good. I'll try it. Is that what you're doing, raising money?"

"That's it. Though sometimes it's not the money but the contacts that are most valuable. You know—restaurant owners, store suppliers. I'm still trying to negotiate for space in White Oaks Park.''

"You want to talk to Bob Collins," he said. "I can take you over, introduce you if you want."

Her eyes, her whole face, glowed. "Would you?"

"Sure, why not?" He rocked back on his heels, enjoying her reaction. "You working me, Clare?"

She flushed. "No, I—" He watched in admiration as she caught herself and the chin angled up. "I don't know. You think if I'm really nice to you it'll get me anywhere?"

Frankly, he answered, "Sugar, you have no idea."

She laughed.

Satisfied, he took her to meet Bob Collins, the head of Parks and Recreation, enduring the usual effusive comments about the holdup until Clare could change the subject.

Smoothly, she launched into her pitch. Matt half listened, content to let the inflections of her voice and the animation on her face wash over him. She was good at her job. He respected that, admiring her poise as Collins agreed to something or other. Clare nodded, smiling, and took Matt's arm.

"Okay?" he asked as they walked away.

"Very okay. He's meeting me Monday." She tipped her head back, regarding him with a look of feminine challenge that burned to the soles of his rented shoes. "So, who else do you have for me?"

He surprised both of them by offering. "You want to meet Will?"

"Your partner? Yes, of course."

He took her elbow to guide her across the room, even as experience warned him he was making a mistake. Will still hadn't forgiven himself for hesitating at the shootout in the convenience store. Matt still hadn't forgiven Will for leaving the force, for choosing his wife over his partner. Logically, Matt knew both he and Will were wrong. But guilt and defection had strained their once-tight friendship to a tenuous strand, thin and sticky as taffy.

Will was in uniform tonight, Matt saw as they approached.

Dress blues. Tall, dark Renee, in red beside him, hung on his arm. He turned and saw them. Warmth suffused his face before it went carefully blank.

"Matt. Looking good."

He shrugged. "It's the monkey suit. Chief's orders. I'd rather be in uniform."

Like you. Without his meaning to, the words hung unspoken between them, a silent reproach. From now on, Will would only wear his uniform on occasions like this one. For show.

Clare held out her hand, covering the awkward moment with her warm charm. "I'm Clare Harmon. You helped my boys out the other day with some paint."

Will's big hand engulfed hers. "Pleasure, ma'am."

"No, the pleasure's mine. Matt speaks very highly of you." She ignored Matt's warning hand on her arm to beam at Renee. "Of both of you. You must be very close."

Will shuffled, clearing his throat. Matt knew the embarrassment his partner must be feeling and exchanged a glance of masculine camaraderie.

Renee smiled sadly. "Not as close as we were once. We've missed you, Matt."

Matt remembered the times this woman had opened her home to him, the Friday night dinners, the Sunday ball games. The five girls flirting through the living room, asking for his help with homework, dragging him outside for fast-pitch softball. Will's daughters. His family.

"I've missed you, too," he said honestly.

"It would be nice to get together sometime," Renee offered tentatively.

Matt stiffened.

"Honey, I don't think—" Will began.

Clare's quick glance darted from face to face. "Yes, it would." She dug in the silly little bag hanging over one arm. "Next weekend? Something simple, I can't cook at all."

And before Matt quite knew how it had happened, his un-date and his ex-partner's wife were exchanging phone numbers and admiring the pictures of Will's pretty daughters Renee just happened to have in her purse.

Matt rocked back on his good leg, torn between irritation and admiring Clare's technique.

"Your new lady's really something," Will observed quietly beside him.

"She's something, all right," Matt muttered. He looked over to find his former partner grinning. After a moment, his own lips curved in a smile. "She doesn't take no for an answer."

"Do you good," Will offered.

"Maybe."

"Good to see you, Matt."

"Yeah." He meant it. "If she calls, I hope you and Renee can make it."

"Count on it," Will said.

It was a promise, Matt realized. It was a start. And he owed it to Clare. The ladies finished their chat and parted in a flurry of pattings and promises. Clare was flushed and smiling as they walked away.

"Pushy, pushy," Matt said out of the side of his mouth.

She gave him a bright, guilty look, saw that he was smiling, too, and elevated The Nose. "So, you owe me."

He liked her attitude. "Yeah? What do I owe you?"

"A dance?" she suggested.

He looked over her head at the polished, nearly empty floor. Did he really want to risk humiliating himself in front of his boss, most of the Chamber of Commerce and a dozen or more of Buchanan's finest?

"Aren't you afraid I'll trip and embarrass you?" he asked, unsure which of them he was taunting with the question.

Understanding softened those gleaming eyes, but she didn't even acknowledge his wounded leg. "I'm in your hands, cowboy."

Heat flashed through him. He'd like nothing better than to get his hands on her, to span that neat, narrow rib cage and run his fingers over that pale, smooth skin.

"We'll take it easy," he promised hoarsely, and something of what he was feeling must have escaped in his voice, because she turned bright red.

He held out his arms. She flowed into them. Thankfully, the band chose that moment to play something slow, with a strong one-two beat. He could count. Once he could even dance. He might not disgrace them both.

He knew she must sense his stiffness, must feel his right leg drag the first time he brought them around. Grimly, he waited for her to object, to say something, to offer him the soul-scorching pity he'd schooled himself to expect.

But she didn't say anything, just clasped his hand a little tighter, settled her slight, strong body a little closer and followed his lead. Gratefully, he stepped in time to the music.

She was a good dancer, he thought, when he'd gotten over the shock. She made him look good. And the brush of her legs against his thighs, the press of those small, firm breasts against his starched shirtfront, was better than good.

There was even a smattering of applause around them when the dance was done. Matt held her hands a moment longer, reluctant to let her go, giving himself time to recover.

Maybe she needed time, too. The shiny stuff over her breasts rose and fell with her breath. Her eyes looked more enormous than ever.

"About that quick, cheap thrill?" she said. "I might be tempted to reconsider."

His breath whooshed out. "You picked a hell of a time to mention it, sugar."

Her expression was rueful. "I know."

"Clare! I've been looking all over for you."

The man appeared at her elbow, exuding superficial confidence and expensive cologne. He was the type Matt might have pegged as suitable for Clare: well dressed, well fed, well spoken. He put his hand high on her back, where the smooth silk parted to reveal smoother skin, and Matt's hackles rose.

He looked at Matt. "And you are…?"

Gracefully, Clare performed the social ritual. "Sergeant Matt Dunn, Gary Shepard."

"Clare's date," Shepard clarified, extending his free hand. "We go back a long time."

Faint parallel lines of annoyance appeared above Clare's nose. Matt felt better. If this guy knew her as well as he wanted Matt to think he did, he wouldn't be so quick to lay a claim.

Matt bared his teeth. "Nice to meet you."

So, he lied. He figured Clare wouldn't appreciate it if he threw the guy into the punch bowl.

Clare didn't trust Matt's bland tone of voice, but when she glanced at him, his face was straight as a plank. Murmuring an apology, she allowed Gary to lead her back onto the dance floor.

After the heat that had built and flashed between them, she half expected Matt to prop up the ballroom wall and glower after them like a brooding hero in a Regency romance.

He didn't, of course. Well, he was probably used to women melting all over him. She was the one left dazed by the profound pull of sexual attraction, disoriented by the feeling that she'd just left the only person in the room who truly saw or understood her.

I might be tempted to reconsider.

Stumbling over Gary's polished Italian shoes, she smiled apologetically. "Sorry. I guess I'm out of practice."

Was she ever. What on earth had possessed her to blurt out that little admission on the dance floor? Repeatedly, her gaze returned to Matt. He was dressed no differently than the majority of guests. He talked and smiled and mingled with the rest. And yet with his height and aura of contained energy, his broad shoulders barely disguised by his elegant jacket, he made every other man present look like a cardboard cutout. She shook her head in disbelief. The place was packed with educated, articulate, wealthy men, and she wanted to be with Sergeant Strong and Silent.

Was she kidding herself, imagining she could handle a relationship with a man who only wanted to be a temporary indulgence in her life? She knew Matt was eager to return to detective work. His assignment in her neighborhood would be over in another month. She could be pretty sure once he left he wouldn't be back.

You're a nice girl, sugar. You've got girlfriend *written all over you.*

Her chin lifted in resolution. Obviously, she wasn't his usual type. Well, he wasn't hers, either. But tonight had demonstrated she didn't belong with smooth, assured, ambitious Gary. She didn't belong with any other man here. She belonged with Matt. What would it take to convince him of that?

She watched over Gary's padded shoulder as another tall man in evening clothes claimed Matt's company, drawing him over to a group that included the chief of police. She looked for him when Gary took her into dinner, but he was seated on the other side of the room. She heard a roar of masculine laughter as he was absorbed into a huddle of navy blue. Over the prime rib and piped potatoes, he seemed to be flirting casually with his dinner partner, a sleek brunette in elegant black. Clare set her teeth and made an effort to be pleasant to her date.

Gary was drinking. With her awareness focused on Matt, it took Clare a while to notice that wine made her escort amorously attentive. He began to emphasize his conversation with little pats on her forearm, her shoulder, her knee. Clare was more amused than annoyed. She could handle it. She could handle him. She'd dealt with much more aggressive attempts on the lot.

Redirecting his wandering hands, she returned her attention to the dais, where the after-dinner speakers were being introduced. After a brief, convincing speech about the importance of community involvement in law enforcement, Matt sat down to enthusiastic applause.

She knew the attention made him uncomfortable. She knew he wanted nothing more than to return to the detective division. His ability to set aside his own preference for the good of his department and her neighborhood made her chest swell with peculiar pride.

He glanced over at their table, his dark eyes seeking. Their eyes met and held. She nodded once, in reassurance and acknowledgment, and he responded with a flickering smile of surprising sweetness. Her heart stumbled.

"You didn't tell me you knew Supercop," Gary complained.

Clare shushed him.

She looked for Matt after the program, but he had disappeared. Retrieving her coat from the check room, she braved the flow of guests spilling through the hotel foyer. When Gary caught up with her, fumbling for his key ring, she could smell the wine on his breath.

That settled it, she thought. She couldn't let him drive.

As he bumped through the departing guests toward the valet parking, she pulled gently at his arm. "Gary, why don't I drive us home?"

"Drive the Lexus? I don't think so."

She knew better than to argue with a drunk. "Well, then, why don't we take a cab?"

"Don't want to take a cab. Don't need to take a cab."

"Oh, yes, we do."

"No, we—" Comprehension gleamed in his swimmy eyes. "Oh, yeah. Yeah, we do. Don't want the car parked out front all night, do we?"

She certainly did not. But not in the way she suspected he meant. She steered him toward the cab line.

"That's right," she agreed smoothly. "Over here, Gary. Put your keys away."

She gave the driver a twenty and directions to her house. Gary slumped in the back seat, fingering the neck of her gown.

"Like your dress," he said. "You know, I always thought you could be attractive."

Capturing his roving hands, Clare nudged him into his own corner. "Gee, thanks."

"I mean it," he insisted. "Of course, you were always so

quiet in those days. Cool, quiet Clare. If I'd figured you were so hot, I would have made my move years ago.''

Clare stared, torn between laughter and the desire to push him from the car. "If we hadn't both been married to other people at the time.''

"What? Oh, yeah. Yeah.''

They rode a while in silence. She shrugged off his hand, which kept returning to her shoulder. To divert him she asked, "How is Janie these days, anyway?''

He blinked, apparently trying to focus. "Fine. Just fine. I hear she's got a little thing going with her trainer.''

"Really?'' Clare asked. Surely they were almost to her place by now?

Janie's former husband nodded solemnly. "'S all right. I understand. A woman's got needs. A man's gotta understand that.''

"That's very—'' words failed her "—understanding of you, Gary.''

The cab turned onto her street and pulled up in front of the house. Meeting the driver's eyes in the rearview mirror, Clare collected her coat and her purse and got out.

"Needs,'' Gary repeated firmly. "I'll see you to your door.''

"Oh, I don't think—''

"You want me to wait, ma'am?'' asked the cab driver.

Clare drew a deep breath. "Yes. Please.''

Gary threw his arm around her shoulders as they went up the walk. She would have thrown it off if she hadn't feared he would fall without her support. The porch was dark. Darn. She must have forgotten to turn on the light. She really wasn't used to the dating game.

"How about a nightcap?'' Gary said at her door.

But she knew enough to guess where that might lead. "I don't think so, Gary. Good night.''

He made a face, more guessed at than seen in the dark. "Coffee?''

It was late, and she was tired. She no longer found the blond lawyer attractive or even slightly amusing. She might have asked him out, but her sense of what she owed him didn't extend past her front door.

She bent her head to dig for her keys. "We don't want to keep your cab waiting."

Rummaging in her purse, she just never saw his next move coming.

He grabbed her shoulders. Trapped by her evening bag, her hands were squashed between their two bodies. A blast of alcohol assaulted her face as his mouth, wet and hungry, sought hers.

"Oh, Clare," he moaned. "Beautiful Clare."

Oh, hell, Clare thought.

She wasn't frightened, not really, even when he ignored her efforts to turn her head and his hands got rough. The cab was parked at the curb ten yards away. If she screamed, the driver would hear her. But she was reluctant to expose either of them to the resultant embarrassment and explanations. Surely she could handle this? Wriggling, she tried to push Gary away as his tongue stabbed her mouth. She stepped on his foot. He slobbered on her neck.

A beam of light swept across her eyes, blinding her. Gary swore and released her as the light swirled and steadied on his face.

A voice came out of the darkness beyond the porch. An official voice. A voice she knew.

Matt's voice.

"Ma'am? Is everything all right?"

Chapter 9

Clare's initial surge of relief was followed by a spurt of annoyance. Squinting over the flashlight's bright beam, she could make out Matt's broad shoulders and the sharp silhouette of his policeman's hat. What was he doing in uniform?

"Yes, officer. Thank you. Mr. Shepard was just leaving."

He approached the porch. "Come on, sir. I'll help you to your cab."

Gary made an effort to straighten up. Befuddled by alcohol and fooled by the change of clothes, he apparently didn't recognize Matt in the dark.

"'S all right, officer. Just seeing Miz Harmon to her door."

"Yes, sir," Matt said in heavy disbelief. "This way."

Gary shrugged petulantly, adjusting the lapels of his jacket. "I'll call you," he told Clare.

She watched as Matt escorted him down the darkened walk and into the waiting cab. The door slammed. The headlights arced as the car pulled away from the curb and accelerated up the street. Unlocking the door, Clare leaned against it as Matt clicked off the light and paced silently back.

She had this funny, shaky feeling under her rib cage, an unstable compound of embarrassment, anticipation and fear. She crossed her arms under her breasts to hold it in.

"Tell me you just happened to be walking by—in your uniform—the exact moment we got home."

He stopped one stride shy of the porch. She still couldn't see his face. "Is that what you want to hear?"

"I don't know. Is it true?"

"Would I lie to you?"

Reluctantly, she laughed. "No, you just won't say." With unexpected bitterness, she added, "I should be used to that."

He stepped up, closed in. She refused to look away, to acknowledge how his nearness affected her.

"I got home about half an hour ago," he volunteered abruptly. "Went on patrol, like I usually do. Put on the uniform, like I usually don't, and kept your porch in sight. I didn't trust that joker you were with. He was tossing back wine like Cherry Coke all through dinner. Okay?"

Her throat closed with appreciation. He'd kept tabs on her, watched out for her. She nodded, forgetting he couldn't see her in the dark.

"You all right?" he asked again, a deeper, personal note in his voice.

Again, she nodded. But annoying tremors shook her arms and shoulders. The various strains of the evening had finally taken their toll.

With a stifled exclamation, he pulled her to him.

Clare wasn't sure what she expected. Not a reprise of Gary's greedy fumbling, perhaps, but some form of masculine demand.

Instead, he held her. Just held her. For quiet, for closeness, for warmth. His arms were strong and comforting. Her palms slid up the long, strong planes of his back as her body unthinkingly aligned itself with his, seeking the solace of a man's warm, living body.

"He said he wanted to come in for a nightcap," she mumbled defensively.

"And you were the chaser?"

Secure in his arms, she shrugged. She listened to the steady thump of his heart as the tension bled slowly from her muscles. Her neck relaxed.

He probably thought she was an idiot. She never should have let her hurt and frustration spook her into asking out a man she had no real knowledge of or interest in. She didn't want Gary Shepard. But how could she have guessed he would show so little restraint?

"He knew my husband," she offered.

Matt's voice rumbled over her head. "Your husband probably knew a bunch of jerks. That doesn't mean you have to date them."

She could have been offended. Instead, his blunt assessment made her smile into his starched blue shirt. For the first time since she'd left his arms at the dance, she felt she could relax and be herself. He felt good. Broad, strong, hard. Her body nestled closer in unconscious recognition that this was what she needed. So good.

"Do you want to come in?" she asked, the words muffled.

"It's a little late for coffee."

"I'm not offering you coffee."

The arms around her tightened and then eased.

"Beer?" he ventured.

"Don't be dense, Detective."

Her implication burst on Matt like gunfire. While his mind wrestled with possible motive, his body concentrated on the feel of hers snug against his front. She was lonely, he reminded himself. It was late. She was vulnerable.

She stood on tiptoe to press warm lips to his chin, and his body won.

He thrust his fingers into her hair to anchor her head, but she was already raising, angling, opening for him. She tasted as spicy-sweet as he remembered, and twice as hot. Twining slim, strong arms around his neck, she pressed close. Blood pounded in his head, surged low in his body.

An enthusiastic, assenting sound escaped her before his

mouth plundered hers again. He filled his hands with her, running them down her supple back over ivory silk to her taut little butt. They rubbed together, belly and thigh, as he swelled with impatient desire.

"This feels really good," she gasped. "Is it illegal?"

He ran his lips along the curve of her jaw and over her ear, delighting in her shiver. "Probably."

"Sexual license without a license?" she suggested.

How could she make him shake with need and quake with laughter at the same time? "Nothing that interesting. Violating public indecency statutes, I think."

Her small, competent hands tugged at him. "Is that all? Come inside."

The invitation jolted through him. He could follow her into the house, through the shadowed hallway and up the narrow stairs to her empty, scented bed. He could take what she was offering. It was what he was used to.

A quick, cheap thrill.

It wasn't what he wanted any more. Not from her.

The realization opened a black pit of possibility under his feet. He stepped back from the edge.

"Clare—"

"Mm?" Her soft, warm mouth opened on his throat, searing through his resolution.

He needed to think. He needed to breathe. He struggled not to groan as her lips reached his collarbone and her tongue flicked out to taste him. *Damn.* He wasn't Mr. Sensitive, but even he could see they needed to slow things down. Didn't she realize how vulnerable she was?

"I don't want to take advantage," he said.

She laughed. "Right."

Frustrated beyond belief, determined to made her understand, he captured her hands and held them.

"I don't want to sell you short."

With regret, Matt watched his words cut through Clare's sensual fog. She tipped her head back against the door, running a hand through her hair.

"What are you talking about?"

"Clare, I'm a cop."

"You want me to compliment you on your uniform now?"

Her brittle mockery flicked him on the raw. After her little adventure with Gary the Human Slug, he must look like a port in the storm to her. He had to make her see his job made him unfit to be any woman's permanent refuge.

"I don't want to hurt you," he said.

Too late, Clare thought. Her disappointed body throbbed, her mind was a muddle, and her heart was one big ache. She'd thought with Matt she could break through the walls of her isolation and end her self-imposed celibacy. Obviously, she'd thought wrong.

She spoke flippantly, to cover her distress. "Big of you."

His breath hissed. "That's one hell of an attitude you've got, sugar."

"Look who's talking, cowboy."

"Listen, Clare—"

"No." She spoke quickly, carefully, picking her way through a quagmire of emotion while confusion dragged at her like mud. "You're right. We moved too fast." Painfully, she corrected herself. "I moved too fast. I'm not sure what I want yet, and you've made it pretty clear that whatever you want it's not me. So, we'll just say good-night now and—and be friends."

He pushed up the brim of his hat with one thumb. "Friends?"

Repeated in that deep, sexy voice, it sounded ridiculous. It was ridiculous. If he laughed she would punch him.

She crossed her arms defensively. The door frame dug into her spine. "Do you like 'neighbors' any better?"

"Well, now, I don't know." He leaned closer, pretending to consider. She was mesmerized by his voice, riveted by the quirk of his mouth as his face approached hers. "I guess you could say I feel pretty neighborly where you're concerned."

His head bent, closing the distance between them. Her heart fluttered in her throat. His breath brushed her lips an instant before he kissed her, soft, considering kisses that tasted, without meaning to, like promise.

"Even friendly," he whispered against her open mouth.

And then he straightened and stepped back, and the night was cold where his body had been.

"Lock your door when you go in," he said. "You're not safe at night."

It was a warning. For her? Clare wondered. Or to himself?

In her dreams, she was there.

In her dreams, she saw it all, the narrow streets two blocks over from this very house, the sedate blue Camry parked in evening shadow. She stood frozen in imagination as Paul ambled toward his car, jingling his keys in his pocket. Had he been satisfied after speaking to his elusive witness? No one would ever know. Because the police report only recorded that a hooded figure jumped from between two buildings, shouted something—What? the witnesses were unclear—and opened fire. Paul slumped against the car, his dark blood spilling on the curb. The keys clattered from his lax hand onto the street.

In her dream, she screamed, as she hadn't screamed when the quiet-voiced policewoman came to the pretty little house on Claridge Street with the news. She wept, as she hadn't wept when the organ played "Now the Green Blade Rises" and she'd sat erect in her pew with numb heart and icy hands.

She screamed and she wept and she woke up.

Clare opened her eyes on darkness. The green numerals of her bedside clock blinked: 3:43. She lay still a moment, waiting for her heart to slow.

She'd hoped the recurring nightmares, with their burden of helplessness and guilt, were a thing of the past. How long since the last one? Six months? Seven? The strain of seeing Paul's old colleagues, the confrontation with Gary and her confused reactions to Matt must really have wakened some ghosts.

Thank God, Matt hadn't taken advantage of her uncharacteristic moment of weakness on the porch. She must have been out of her mind to risk getting involved again, even on a temporary, physical basis. She was grateful for his restraint.

Sure she was.

Sweat dampened her nightshirt. She stumbled out of bed to get a fresh one. From the top of her dresser, Paul's picture smiled at her with wry understanding. Leaning against the open bureau drawer, she reached with one finger to trace the tiny lines of his crowsfeet through the glass. When he'd died, her heart had died, too, and her libido had just shut down. She'd concentrated her energy on her work, trying to satisfy her frustrated maternal longings with the kids she hired.

It was disconcerting to find both heart and body showing signs of life again.

She lifted her clammy nightgown over her head, dropping it to the floor. Her flesh goose-bumped. Her nipples puckered. It was the cold, she told herself. Of course it was the cold. And slammed the door on the memory of Matt's hard, warm chest moving with debilitating effect against her breasts.

She grabbed for another nightshirt, cotton, short-sleeved, faded like the rest. It had been ages since she'd bought anything new to wear to bed. What was the point? she demanded with brisk practicality whenever her mother brought the subject up. She was comfortable just the way she was.

Tugging the sagging hem down over her thighs, Clare climbed back into bed.

And dreamed of Matt.

The Dumpster sat right where Matt had requested it, close by the curb where he'd tied the dog. His turf, Matt thought wryly, dragging a broken chunk of sidewalk through rutted clay. The cleanup of this empty lot at Alston and Magnolia marked the kickoff of his Neighborhood Pride campaign. A crew from city works had come around twice, once to haul rubble and once to grade the lot, but a lot of debris remained to remove by hand. The volunteers started arriving midmorning, more than Matt had expected. His neighbors.

It was mostly men, six or eight. Matt supposed the excuse

of creating a neighborhood playground allowed them to beg off Sunday worship. He recognized a couple of the crew who'd helped him move in, Isaac and the short guy, Benny. If Clare was miffed about losing the lot for garden acreage, she hadn't let her disappointment discourage her project's employees from lending a hand.

Isaac settled his navy cap back on his head and picked up the other end of the ragged concrete slab. Together they hauled their burden down to the metal Dumpster and heaved it in.

"How's the eye?" Matt asked.

Isaac squinted at him. "Okay."

"I had a chat with Eddie Boothe down at the station house the other day. He says he knows you."

Slowly, Isaac lowered his arms. "Eddie knows a lot of people."

Matt rubbed his jaw with the back of his hand. "So he says. You two tight?"

"Once," Isaac admitted. "I ran with his posse for a while."

"And now?"

Isaac's slow grin spread across his face. "Don't guess Clare would much like it."

"No, I don't guess she would," Matt agreed. "You think your working for her ticked Eddie off?"

"Might have."

"Enough for him to…make his feelings known?"

Isaac looked away. "Yeah. Maybe."

They worked together in silence for long minutes. Red dust rose in spurts from the hard ground, powdering work boots and jeans. Slowly a rhythm and a bond developed out of shared sweat and a common goal.

"Ticked enough for him to take those feelings out on someone else?" Matt asked at last, getting to the heart of his questioning. "On Clare?"

Concern roiled his stomach as Isaac pondered his reply. "I don't know," the crew chief said at last. "Might be he holds a grudge, seeing it was her husband was prosecuting him when he got put away."

Matt practically dropped a rock on his foot. He should have known. Stewart should have told him. Hell, Clare should have told him. First thing tomorrow, he was going after some answers. And then he was going after Eddie.

Isaac hefted another chunk of concrete. "He could've had me killed, though, and he didn't. It might not have been, you know, personal against Clare. Maybe he just had to, like, get some respect back on the street. Me having run with him for a while."

And Matt had to be content with that answer. For now.

The pale sun climbed higher, sharpening shadows and warming the air. Used to the society of the station house, Matt relaxed in the company of the work crew, in the joint tasks, the off-color jokes. His leg didn't cripple him, at least not much, and the exertion took his mind off Clare and his troublesome response to her last night.

With the ground cleared, they began to set landscape timbers along two sides of the empty lot.

Matt hadn't figured out where his relationship with Clare was headed. That bothered him. He liked to know things, to be in control, to have all the little pieces of a puzzle and put them together. It was one of the reasons he was a good cop. To reconstruct a crime, a detective needed both logic and imagination. But where Clare was concerned, Matt admitted, logic failed him and his imagination went too far.

She kissed him, and his body took off like a patrol car on a high-speed chase—lights, sirens, the works. She looked at him with those whiskey brown eyes, and wild visions of Little League and white frame houses filled the empty space between his ears where his brain was supposed to be.

Wrestling a twelve-foot timber into place, Matt stamped on it for good measure. The unthinking movement shot pain up his thigh.

He couldn't afford, he didn't want, some big romantic complication in his life. If he opened to her... Matt shuddered. He couldn't. Time and again, his mother's uncomprehending demands on his father's time and attention and emotions had broken against a wall of uncompromising professionalism. He'd seen his father's frustration and his mother's tears. He'd watched his own partner falter under the weight of a wife's concern.

"We're too much alike," Shirley Dickson had said when she broke with him. "We don't let anybody in, and we don't give anything up. Not a case, not control, and not the way we feel. It's better if we stay just friends."

Friends. Matt spat into the dust. Clare wanted to be friends, too. Maybe that would be better. Simpler for him, and kinder to her. She was still getting over the loss of her husband. A walk on the wild side with a broken-down cop who ducked emotional involvement might not be what she needed just now.

And then, as the sun caressed his back, the memory of her small, quick hands racing over him temporarily stopped his breath. Exhaling, Matt tamped earth around the base of the timber. Yeah, better, maybe. But not nearly as much fun.

He knocked off work around noon to pick up a sackful of burgers and soft drinks for the volunteers. When he opened the truck door, Trigger leapt for the bench seat, big black nose quivering.

Matt eyed the mutt with disfavor. Even the dog had expectations. "I'm not going hunting, you know. The meat comes already cooked."

Trigger watched him hopefully, a thin rim of white appearing around the bright gold eyes. Matt sighed and started the truck.

By the time he got back to the lot, the church-going contingent had arrived, led by Reverend Ray in a white baseball cap and a sweatshirt that read Grace Saves. Matt scanned the Grace Church volunteers: three more men, twice that many women, and a handful of teens mobilized by Alma, the minister's formidable wife. Richie was among them. Tyler, too, Matt noted with a frown. He climbed stiffly from the truck.

He sensed Clare before he saw her, with that peculiar new hyperawareness he'd developed where she was concerned, like the hunch that used to warn him of trouble. He rubbed his jaw. Come to think of it, maybe it was the same old instinct at work after all. Because, striding toward him over the fertile red ground in her slim-hipped boys' jeans, the woman was definitely Trouble.

The temptation she'd posed for him last night still made him sweat.

She smiled when she caught his eye, deliberately pleasant, carefully casual. Friendly, Matt thought with a lick of temper that surprised him.

"I brought help," she said.

Propping back against the truck, he held up the big white bag. "I brought lunch."

She parked her tempting butt beside his against the warm cab of the truck and gazed over the lot. Her head barely came to his shoulder. He could smell the sun on her hair. "It looks good."

He lifted an eyebrow. "I didn't figure greasy burgers were your style."

"I told you I can't cook. If it weren't for fast food, I'd starve. But I was talking about your playground, actually."

"I thought you wanted this lot to grow more cabbages or something."

"Tomatoes. That's all right. You were right when you said the kids need a place to play. And the lot is a little small to cultivate anyway." She looked at him sideways from under blond-tipped lashes, a faint smile touching her lips. "But if you still want to help me acquire that park space in White Oaks…"

He felt an answering grin tug at his mouth. God save him from a hardheaded, softhearted woman. "I'll put in a word for you with Collins."

In the warm glow that spread over her face, he saw that he'd pleased her, and tried not to like it so much.

She bounced from her perch, breaking the tenuous connection between them, and held out her hand. "Can I help you pass out those sandwiches?"

He gave in to impulse. "Yeah, sure. As long as you eat with me."

Awareness jittered between them as her eyes met his. "All right."

He handed her the bag he held and turned to pluck another through the open window of the truck. When their sacks were nearly empty, she came back to him. Matt lowered the tailgate, and they sat in the bed, finding space alongside three old tires and a stack of treated four-by-fours.

"What's all this?" Clare asked.

Matt cleared his throat. "Playground equipment," he explained. "I know a guy who runs a hardware store, practically gave it away."

Her eyes were warm and amused. "And of course you couldn't say no."

He took refuge behind his burger. She took a bite of hers, chewed and looked away.

"I wanted to thank you. For last night."

Uncomfortable with her openness, he tried to joke. "Sugar, I don't usually get thanked unless something happens. Nothing did."

"Well, I wanted to thank you for that." Her face was scarlet. "I don't know what got into me. I acted like a— I didn't act like myself at all."

Matt couldn't let her think there was a single thing wrong with her behavior last night. Hell, he'd probably carry the impression of her sweet little body to his grave. He chose his words carefully.

"You're being kind of hard on yourself, aren't you? Seems to me if a woman has a right to say 'no,' she sure as hell has a right to say 'yes.'"

Her soft lips pressed together. "Oh, great. Is that another variation of 'a woman's got needs'?"

What was she getting at? "I guess she does, same as a man. You've been alone a while. It's perfectly natural for you to be looking to go out with somebody now."

"Somebody like you?"

Matt marshaled his good intentions. "Not exactly. No. I'm not right for you."

She crossed her arms in the defensive posture he was beginning to recognize. "So, who died and made you the big authority on what's right for me? What's wrong with you, anyway?"

He was trying to protect her, and she was making him feel like a chump. He started to get angry, and stuffed his burger in his mouth before he said something rash. "You can do better, that's all," he mumbled.

"Oh, this is interesting. Better how?"

He swallowed. "Come off it, Clare. You were married to a lawyer."

Putting her head to one side like a bird, she regarded him brightly. "Gary's a lawyer."

Even with his blood pressure rising, he had to smother a laugh. "Gary's a horse's ass."

"Finally, something we can agree on. I never should have asked him out."

"Wait a minute. You asked him?"

"I said it was a mistake."

"But why him? Why not me?"

For a minute, he didn't think she would answer. She sucked on her drink. Putting it down, she dried her hands on the thighs of her jeans. "Because he was safe," she said.

Drop it, his mind warned him. But he couldn't let it go. "Safe like familiar-safe?"

Crumpling her sandwich wrapper, she tucked it away in the bag. "That, too, I'm sure. More like safe-I'm-not-attracted-to-him-safe."

As simply as that, she destroyed his emotional balance and rocked his self-control. She wanted him. He sure as hell wanted her. But not at the cost of her unhappiness. He'd never left a woman crying, and he wasn't about to start with her. Even if she recovered, his self-respect wouldn't.

"I don't like to take risks," she added.

Matt studied her as she sat cross-legged in the bed of his

truck, still pleating the top of the paper bag. The sun reflected off her bent head, making a halo of her red-gold hair.

He was no monk, never had been. The women he'd taken to his bed were generally no saints, either. What could he offer a woman like Clare, who deserved a safe future and a man's whole heart and attention, a woman who'd already lost one husband to an assailant's gun? But he couldn't let her remark go unchallenged.

"Sure you do," he said.

She shook her head.

"Starting the Project was a risk. Living here is a risk. That kid, Tyler—" He jerked his chin toward the back of the lot where the teens were making jump shots with their napkins into the other paper sack. "He's a risk."

"That's different."

"Different, how?"

She ignored him, climbing to her feet in the truck bed, wadding the trash in her hand. "We ought to get to work."

He caught at her wrist. Under his fingers, her pulse beat furiously. "Seems to me you've got your priorities backward, sugar. Maybe you should stop doing stuff that could get you hurt and take a chance on life for a change."

Matt knew the minute he'd said the words that they were a mistake.

Clare's whiskey colored eyes blazed like flamed brandy as she tugged her hand free. "Oh, that's really something, coming from you. Are you implying that just because I'm grateful you didn't jump into my bed last night, I'm afraid of life?"

He reddened but would not back down. Maybe that made him the reactionary chauvinist Marcia had called him, but it was a crime a woman as warm and sweet and sexy as Clare should bury her heart with her husband. "Afraid of sex, then. Love."

"At least I've been in love," she retorted. "In love and loved, Mr. Single Cop Afraid of Commitment."

Warm, sweet, sexy...and quick as a wasp. Awkwardly, Matt stood. In a minute he was going to either yell or kiss her, and they weren't anywhere that would allow him to follow this argument to its natural conclusion. He was, he noted with disgust, already half-aroused. And their raised voices were beginning to attract an audience.

Before he could figure what to say, Clare jumped from the truck and buzzed off toward Alma and the reverend. Matt watched her go with regret.

"She sure is something to see when she gets going, huh?" Isaac commented, leaning on the handle of a shovel a few yards away.

Matt glared, giving up when the other man only grinned. He rubbed his jaw. "I think I made her mad."

Isaac nodded. "But she'll get over it quick."

If she did, Matt reflected a couple of hours later, she made sure he was the last to know. Clare worked with her crew banking the sides of the lot, putting in one-gallon pots of juniper and a triad of crepe myrtle trees. She attacked the dirt like a fenced-in puppy, fueled by nothing more than one greasy burger and indignation. Digging fence posts and drilling holes for the new playground equipment, Matt might as well have been invisible.

He tolerated her avoidance policy for as long as it took to assemble a fourteen-by-four-by-twelve-foot climbing structure of treated wood. After screwing together the last platform, he and Isaac hoisted it between the play tower's uprights while Reverend Ray grunted and secured it.

Wiping his face with a dirty forearm, Matt stepped back to check the level.

"Looks good," he said.

"It's very good," the reverend concurred. "Thank you, Matthew."

It was the first time Reverend Ray had used his Christian name. "Just doing my job, Reverend."

"I'd say you were doing the Lord's work."

Matt shrugged, uncomfortable with the praise, uneasy with the satisfaction that spread through him. He was a detective, not a blasted social worker.

He glanced across the lot to where Clare, on her knees, pressed dirt around the roots of a low-growing evergreen shrub. Straight, fine hair flopped forward onto her intent face. Denim stretched enticingly over her behind. It was a good thing the reverend couldn't read his mind right then, because his thoughts were hardly godly.

"Only for another month," Matt said. "This is a temporary assignment, remember?"

"I remember that's what you told me."

Clare stood. And swayed.

Matt's jaw set. "Dammit. Doesn't she knew when to quit?"

Striding stiffly across the pockmarked ground, he never heard the reverend's reply.

"You should get something to drink," Matt said harshly behind her.

All afternoon, he'd loomed on the edge of Clare's vision like a storm cloud. So, why should his rumbling voice startle her now? The electricity that crackled between them dizzied her.

Oh, for goodness sake, Clare thought crossly. Of course she was dizzy. She'd been in the sun for hours. Trying to immerse herself in work, she'd ignored her body's need for fluids. But just because Matt was right about what she needed didn't mean he could tell her what to do.

She straightened her shoulders and lifted her chin. "Do you have a problem, Matt?"

"No. You do, though. You're dehydrated. Richie!" The boy, knotting rope to a tire, stood and turned at his command. "Get Clare a drink, okay?"

Richie ran for the shade of the white oak tree where Alma had set out gallon jugs of sweet tea and a bag of cups. Clare watched him go, pressing her lips together.

"Are you this bossy with everybody? Or is there just something about me that brings out that guard dog instinct?"

Matt's slow grin surprised her. "Both. You should sit down."

"I'm fine. I'm tougher than I look."

"Yeah, well, you look like the next puff of wind's going to blow you over." His hand, callused, warm and gentle, cupped her arm. "Here."

She let him support her as she took the cup, her indignation sapped by his concern. Oversweet, almost cool, the liquid felt delicious in her parched mouth. Matt stood over her as she drained the cup. She felt his gaze on her throat as she swallowed. Clare flushed, heat rising in her cheeks and swirling low deep inside.

"More?" he urged.

"No. I'm all right now, really. You should have some."

"I'm okay," he said dismissively.

She was going to have to watch this macho guy pose of his if they became lovers, Clare thought. And then realized that the idea, once planted, was as tenacious as bindweed. *Lovers.* The images the word evoked poked through her consciousness and twined delicate tendrils along all her nerve endings.

"Richie, could you please get another drink for Sergeant Dunn?"

The boy made a face. "What do I look like, your water boy?" But he took the cup and ambled back toward the jugs.

Her head swam. Giving in to the lure of Matt's strength, Clare rested her cheek briefly against his hard, muscled arm. He smelled of sweat and sun-warmed clay. Under her cheek, his cotton sleeve was damp. She saw the sudden rise of his chest, and then his broad, blunt fingers threaded through her bangs, stroking back an errant strand of hair. The tiny tug on her scalp made her close her eyes with pleasure.

"What's he doing here, anyway?"

Her eyes popped open. "What? Who? Richie?"

"No, the Boothe kid, Tyler. What's he doing?"

Clare stiffened and pulled away. She wasn't used to her own unsettling sensual response, to Matt's lightning quick changes of mood. It was disconcerting, contemplating sex with a man who could shift so quickly into professional mode.

"Working," she said. "It's a condition of his probation. He

and Richie have appointments with the court counselor tomorrow afternoon.''

Matt nodded, staring over her head at the boy by the fence with Alma. The Big, Bad Detective was back in force. She wondered if he even remembered she was there.

"It's a good idea, if you can trust him." His voice implied he did not. "Keep an eye on him."

She tried to feel amused by his protective preoccupation and almost succeeded. Straightening, she brushed her palms over the seat of her jeans. "I will. I thought he could paint the fence."

"Uh-huh. Kid's had a lot of experience painting things. Tell him no snakes this time."

She planted her hands on her hips, both entertained and exasperated. "Tyler's not about to paint gang graffiti on a neighborhood project!"

"No? He did on your shed."

"You need a course in art appreciation. Or glasses. He and Richie painted produce. Tomatoes, remember? Peas, carrots. You got the paint."

"And who vandalized the shed in the first place so that you had to cover it up?"

"I don't know. It doesn't matter."

"Sure, it matters. Somebody's got it in for you, Clare. You need to be careful."

She shook her head. "Are you always like this? Looking for the bad stuff, thinking like a cop? Tell me something, if and when we finally do make love, are you going to stop and check for burglars under the bed?"

She was joking. She thought she was joking. But Matt was looking at her somberly, seriously considering his reply.

"Yeah, I think like a cop. I act like a cop. All the time. So, if and when, sugar, I'll check for the burglars first. And after that..." The expression in his dark eyes, hot and heavy-lidded, arrested her breath. "After that you've got my undivided attention."

Chapter 10

The air contracted and thickened, enclosing them in a bubble of awareness. Details assumed huge proportions: the dark prickle of beard along Matt's stubborn jaw, the tender hollow just below his strong throat, the lines of pain or humor that bracketed his sensual mouth. Clare drew a deep breath. Her blood drummed in her ears.

Vaguely, she was aware of a long white sedan cruising around the corner, a pair of teens shuffling and shoving, and Reverend Ray moving out of sight behind her to get a drink. Dimly, she heard a man joke and a woman laugh and a car backfire.

And then Matt's face changed and hardened, and a second pop followed the first, and the bubble around them shattered.

"Down! Get down!" he shouted.

His shoulder caught the middle of her chest. She fell flat, his hard arm pinned between her and the churned-up ground. The sky spun. Someone screamed. An engine roared as a car accelerated away.

Clare struggled against Matt's weight, trying to sit up. She didn't have to understand what had just happened to know it was bad.

"Dammit, stay down! Are you okay?"

"I'm squashed. You're squashing me. Matt—"

He scrambled off her, his knee connecting painfully with her ribs as he pushed himself over her shoulder and away. Clare rolled to her side and up on her elbows, tracking his ungainly sprint toward the white oak tree and the tall black man lying on the ground. Reverend Ray.

The minister had his hand pressed to one shoulder and a surprised look on his face. Between his fingers, dark blood seeped and stained his white sweatshirt.

A woman sobbed quietly. Other voices drifted to Clare like smoke on the wind.

"Oh, God. Oh, God."

"Did you see the son of a bitch?"

"Ray!"

Alma, her proud face contorted, pushed through the milling bystanders and fell to her knees beside her husband.

"It's all right," Matt said, reassuring her. He was already bending over the reverend, turning him, lifting him gently. "Give me your shirt."

The minister's wife stared at him for a moment before tearing her matching white sweatshirt over her head. Her dark hair tumbled as she mutely handed it to Matt.

It was not all right, Clare thought numbly. It was like her dream, only worse. Because this time she didn't have to imagine the shock and the noise. She didn't have to close her eyes to feel the confusion. This time the blood was real.

But Matt, with quick, competent movements, was already folding the shirt and pressing it to the wound. "Okay, Reverend, we'll have you fixed up in no time. I'm just going to call for an ambulance, and you'll be fine. You understand me?"

Face gray, he nodded. "Yes, I do."

"Well, that's fine. That's good." Matt braced the older man's barrel-shaped torso forward. "Mrs. Carter?"

Alma, tight-lipped, looked up.

"Would you hold your husband just like this, ma'am? That's right. Let him lean back against you. And you need to hold this now—press it—against the wound. Just like that."

The minister groaned, and Clare's heart stuttered.

"I know that's not too comfortable," Matt said calmly. "But you're doing great. You're both doing great. Clare?"

She flinched. She couldn't. She just couldn't move. There was blood on his hands, on his shirt, on the ground.

Without turning his head, he called her again. "Clare!"

His confidence in her propelled her forward. She swallowed the bile that burned her throat. "Here."

"I need you to apply pressure to the entry wound," he instructed her, "while Mrs. Carter holds him and stops the bleeding from the back. Got it?"

She couldn't do it. Images of Paul, pale on the ground, swam in her vision. But she didn't want Matt to see her weakness. Not if he needed her strength.

"I need a bandage. A towel or something."

Glancing around at the immobile church members, Matt swore softly and stripped off his own T-shirt. "Here. Like that. Down here. Come on, Clare!"

His tone, matter-of-fact and edging into impatience, prodded her forward. She stumbled to her knees, wedging her small hands in beside his big ones, overcoming her involuntary wince at the dampness and smell of blood.

"Good. Now you just take it easy a second, Reverend. I'll be right back. Come on, folks, stand back. Move back, please."

Lumbering to his feet, Matt ran stiffly in the direction of the truck. Concentrating on maintaining steady pressure on the wound, Clare was only dimly aware of him rattling off a string of numbers and the street name.

She reminded herself to breathe. Through her mouth, slowly. Looking up, she met the reflection of her own fear in Alma's eyes.

"Is he going to die?" the minister's wife asked.

Clare's stomach lurched. Under her hands, she felt the ominous wet spread of blood.

"No."

"Of course I'm not going to die," Reverend Ray scolded gently. "You heard the Sergeant. I'll be—" a spasm crossed his face "—fine."

"Shut up, Raymond," Alma said tenderly. Her straight dark hair swung forward as she laid her cheek against the top of his head. "Just shut up."

Unwilling to intrude, unable to take her hands away, Clare glanced over her shoulder for Matt. He strode back from his truck, swinging his straight right leg awkwardly from his hip. Had he hurt it when he'd tackled her? Limping, bare-chested, bloody, his face streaked with grime and his eyes blank with professional preoccupation, he looked like an avenging action hero.

She'd never been more glad to see anyone in her life.

"I don't know how hard to press," she said worriedly as he knelt beside her. "I don't want to hurt him, but he's losing blood."

"Here." His hands nudged hers aside. "Mrs. Carter, can you lean forward a little? We want to keep that shoulder elevated until EMS gets here."

Alma shook back her hair and complied. "How long?"

"Not long now. Couple minutes. How are you doing, Reverend?"

"I've done…better."

"Yeah." Matt's grin flashed. "Getting shot is way down on my list of favorite things."

Of course, Clare thought, wiping her sticky palms down denim-clad thighs. He'd been shot, too. It was practically part of his job description. How many months since he'd lain, bleeding, in pain and shock, waiting for the ambulance, waiting for relief? No wonder he knew what to do and what to say. He was familiar with all the things that terrified her.

She couldn't stand it.

She pushed to her feet. "What can I do?"

Black eyes met hers briefly in unspoken complicity, with unquestioning confidence. "Ask everybody to stay put. We're going to have some questions in a minute. I don't want to lose any witnesses."

She nodded. And this was the other side of what he did. Succor the victim, and then chase the bad guy. The police had failed to obtain the evidence to convict her husband's killer. She'd lost faith in the legal system after that, preferring to fight her demons and her battles in her own way. But this... She was grateful for Matt's competent, solid presence.

Reverend Ray coughed, squeezing his eyes shut in agony. Alma soothed him as Matt talked, calming and encouraging. Clare pressed her lips together. She would do whatever she could to help.

The sirens began, first one, then others joining in like a pack of hounds on the hunt. Trigger howled in response. The rising noise rippled through the milling bystanders. Unexpected violence had broken their cheerful, sweaty workforce into distinct knots of shocked, grieving, angry onlookers. But no one seemed about to leave.

By the nearly completed swing set, one of the church moms had an arm around Richie. Two girls held each other, openly crying. Clare's gaze went from Tyler, pretending nonchalance, to Isaac, twisting his navy cap in his hands.

She threaded through the fringes of the crowd to approach her crew leader.

"Isaac," she said gently, "did you see anything?"

He looked down and away. "It happened real fast."

Too fast, Clare thought. Just like the last time. Always too fast.

A patrol car swung in by the curb, an orange-and-white Emergency Medical Service vehicle screeching behind. Lights blinked on two sides of the lot, blue and orange. Doors opened. A patrolman in navy, paramedics in blue and gray, rushed on the small group huddled by the tree. Dimly, under the wail of approaching sirens, Clare heard Matt's terse explanation as he slid his big body out of the way.

"I have a male in his forties, conscious, shot in shoulder, possibly with a twenty-five caliber automatic pistol."

"Okay, we've got it."

"This is Mrs. Carter. She'll ride with you to the hospital."

"Right. On my count. One. Two. Three."

Through the boil of activity, Clare watched as they loaded the reverend onto a gurney and into the ambulance. Clear lines of oxygen and fluid were already being fitted to him as they wheeled him away. She remembered the tubes, the useless tubes, the silent machines, by Paul's bed in the hospital room. DOA, they'd told her, in hushed, oddly impersonal tones. Dead On Arrival. She shivered, clutching her elbows.

An officer's voice cut through her momentary abstraction. "Hell, Dunn, you look lousy. You okay?"

Her attention jerked back to Matt, hauling himself painfully to his feet on the other policeman's arm. Recognizing the officer who'd questioned Tyler and Richie, Clare looked around for the boys. Tyler hung back behind Benny. Richie knelt by Trigger, giving and receiving comfort.

"Fine. You the primary officer, Stewart?"

"Looks like it. My beat. You see anything?"

"Not a damn thing. My back was to the street."

"Drive-by?"

"Yeah."

Three more black-and-white patrol cars pulled up, circling the lot, blocking the street. Uniforms jumped out, voices raised, radios crackling. Beside her, Isaac shifted from foot to foot, hunching his shoulders to his ears. A perfectly understandable reaction, Clare thought. He'd been detained before, chased off and moved along often enough to be wary around so many cops.

But when he pulled his cap down almost to his eyebrows, she put her hand on his arm. "What is it?"

"Nothing."

"Isaac?"

"I got nothing to say."

She'd missed the officers' brief conference under the oak

tree. A blond patrol woman started unrolling yellow crime scene tape. A fresh-faced male officer took pictures. Officer Stewart and another policeman were already moving through the bystanders, talking, asking questions. Phrases buzzed around her, laden and persistent as wasps in autumn.

"We've got one shell in the ground."

"Who saw the whole thing?"

"Give your name to the officer."

Clare brushed her hand over her face, as if she could shoo her doubts away. "I think I saw the car," she volunteered.

Matt loomed beside her. He'd borrowed a jacket from someone, she saw, hanging open over his naked chest. "Stewart! We got a description of the vehicle." He turned back to Clare. "Did you notice the make or the model?"

Clare shook her head, feeling foolish. "No." At the time of the shooting, she'd been focused on Matt. Engrossed. Enthralled. Stupid.

"Don't worry about it. Nobody does. Well, twelve-year-old boys, maybe."

She forced herself to smile, appreciating his attempt to make her feel better.

"How about the color?" he prompted her.

"White."

"Yeah? All white?"

"No." She closed her eyes, remembering. "It had a black vinyl top. And those shiny strips, chrome, on the sides."

"Good. How many doors?"

"Four."

"New car?"

"No." She couldn't quite explain how she knew. "It was dirty. Not beat up. It just looked...long."

"Okay, that's good."

Officer Stewart murmured, "We can make a sketch. Did you see anything special, any distinguishing scrapes or dents, any features on the wheels or tires, ma'am?"

"No, not really." She tugged a hand through her hair, hating her inadequacy. "I'm sorry."

"The driver? Passengers?"

"Sorry, no."

"Were the windows open or closed?"

"I didn't notice." Her voice shook. She bit her lip.

"It was a Buick." Isaac spoke up suddenly beside her. Both officers turned to him.

"You recognize the car, Isaac?" Matt asked softly.

"Nope." The crew boss pulled off his navy cap, rolling it in his hands. "I saw it go by on Alston before it turned the corner on Magnolia. Passenger window was down in the front." He stopped fussing with his hat to meet Matt's gaze directly. "I recognized the shooter."

Clare's heart thumped. She felt the policeman's increased intensity, but Officer Stewart never looked up from his notebook. Matt's voice was almost casual.

"Name?"

"Real name's Kenny something. He goes by Sidewinder."

"He's a Viper?"

Isaac shifted. "Yeah."

"How do you know?" Stewart asked.

Clare stiffened. She knew how hard her crew chief had worked to put his past behind him. If they tried in some way to implicate Isaac...

"He knows," Matt said. "That's good enough for me."

Gratitude flooded Clare as the other cop shrugged. "Okay, Sergeant. Your call. You know where this Kenny guy hangs out?" he asked Isaac.

Matt looked up from zipping his jacket. "Try the storefront behind the gas station over on Jefferson. Used to be Willard's. Know it?"

Stewart grinned, flipping his notebook shut. "Oh, I know it, all right. Thanks, Mr...?"

"Do you need his name?" Clare intervened.

"Got to have it, ma'am. Doesn't mean we're going to use it."

She nodded to Isaac. "All right."

"Mills. Isaac Mills," he said, and watched while the officer wrote it down with his address.

"And yours, ma'am?" Stewart asked politely.

She gave it to him. "Can we go now?"

"Yes, ma'am. And thank you for your cooperation."

Her cooperation? Clare stared back at the officer, cold settling in her stomach. Her husband had been killed during the pretrial investigation of the Vipers leader. Clare had blamed herself then for not knowing enough, for not caring enough, for not being involved enough in his work. But what if all her knowing and caring had accomplished now was to involve another human being, to put at risk another man's life? Isaac had spoken up in part for her sake. What if the gang came after him now?

Matt touched her arm. "Come on, Clare. You're done here. Let me take you home."

"No. I can't go home. I need to know if the reverend's all right."

His hand, warm and strong, urged her toward his truck. "I'll call the hospital."

She stopped. She would not let him make her decisions for her. She could not let her longing for his strength undermine her hard-won self-sufficiency.

And her heart cringed inside her at the memory of Alma's fearful eyes. She remembered too clearly what it was like to lose the one you loved and depended on.

"I'm going to the hospital," she insisted. "Alma might need me."

He never let up his gentle pressure on her arm. "Fine. Then I'll take you. Richie can walk the dog home. Get in."

She found herself swinging obediently onto the seat as Matt untied the dog's leash and tossed it to Richie.

The boy's face lit. "Do you mean it?"

The creases around Matt's eyes deepened, but he didn't smile. "Yeah. Take him to Clare's, put him in the shed, and make sure he's got water." Richie gathered the leash up eagerly. "And Richie?"

"Yessir?"

"Don't get lost on the way home this time."

Don't get lost? It was only two blocks to her house. He couldn't possibly lose his way.

But Richie nodded. "I won't."

In his solemn response Clare recognized the man's implicit trust and the boy's underlying promise.

Apparently satisfied, Matt rounded the hood of the truck. Limping, she noticed. He grunted climbing in, and she left off messing with her seat belt to stare at him.

"What did you do to your leg?"

Matt started the engine. "I'm fine."

Clare frowned. He didn't look fine. His eyes appeared sunken under those formidable brows and, in spite of working in the sun all day, his color was lousy.

She bolted upright at a sudden, horrible thought. Everything had happened so fast. "You weren't hit, were you?"

"Do you see any blood?"

Somewhat reassured by his wry tone, she settled back against the hard blue seat. "Lots, actually."

He glanced down at his chest before turning the pickup onto a major road. "Not mine."

"Oh, right. I forgot. Bullets bounce right off you."

"Uh-huh."

"Like some superhero."

He winced slightly. "Yeah."

She didn't buy it for an instant. Polite demurrals worked well enough in her parents' world. Paul's soothing evasions had satisfied her for years. But if Matt thought he could hide his hurt or push her away, he didn't know how determined she was prepared to be.

"I think when we get to the hospital you should let someone look at your leg."

"They've seen it."

The hospital intersection came up on the left. An ancient Dodge in the right hand lane lunged in front of Matt's pickup and then braked for the yellow light. The Chevy jerked to a stop. Automatically, Clare braced her hands on the dashboard.

"Sorry," Matt muttered.

It sounded like a curse. Clare glanced at him, gauging the level of his tolerance, noting the fatigue lines around his mouth and eyes, the faint sheen of sweat on his upper lip. "It's okay."

As the light turned green, she watched as he let up on the clutch and saw his right thigh strain as he wrestled his foot from the brake to the accelerator. He hit the gas too hard, and the pickup lurched and stalled in the middle of the intersection. Clare pressed her lips together. He was hurting, dammit.

She waited until he'd restarted the truck and turned into visitor parking before she said, "Well, maybe they should check it again."

Muscling into a narrow space, he cut the engine and shot her an unfriendly look.

"Please, Matt. We both hit the ground pretty hard. I don't like thinking you got hurt protecting me."

His fingers drummed the steering wheel. "You are one pushy woman, you know that?"

"Yes," she answered promptly.

One corner of his mouth pulled up. Getting out, he slammed the door, speaking as he came around the cab of the truck. "Okay, fine. I'll get it looked at after we check in. Satisfied?"

Hope and relief made her incautious. She smiled back, knowing her heart showed in her eyes and not caring. "For now."

She thought he might grin at her silly innuendo. Instead, he stopped on the sidewalk and just looked at her. The laughter drained from his face, leaving it tired and a little sad. His lips parted. Afraid of what he might say, she half-lifted her hand to his mouth.

And then the wide steel-and-glass doors swished open, and an orderly wheeled out a young woman, balloons jerking and bobbing in their wake. Closing his mouth, Matt pivoted on his good leg and strode ahead. Clare followed, stepping from dirty rubberized carpet onto immaculate gray linoleum. Fluorescent lights and the sharp, remembered scents of alcohol and disinfectant assaulted her.

She hugged her elbows, suddenly cold.

Matt approached the long veneer counter to confer with a gray-haired volunteer in a pink cardigan.

"They've already moved the reverend up to the OR," he said, returning. "Alma's in the waiting room on the second floor. Do you want to go up?"

The cold spread. Of course she didn't want to go up. She just couldn't live with herself if she didn't.

"Second floor waiting room," she confirmed. "See you later?"

"Yeah." He hesitated, his dark gaze intent on her face. "You want me to take you?"

She squeezed out a smile, pretending for both their sakes that nothing was wrong. "Don't be silly. I can find it."

"Right." He didn't move.

Wiping her damp palms on her jeans, she forced herself to the elevator. For three years, she'd avoided this hospital. Now she wished some small emergency—a stitch or a sprain—had pushed her here sooner.

Dead on arrival...dead on arrival...

The automated doors whispered it. The lift machinery hummed. Muffled voices from the corridor blended into the remembered chorus. Paul had died before either one of them ever reached the hospital, before the policewoman came to tell her he'd been shot, even before the ambulance arrived, wailing, to rescue his body from the street.

She'd stood by a steel bed rail in this very building, pressing her husband's cold, slender hand, waiting for him to open his eyes so they could laugh together over someone's stupid mistake. And he never had. They explained it to her, over and over.

Dead on arrival. There was nothing they could do.

Stop it, Clare commanded herself, getting off the elevator. The situations weren't the same. She wasn't the same. After the shooting this afternoon, Matt had been there to staunch the blood and radio for help. He'd been there, strong and supportive and knowing in a crisis. Raymond Carter was not dead. And Ray's wife needed Clare's strength and reassurances, not morbid memories of tragedy.

A rectangle of flecked commercial carpet defined the waiting room area, a windowless alcove on the right of a wide, well-lit hall. Black-and-white portraits of prominent dead doctors hung on the walls. The square, upholstered chairs were nearly empty. Later, Clare knew, the room would fill with supporters as Grace Church mustered to care for one of its own. But Matt's truck had outstripped the family cars and the infrequent city buses. For now, Alma kept vigil alone.

Her arms folded protectively over her stomach, the minister's wife stood sentry in the middle of the room. Dirt marked the knees of her ironed jeans and her usually immaculate hair tumbled on her shoulders.

"Alma? How is he? Is there anything I can do?"

"Hey, Clare." Alma smiled, but the courtesy faded before it reached her eyes. "He's in surgery now. They said they'd tell me as soon as… Well."

"That's good," Clare said, and hoped Alma couldn't hear the false cheer in her voice. "Can I get you anything?"

"No. No, I'm fine."

Another one, Clare thought. We're all *fine* this afternoon. "How about the children? Do you want me to call anyone?"

"No. My sister Gloria's going over. She'll bring the girls this evening, maybe. I don't want to call James at school until—" She bit her lip, her dark eyes filling with tears.

"Until you know," Clare concluded for her.

An awkward silence fell. Under the flat gaze of some long gone medical department head, Alma straightened, pushing a loop of dark hair behind her ear.

"He's a sophomore this year."

"James?" Clare ventured. She'd met the Carter's oldest son over the Christmas holiday, a tall, well-spoken youth with his mother's pride and his father's smile. If Alma needed the comfort of distraction of discussing the boy, Clare was happy to oblige. She cleared her throat.

"Has he chosen a major yet?"

"Computer science."

"Lots of job opportunities there."

"Oh, yes. Though his father says—" Alma faltered.

Clare squeezed her hand. "What does his father say?"

"Ray says James will do well at whatever he wants, as long as he loves whatever he does."

Clare flinched. She thought of Paul, whose keen mind and sense of justice had led him to the law, and Matt, whose uncompromising courage and unexpected compassion made him a cop. What if doing what you loved put you in the way of some lunatic with a gun?

It wasn't a thought she could share with the preacher's wife. Shaking it off, Clare led Alma over to the row of chairs.

"We should sit down. I'm sure we'll be here awhile."

An hour passed, measured by the ping of the elevator doors and the quick steps of soft-soled shoes in the hall. The smells of fear and hope, of sweat and antiseptic, saturated the carpet and permeated the air. Leaning her head back against the cinder block wall, Clare closed her eyes to shut out the room and her memories.

A new scent cut through the hospital smell. Hot, bitter coffee. Her lids opened reflexively.

Matt stood before her, a paper cup in each large hand. Big and solid, reassuring and blessedly alive, he filled her senses, filled the waiting room.

"I brought you some really bad coffee." Handing it off, a cup to her and one to Alma, he fished in the pockets of his borrowed windbreaker for little paper packets. "Sugar?"

As his dark eyes met Clare's, she felt a heat and sweetness flow through her that had nothing to do with the coffee. "No, thanks. Just the 'powdered nondairy crud.'"

He grinned. "You remembered."

She looked cautiously down at the tan, chalky surface of

her coffee. He'd already added creamer to her cup. "So did you."

He took a seat beside her, leaning across her knees to speak to Alma. "I talked to the ER doc. He said your husband was looking good when they brought him upstairs."

Alma's grateful expression thanked him. "Did they catch him yet? The man who shot Ray?"

"No, ma'am. Not yet." He hesitated, as if wondering how much to tell her, before he offered, "They're investigating the possibility that the shooting was gang related."

"But why would the reverend be a target?" Clare asked.

"Community leaders are always at risk," Matt replied.

Alma's mouth twisted. "I liked it better when the most we worried about was gossip."

Clare's vigil with the preacher's wife continued, relieved now by Matt's strength and energy. He chatted with Alma about her preschool. He made forays, despite his limp, to the vending machines and rustled up a morning paper. Supporters from the church drifted in, a teacher from the school and a pair of elderly sisters who hugged Alma tight.

But the surgeon didn't come, and the worry couldn't be held at bay forever. Two hours later, strain lined Alma's face, and Clare's stomach churned with anxiety and bad coffee.

She turned in relief at the sound of new arrivals coming down the hall. She recognized the preacher's two daughters skipping ahead. The woman with them must be Alma's sister. And the tall boy in the red jacket, surely that was...

"James!" his mother cried, and fell on her son.

Clare felt a catch in her throat. Matt's hand rubbed a circle on the back of her neck. "Did you know he was coming?"

"Yeah."

She turned her head. "You sent for him."

"I talked to the aunt. She sent for him."

"Because you knew his mother needed him."

His hand fell away to scrape at his jaw. "I knew he needed to be here."

Not only a cop, she remembered suddenly, but a cop's son.

It explained so much. His understanding, his kindness, brought tears to her eyes. "Was your dad ever...?"

"Shot? Yeah. Twice." He shrugged away from her sympathetic touch. "He's still with us. Ornery old bastard."

His tough-guy routine couldn't fool her any longer. She heard the depth of love in his voice. "You take after him, then."

His acknowledging grin sizzled clear down to her toes. The man had no business looking at her like that in a room full of people.

Before she could tell him so, the doctor emerged, tired in pale green scrubs, and Clare felt cold again.

"Mrs. Carter?"

Alma's hand tightened on her son's arm. "Yes?"

The news was good. The bullet had missed the lung, missed the aorta. Reverend Ray was resting in recovery and could see her in a while.

Clare turned her head into Matt's broad chest and let relief take her.

Chapter 11

"**Y**ou need to eat."

They were in the elevator, going down. Matt braced his weight on the handrail, chafing at his bum leg, furious with his failure to take better care of his beat, of the reverend, of Clare. Standing beside him, she swayed with exhaustion. Her freckles stood out starkly against her white face.

She rallied, as he'd known she would, at his attempt to help her. "I'm not hungry."

"I am. You going to make me eat alone?"

"Well, I... Well, no."

He pressed his advantage. "Besides, I can't drive the truck."

"Oh, Matt." Her eyes rounded in dismay. "I didn't even ask. What did they say about your leg downstairs?"

"I'm fine," he said hastily. He wanted her to feel cooperative, not guilty. "I'm supposed to rest it some, that's all. And the pain pills they gave me make me loopy."

Her gaze turned speculative. "Is that a fact?"

He hid his grin at her implicit challenge. "I haven't taken any yet."

"Why not?"

"I can't take them on an empty stomach," he said craftily, counting on her overdeveloped sense of compassion to kick in.

She capitulated, running her hand through her hair. "All right, we'll go get something to eat. Do you want to stop for a burger?"

"I've had a burger." And he'd gladly eat another one, but he didn't think that was what she wanted. She needed something to restore the color to her lips and cheeks. Maybe that rabbit food she was so fond of? "Why don't we go out for Italian?"

The elevator doors swished open, and they stepped into the lobby. "Not if you need to rest up and take your pill. Besides—" Just for a moment, her smile glinted, and his insides ached. "We're not exactly dressed for dining. Come home with me. I'll make you something."

"I don't want you to cook."

"Come off it. My cooking's not that bad."

She looked almost hurt. He gritted his teeth. How could a woman so competent have such unexpected insecurities? He was trying to take care of her, dammit.

He waited for her to precede him out of the building into the damp twilight before he said, "Sugar, there's not a damn thing wrong with your cooking. Your cooking is fine. Your cooking is great. I don't want you putting yourself out, that's all."

She blinked at him. "You are loopy. Are you sure you didn't take one of those pills?"

"Sure. And I'll do the cooking."

Her smile spread. He wanted to cup his hands around its warmth and coax it into full life with his breath and mouth.

"We could do it together."

He could think of dozens of things he'd like to do with her, on her, to her. Preparing dinner was miles down on the list.

But there was no way he was acting on his impulses tonight. He was still pumped from the attack on the reverend. With his adrenaline already high and his control already stretched, he wouldn't last five minutes with this woman.

He leashed his tension, smiling at her. "You mean, cook?"

"You've got a dirty mind, cowboy."

She didn't guess the half of it. "I knew there was something about me you had to like."

Clare sniffed. When they reached his truck she held out her hand for his keys. Will had always let him drive. It was something else Matt had to get used to, being driven by another person. By Clare, he corrected himself. He eased in beside her, and she reached under the seat to adjust it. As the bench slid forward, he bent his leg sharply to avoid banging his knee on the dashboard, sucking in a groan.

The parking lot lights sparkled through the windshield, lighting Clare's pale, concerned face. "Are you all right?"

Sweat broke out on his upper lip. "Yeah."

Her look said she didn't believe him, but she didn't press. He appreciated her restraint.

The streetlights glowed in misty orange moons. The wiper blades beat an intermittent rhythm as Clare drove carefully along quiet, empty streets. She'd left her porch light on, Matt noted with approval. He really wasn't up to beating burglars out of the bushes tonight.

He limped up the slick walk behind her, listening to Trigger challenge their approach from inside the closed shed. Good dog. Opening the door, Clare led the way to the back of the house, flipping on lights as she went. Thin shafts of damp, cool air slid under the old windowsills as easily as a jimmy blade. But at the heart of the house, the kitchen glowed with ferns in pots and ripening fruit in baskets. The brightly colored dishes and vegetable-faced clock masked the dingy walls and old countertops. The short row of plants on the windowsill scented the air with aromas he recognized from his mother's cooking, basil, sage and rosemary.

He felt like the Big Bad Wolf calling on Red Riding Hood.

"Omelettes and a salad?" Clare suggested, turning from the refrigerator.

Remembering the red-and-green concoction she called a salad, Matt opted for something that fell within his area of expertise. "Fine. I'll do the eggs."

She pulled out bowls and opened drawers while he grated cheese and beat eggs with a fork. He circled around her as she splashed water in the stainless steel sink, drawn by her competent hands, her delicate wrists, her intense concentration as she measured oil and vinegar into a bottle. He imagined those hands on his body. He pictured her face as he moved strongly inside her.

He drew a breath. Held it. As soon as they ate, he was getting the hell out of here.

The trauma of the day had left him keyed up and on edge. He throbbed with pent-up energy and steamed with heat. He needed to unwind before he was fit for civilian company. Given the slightest encouragement, he'd fall on Clare like a slavering dog on a piece of meat. She deserved different, she deserved better, their first time together.

Besides, the incident that pumped his adrenaline had clearly disturbed her. In spite of her brave assistance, he'd seen her shock when the reverend was hit, the memories that crowded her eyes and tensed her shoulders. However much he admired her calm competence at the scene, he knew she was too shaken to take him tonight.

They sat at the battered kitchen table with its pretty woven place mats and flowery napkins and ate. Squelching his body's restless want, Matt derived a certain painful satisfaction just watching her, amused by the contrast between her hearty appetite and her neat, almost dainty handling of knife and fork.

As she ate, the color returned to her face. Her nose was faintly sunburned. He wanted to test the temperature of her pink skin with his fingers. Hell, he'd take any excuse to touch her at all. The imagined feel of her warm, smooth flesh made his blood pressure build.

Doggedly, he plowed through his omelette and chomped on

his salad, hardly registering the alien vegetables that lurked amid the lettuce. After today's events, he told himself, Clare needed care and cosseting. He could only give her hunger. His demand was too great, his desire too raw, for the patient seduction he figured she required.

She looked up from her plate, and the tentative invitation in her eyes made him bite his tongue.

He pushed back from the table. "I ought to go."

Clare didn't want him to leave. She wanted the reassurance of his warm, living presence. She knew her need was partly a reaction to the afternoon's violence, an instinctive affirmation of life after a reminder of death. She knew, too, that her feelings went deeper than that.

What she didn't know was how to make Matt stay.

"Have you taken a pill yet?" she asked, to delay him.

"What?"

"Your pain pills. Where are they? I'll get you one."

He stood, moving restlessly, hands jammed in the pockets of his borrowed windbreaker. It strained across his broad shoulders, emphasizing his size and power and muscle.

"It can wait. I'm fine."

His masculine energy had sustained her all day. She'd admired his calm, depended on his decisiveness and control. Now he looked tired and edgy and in pain. Concern over his injury sharpened her reply. "You're limping. And no offense, but you look rotten."

He laughed shortly. "I don't think a pill is going to help either one of those conditions, sugar."

"Well, it can't hurt. Sit down."

Somewhat to her surprise, he sat. She jumped up to get him a glass of water, glad to help, relieved to have something to do with her hands. He fished a brown plastic bottle from his pocket and shook out two small white tablets.

Filling a glass at the tap, she stood over him while he drank. His close-cut hair curled slightly into the strong nape of his neck. She itched to touch it.

"Clare." His voice was restrained.

"Mm?"

"You're making me nervous."

She laughed and ran her hands down the thighs of her jeans. "I know," she admitted ruefully. "I'm even making *me* nervous. Can I get you something else? Coffee, anything?"

He leaned back to look at her from under half-closed lids. The expression in his eyes made her pulse race. "Coffee would be fine."

She hovered an instant longer by his chair and then darted for the coffeemaker. Pouring water into the well, she offered suddenly, "You were wonderful this afternoon. I didn't tell you before."

"Not so wonderful. The shooter got away."

She turned, indignant he could think that way, could value himself so little. "You saved Reverend Ray's life."

He shrugged. "Maybe. The bullet missed the major organs."

"He still could have bled to death."

"Yeah." He met her eyes again, and she warmed at the appreciation in his gaze. "You didn't do so bad yourself. It can't have been easy for you, dealing with the gunshot back there, reassuring Mrs. Carter. You did good."

The warmth spread, settling low. His opinion mattered far too much. She ducked her head, spooning coffee grounds into a paper filter, counting carefully.

When she thought she had herself under control again, she said, "You really should take that jacket off. I might have a T-shirt or something you could borrow."

"Trying to get my clothes off, sugar?" He sounded amused.

Her hands shook as she fitted the filter into the basket. She was afraid. Afraid that he could breach the walled garden of her heart and bring it to ruin. More afraid of the strength of her own feelings than she was of his rejection. But all day she'd had practice in facing down her fears. She wasn't backing down now.

Baldly, she answered, "Yes."

Silence settled in the kitchen like thick honey. The scrape

of his chair clawed through it. She imagined him standing, and pulled a deep breath into her lungs.

"Clare."

She gripped the cool plastic handle of the coffeepot.

He said her name again, soft, insistent. She turned, her back to the counter.

His hands waited at the zipper of the navy windbreaker. Her mouth dried. She couldn't speak. While she watched, he pulled it down, the sound rasping the silence. She could hear it even over the pounding of her heart. Without embarrassment, he stripped the jacket from his shoulders and dropped it on his chair.

The sight of his broad body, all hard planes and slabs, closed her throat. A thin rug of dark hair swirled over his pectorals and stomach. A small medal on a thin gold chain rested on his chest. A white scar cut across a lower rib.

He paced toward her across the linoleum and reached behind her to pull her clenched hands from the rim of the countertop. Gently, he smoothed them open. One by one, he placed them high on his chest, against the warm muscle and springy hair. She could feel the suggestion of sweat against her palms, see it on his upper lip. Her hands rose and fell with his breath.

"All you had to do was ask, sugar," he said in his brown velvet voice. "All you ever have to do is ask."

She looked up then. "I have. Before. You turned me down."

Her honesty humbled him. "I just don't want you to regret this."

"Why don't you give me a chance to find out?"

He inhaled once, sharply. And then his mouth took hers. Warm and patient, it coaxed a response she was eager to give. He kissed her with a slow thoroughness that sapped her doubts and burned away her fears. Through the thin cotton of her T-shirt, she could feel the hot imprint of his flesh. His breathing was deep but steady. His arms were strong and comforting.

Comfort wasn't all she wanted tonight.

She stood on tiptoe to twine her arms around his neck and opened her mouth wider. His instant response jolted through her system before he controlled it, channeling the urgent heat that threatened to consume them into long, lush, leisurely kisses. Warm, gentle kisses. Ultimately frustrating kisses. Making an impatient sound in her throat, Clare wriggled closer.

His hands clamped on her shoulders and then released. "We'd better stop here."

Disbelieving, she tilted back her head. "Why? Better for who?"

"Just better. For now." His callused fingertips trailed down her cheek, sending ripples of delight along her nerve endings.

She didn't understand. Admittedly, it had been a long, dry while, but she still knew when a man was aroused. And he was, heavily, gloriously aroused. But there were other considerations that might stop him, she realized, concerns she hadn't had to worry about in years.

"Is it birth control? Because I've got condoms. I mean, I probably should check the expiration date or something, but—"

He continued to touch her face, her hair, with broad, strong fingers that teased and trembled. "No. Sugar, no."

"What, then?" she demanded. "You said all I had to do was ask. Well, I'm asking."

A muscle ticked in his jaw. "Clare…"

She fanned her anger, preferring it to the hurt that burned the back of her eyes. "What am I supposed to do now? Beg?"

"Dammit, no!"

His obvious frustration soothed her resentment, but not enough. "Maybe you could tell me what I'm doing wrong," she suggested. "I'm a little out of practice."

He shook his head impatiently. "Maybe I'm not the guy you should practice on."

"Why not?" she snapped.

"I can't make you promises."

Deliberately, she held his gaze. She could see his struggle to do the right thing, and it only made her want him more.

"I'm not asking you for promises." Paul had made her promises, solemn vows blown to bits by a murderer's gun. "I'm asking for tonight."

Goaded beyond the limits of his control, he swore and reached for her. The anger that had crackled around them coalesced into a lightning flash of passion. Triumph burst in her, drowned almost immediately by a downpour of desire as his hands swept over her, as his mouth crushed hers and devoured her. Shaken by the storm she'd conjured, she could do nothing but ride the wind.

His tongue plunged deep as she ran greedy palms over his damp, smooth, naked back. His rough cheeks abraded her face as they fed on one another, grappling frantically, rubbing like big cats mating. His scent swamped her, and she made a feral sound deep in her throat. Trying to absorb him through her skin, she pressed closer, breast to chest, belly to groin. It wasn't close enough. He stroked her, his touch hard and hungry. Her fingers curled, her short nails sinking into his shoulders, and he groaned into her open mouth.

Her blood pounded in her head as she breathed in deep gulps. She couldn't remember sex ever being like this, not sweetly close or quietly comforting, but raw and elemental. She felt matched. Mated. He dragged his teeth along the sensitive cords of her neck, and she shuddered. He branded her, his touch searing her breasts through thin cotton and insubstantial lace, and she moaned.

When he ripped open the fastening on her jeans, thrusting his hand inside to close over her, she screamed. She was already wet and ready for him.

He staggered, and they banged into the table. Cupping her buttocks, he lifted her onto it and ducked his head to suckle her through her shirt. She gasped encouragement, flinging her arms around his neck to pull him closer.

With hot, dark words of praise, he petted her, burying his lips against her throat as his touch glided surely over, around and between the petals of her flesh. She flowered for him, pushing her hips urgently against his hand.

More, she thought frantically. She needed more.

She was desperate for him, already straining for his hot, full, complete possession. He stripped her jeans down to her knees and off her ankles. She grappled with his belt buckle, fought the buttons of his fly as he stepped between her legs.

His arousal, thick and proud and heavy, sprang into her hands. She caressed him and was rewarded by his groan.

"Birth control," he rasped. "We need…you said…"

"In the bedroom."

His stomach muscles jumped under her wandering touch. Inhaling sharply, he rested his damp forehead against hers. "I'm not in any shape to carry you up the stairs, sugar."

The wry tone couldn't disguise Matt's chagrin. Shocked to momentary sanity, Clare drew back. His wound. Of course. He returned her gaze impassively, the muscles tightening in his jaw. The knowledge that this strong, proud man required her reassurance was surprisingly sweet.

She smiled in invitation, her blood roaring in her ears. "Then I guess you'll just have to race me up them."

The heat in his answering smile warmed her to the soles of her feet.

In the end, Clare figured, it was less a race than an obstacle course. They bumped and slid from step to step, pausing to kiss and play and touch until frustration sent them staggering upward again. They were leaning on each other at the finish, naked as ancient Olympians and breathing deep like runners at the end of a marathon. His hands flowed over her, igniting fires in their wake.

"Here." She tugged his arm impatiently. "Through here."

Her room was like her, Matt thought, with a cop's ability to observe and retain detail even in moments of emotion. Small and neat and deceptively utilitarian with its narrow white bed and big wooden dresser. Around the room, little touches hinted at the sensuality in her nature: the vanilla-scented candle on the nightstand, the soft blue throw at the foot of the bed, the fresh flowers on the table by the window. She must have left the sash open when she left the house that morning because the gauzy white curtains billowed at the bottom, and the air that flowed through the room was fresh and chilly.

His skin prickled.

Clare kissed his shoulder. "Checking for those burglars?"

It wasn't burglars that worried him. He was the intruder here.

Unexpectedly intimidated, he lowered himself cautiously to the edge of her neat white bed. He guessed he was the first man to make it this far since her husband's death. Could he control himself long enough to make it good for her? He hadn't been with a woman since he'd left the hospital. For a while before that, actually. But he was ready for her.

He looked down at his lap, where his body quivered with greed and eagerness. All right, more than ready. And healed enough. His wound had closed to a neat white circle and a ragged pink line. He'd built his muscle until the right thigh was a match, outwardly at least, for the left. She didn't seem disgusted by the slight difference, by the weakness that kept him from sweeping her up and under him and loving her until she cried out and clung. Loving her as she deserved to be loved.

Slim and white, she glimmered before him. She was so beautiful she made him ache. She was so delicate she made him sweat.

"You'll have to be on top," he said roughly.

She stepped forward, her hair pale gold in the dim light from the window, her smile lighting the darkness.

"I think I can take it," she said.

Her innuendo eased the knot inside him, released his rigid control. In this one way, at least, maybe he could be what she wanted. He held out his hand. She twined her fingers with his, and he drew her down onto the soft, quilted cover of the bed.

As he rolled on his side to kiss her, her smooth thighs rubbed his. Need leapt inside him, sharp and deep. He felt the hardened crests of her nipples against his chest. Hoping her reaction was to him and not to the chill of the room, he grazed them with his thumbs, pressed them with his palms. Her sigh of satisfaction filled his mouth.

Her hands and feet were cold. Sliding over him, they warmed quickly. Her mouth was hot and drew on his. Little avid sounds escaped her. She liked what he was doing, he knew it. He felt it in the flex of her muscles, the arch of her back, as his hands explored, as his mouth feasted. Her tension built his, stretching his self-command until they both quivered like trees in the wind. Limbs rubbed. Sheets rustled. A pillow slid to the floor, but he didn't miss it.

Her delicate cheeks were flushed, her slitted eyes turbulent with emotion. He took her up once with his touch alone, for her pleasure, for his. Her head tossed. Her heels dug into the mattress. He did it again, driving her on and on before the strong gale force of his passion, swept up in her gloriously uninhibited response. She poured herself into his hand.

He flung himself onto his back, gripping the disordered sheets on either side.

"Now," he said. "Dammit, sugar, now."

She slid silkily over him and climbed astride. Soft as mist, wet as rain, she took him into herself in exquisite increments. He was sucked into the center of the storm, rising under her, falling with her, until sensation whirled him up and pleasure emptied him.

Her final cry of satisfaction drifted down with him to earth.

Clare woke to rain and the sound of Matt breathing in the darkness.

A cold, fretful breeze stirred the curtains, but under her hand his chest rose and fell in deep, steady cadence. He radiated heat like a furnace.

Comfort, bone deep, flowed through her.

She'd forgotten the peace of lying with a man, the intimacy of sharing a bed and sleep. She didn't know how long she'd drowsed, but she felt she could go on like this forever.

In the intimate darkness, the subtle colors of the room were drowned and glimmering. The faint, sweet scent of daffodils drifted from the table by the window, mingling with the earthy musk of man and sex. Turning her face into the smooth skin of his shoulder, Clare inhaled.

"Your nose is cold," Matt rumbled.

His words, hardly loverlike, pricked her confidence. A little of her satisfaction leaked away.

"Sorry. I thought you were asleep."

"Hey, come here." His big hand pressed against the back of her head. "I like it. Means you're healthy."

"Healthy?" she repeated, tasting the word in her mouth. "Like the dog?"

"Yeah."

She heard his grin in the darkness. Turning her head quickly, she bit at one of his fingers.

"Careful, sugar. You're liable to give me ideas."

Reassured, she nestled her cheek against the hard, smooth curve of his shoulder.

"Big talk," she scoffed.

"You want big? I'll give you big."

She giggled. A genuine giggle, she thought, vaguely astonished at the sound. "You're delusional, cowboy."

"Is that what I am?" Rolling to his side, he pressed against her.

Her breath caught. The muscles in her thighs went lax at the hard evidence of his desire. "Maybe not delusional," she conceded, getting the words out with difficulty as he nuzzled her throat. "Maybe just insatiable."

He breathed in her ear. "How about 'healthy'?"

She laughed, already reaching for him.

The phone rang. Matt swore at the interruption.

"It's all right," Clare soothed. "They can call back. It's not important."

"Nobody calls at ten-thirty at night unless it's important," Matt said as the phone continued to ring. "You better take it. It could be Alma or somebody from the hospital."

He hadn't lost track of the time, Clare noted, sitting up. She stretched one arm out for the receiver and made a grab with the other hand for the sheet as it fell away from her naked breasts.

"Miz Harmon, this is Officer Stewart. Is Sergeant Dunn with you, ma'am?"

Her heart jumped to her throat. She coughed to clear it. Matt, sprawled against the white linens of her bed, looked up in query.

"It's for you."

Frowning, he took the phone.

Her hands were icy again. Hiking up the sheet, she tried to warm them under her armpits while she listened to his one-sided phone conversation.

"Uh-huh...okay." Very sharply, "You're sure?" A longer pause while tension tightened his upper body and his face slowly blanked to a mask of professionalism. "Okay. No, I'll tell her.... Thanks, Stewart. I owe you one."

He hung up, his knuckles gleaming white on the receiver before he deliberately relaxed his grip.

"Is it Reverend Ray?" Clare asked, stomach clenched with foreboding. "Is he all right?"

"Yeah, fine. As far as I know. They picked up the guy who shot him."

His reaction puzzled her. "Well, that's good, isn't it? Did he confess?"

"Sort of. Turns out he wasn't aiming at the preacher."

Clare closed her eyes. So, that was the problem. It was everything she hadn't wanted to see, everything she'd feared. She'd just given herself, body and soul, to a man whose job, whose very identity, made him a target for violence. The fragile partnership they'd forged was already at risk. She forced herself to ask anyway, with no real hope of a positive response. "An accident?"

He seemed as reluctant as she was to admit it. "No."

She picked at it like a child with a scab, knowing it would hurt. ''Who, then? Who was he aiming at?''

He turned his head. The soft gray light through the gauzy curtains illuminated his dark eyes, his grim mouth.

''You, Clare. He was gunning for you.''

Chapter 12

"But why?" Clare asked.

They were sitting at her kitchen table, fully dressed. Matt had used her shower and borrowed an oversized T-shirt she sometimes slept in. In spite of the wet comb tracks in his hair and the wrinkled fabric pulling over his shoulders, he looked wired and ready for action. Clare half expected him to whip out a notebook and pencil and start asking questions. She braced herself for a brush-off.

But he answered her, after a pause, as if he had to sort out first what to tell her. "Your project's encroaching on Vipers' turf. Sidewinder said he was trying to...discourage your expansion."

"Shoot me, you mean," she said bluntly.

Her frankness surprised him. There was a gleam in his dark eyes, of admiration or maybe amusement. "Shoot *at* you," he corrected. "We've got aggravated assault with a deadly weapon, but he's not admitting to malice aforethought. He wanted to scare you, he says."

''Well, he succeeded.'' She got up to pour them both more coffee.

''Clare...''

She pretended not to see his outstretched hand, though she felt the pull deep inside as she swerved past him on her way to the coffeemaker. If he touched her, she wasn't sure what she would do. Whimper, maybe, or cry, or some other disgraceful, vulnerable thing. She wouldn't do that to him. He had enough to deal with.

He was hurt because of her. Not because of his job, not because of random violence, but simply because he'd tried to protect her. He was lucky only his thigh had been strained in that tackle on the lot today. He might have taken the bullet meant for her. Reverend Ray had been shot simply for standing behind her.

Clare didn't want that responsibility. She couldn't take the guilt. For three years she'd sheltered behind the barriers of her heart, and the first man to breach her defenses could have been killed for her sake.

The threat to her own life worried her. Well, all right, she admitted, it scared her silly. But she'd accepted some degree of danger when she'd moved to this neighborhood. It was the price she paid for taking on Eddie Boothe. It was a penance, of sorts, for never really sharing her husband's goals or understanding his job while he was alive. She figured her increased self-respect was worth the risk.

She'd never bargained on the cost to others.

For Matt's safety, for her own peace of mind, she had to rebuild the wall between them. Keeping her back to him, she added milk to her cup.

''It wasn't even a lot on my own project,'' she muttered.

''No,'' he agreed bleakly. ''It was mine. The playground was my idea.''

She hadn't thought of that. Turning to face him, she read the burden of his highly developed sense of duty in his eyes and the grim set of his mouth. The very qualities that made him so hard on himself made her go soft inside.

She wanted to protest his unforgiving commitment to the task he'd set himself, to ignite the laughter in his eyes and tease his mouth with kisses. But the sooner she restored some distance between them the better off they'd both be. She settled for taking the chair opposite his, sliding his coffee mug across the table.

"That was just a coincidence. It could have happened anytime, anywhere."

One corner of his mouth twitched, as if he considered smiling. "That shouldn't make either one of us feel better, sugar. Do you have someplace you could stay for a while?"

Her stomach dropped. She stared at him, hoping she'd misunderstood. "What are you talking about?"

"You should go somewhere safe for a while."

"But...it's over. They caught him, you said."

"Clare, there's a good possibility he wasn't acting alone. I talked to Stewart. Eddie Boothe is out, and looking to get his old territory back. Until we can tie him to the shooting and pick him up, you're in danger."

Her heart constricted. Matt was shutting her out. Sending her away. Trying, as Paul had tried, to protect her, while he went into danger.

"I'm not leaving."

"Just for a while. A couple weeks' vacation. Maybe you could visit your parents?"

Clare could just imagine her wealthy, sheltered parents' reaction if she showed up on their doorstep, a fugitive from gang violence.

She shook her head. "No. If my parents think someone's gunning for me on the streets of Buchanan, they'll wrap me up with the wedding crystal and lock me in storage. I can't abandon my work and my life here and go running home to Mommy and Daddy the minute things get tough."

His jaw tightened, revealing how much his mild tone was costing him. "Let's look at this reasonably. You go, we pursue our investigation, and I'll call you the instant we make an arrest. You stay, you put yourself and everyone around you in danger.''

Now, she ordered herself. Tell him now. With forced casualness, she wrung the words out. ''So, don't stick around.''

His stillness weighted the air. Clare focused on the hand curled around his cup. She didn't want to look in his eyes, to see the hurt reflected there.

''Not an option,'' he said finally, flatly.

Relief settled in her chest. She ignored it. There had to be something she could say to convince him to go.

''Maybe it is. Maybe it would help.''

''Help, how?''

She glanced away to where the rain trailed down the window, tracing the dark outside with silver streaks. ''I never used to have trouble on the lots,'' she said slowly. ''Not like this. You move in across the street, and suddenly I'm vandalized and shot at.''

''Are you saying that's my fault?'' he asked steadily.

She couldn't say that. Even if she believed it was true, she wouldn't add to the load of responsibility he shouldered. ''No. I'm just pointing out that our association might be threatening to someone.''

''Good. Let them be threatened. Let them be scared the hell away. But if they're not, you can't be here to take the heat until they're caught. We've got a statement, Clare, from a known gang member, that targets you. You need to go.''

He was right. Of course he was right. She opened her mouth to agree with him and heard herself say, ''I have to stay.''

''Why?'' His question cracked like a gunshot in the quiet kitchen.

How could she defend her decision? How could she explain? If she told him about her frustration after the legal system's failure to punish her husband's killer, Matt would hear it as a criticism of the police. If she admitted the private war she waged on the Vipers' leader, he'd have one more reason to go after Eddie Boothe and get himself shot.

She shivered, afraid. Pleating her fingers together in her lap, she took refuge in practicalities.

"The project doesn't run itself. Who's going to make the contacts and schedule the crews and pay the bills if I leave? Who's going to write the paychecks? What do you think will happen to the people who work here if I walk out on them, the way everyone they've ever depended on has walked out on them?"

"I don't know, and I don't care," Matt said roughly. "What good is it going to do them if you get shot?"

"None." He was angry. She didn't blame him. But she wished he would stop trying to convince her and comfort her instead. She took a sip of coffee, to steady herself. "But I can't preach to these kids about hard choices and taking responsibility and then shove off the instant I'm threatened."

How could she do it? Matt wondered. How could she sit there, small and indomitable with her quiet, watchful eyes and her calm, reasonable arguments while panic raked his gut and threatened to take control of his voice?

"You're making me crazy, you know that?"

That jolted her, he saw with mean satisfaction. Usually he was the one who ducked the direct discussion of emotion. But her danger pulled it out of him.

"Some gangbanger is using you for target practice," he continued, "and I can't protect you. You're not stupid. Don't you understand the risk?"

"I understand it," she said, her blond-tipped lashes sweeping down to hide her eyes. "I just can't allow it to matter. I owe my kids and crew my loyalty."

Matt curled his fists for control and fought not to punch out a wall in his best intimidate-the-suspect style. He was jealous, he acknowledged. Envious of her dedication to her job, resentful of her devotion to the scruffy street people and sullen teens she employed.

"They don't deserve it," he said.

She gave him that look of patient disappointment, like Saint Joan reproving Buster the Clown. He didn't back down.

"That was no random drive-by this afternoon. The shooter knew exactly when and where to find you. Either he's a regular reader of your little church bulletin, or someone at the project tipped him off."

He saw the doubt that clouded her face, the sickness in her eyes as she realized he was right, and squelched his flash of sympathy. He couldn't afford to worry about her feelings when her life was at stake.

But she was ready with a prompt defense.

"That makes it even more important that I don't leave right now," she said in her certain, well-bred way. "I'm not losing all the gains of the past three years because you think someone from the project *might* be responsible."

His open palm hit the table. Frustrated, he roared, "Do you want to get killed?"

"Of course not. Do you?"

Afraid he knew where this argument was headed, he glared at her. "What the hell does that have to do with anything?"

"Nobody asks you to give up your job because of the risks involved," she argued. "There's no reason why you should expect me to."

"Pack your bag," he ordered. "There's a guy in a cell who's taken one shot at you already, a dozen on the street hot to finish the job and some stooge on your payroll willing to make it easy for them. I've got every reason I need to drive you straight to the airport and sling your cute little butt onto the next flight out of here."

He'd shaken her, he saw. Good.

"Maybe every reason," she conceded. "But you don't have the right."

That stopped him cold.

No right. Not a husband's authority. Not even a lover's influence, apparently, though she'd taken him to her bed earlier this evening with generosity and joy. He'd claimed her with his body, and now she was repudiating his stake with her words.

Her rejection hurt. He felt it like a blow to the chest. With an instinct as old as Genesis and as powerful as the Flood, he wanted to be the man she turned to for defense and support. He wanted to seek his comfort in those slim, freckled arms and see his future in her whiskey brown eyes.

Stupid, Matt thought. And irresponsible. As long as he was married to his job, he wasn't fit or ready for other duty. Hadn't a string of ex-lovers told him so? Cops made unreliable boyfriends and lousy husbands. Even the good ones, like his dad, bought their domestic happiness at the cost of their wives' peace. He'd never been able to make up to his mother for his father's neglect or satisfy the Marcia-Amys. What made him think after Clare's loss that he was the right man for her?

I can't make you promises, he'd told her tonight, and she'd taken him at his word.

He hadn't realized the lack of ties could bind him so closely.

He swore, long and fluently, while she watched with grave, intelligent eyes. The outburst made him feel better, and then silly, like a nine-year-old mouthing off to shock his mom. "Would you at least go to a hotel?" he asked tightly, already knowing her answer.

"No. I won't leave the neighborhood."

"Fine. You can move in with me."

Real consternation disturbed her calm, resolute face. No wonder. His sudden offer had surprised even him.

She scrubbed her hands against her thighs. "No. I don't think we should advertise our...relationship."

He'd known all along he didn't deserve her. He hadn't known how much it would cut when she reached the same conclusion. He raised an eyebrow, mocking them both. "So, I'm okay for a quick feel-good tumble but not good enough to live with, is that it?"

"No!"

Suddenly tired, Matt held up his hand to forestall the compassionate spate of excuses that was all she had to offer him. The pulse in his thigh throbbed violently, the effect of too much exertion and not enough rest. His head pounded in sympathy. And there was an ache in his chest, unrelated to either of these, that he didn't want to examine too closely. So, she didn't feel what he felt when they made love. That wasn't her fault.

"Fine," he said wearily. "Get me a blanket. I'll sleep on the damn couch."

She pressed her pretty lips together. "I don't think that's a good idea."

"I'm not leaving you alone and unprotected in this house," he said through his teeth. "Dammit, sugar, you're in trouble."

"Don't you think I know that?"

"I don't think you have a clue," he said brutally, remembering Boothe's bright, malicious eyes. "Just because you've had some success with good guys like Isaac and boys like Richie doesn't mean you're a match for somebody like Eddie Boothe. You have no idea what he's capable of."

Her face went cold and still. Her eyes glittered.

"You're wrong," she said. "I know exactly what he's capable of. Eddie Boothe ordered the murder of my husband."

As an exit line, Matt figured, it was near perfect. He sat there like an idiot, slack-jawed and sorry, as her slim back faded into the darkness of the hall.

Isaac had said Clare's husband was prosecuting Eddie Boothe when he got put away. Frantically, Matt thought back, casting about for details. An assistant D.A. had been shot a few years ago when he'd gone on his own to interview a witness. It hadn't been Matt's case, but he recalled the investigating officer's frustration. They'd never made an arrest.

And Eddie, Matt remembered now, had plea-bargained his original charge of dealing drugs to possession, serving three out of five years. They'd never proved—Matt hadn't known—the two cases were connected. But obviously the lawyer's widow thought so.

Matt listened to Clare's footsteps going up the stairs. And he'd just told her she had no clue of Eddie Boothe's evil.

Nice going, Dunn, he jeered himself. Why don't you kick the dog while you're at it?

The dog. He rubbed his face. Damn, he still had to feed and walk Trigger, shut up in Clare's shed.

He rubbed the knot of tension at the back of his neck. He couldn't leave her house unlocked. But following their bitter exchange, he wasn't about to go banging on her bedroom door, either, demanding a key. After a quick, professional search, he found an extra key in the most obvious place, on a hook by the back door, where any thief could shatter a pane in the glass and lift it. He'd have a word with Clare about that in the morning, he thought. If she was still speaking to him.

Quietly, he let himself out, seeking relief from his tumbled thoughts in action. The security lights were on in the lot next door. At the crunch of Matt's footsteps on the gravel, Trigger lumbered up from sleep, head low and hackles raised. They did a quick tour of the lot and then scouted the perimeter of Clare's yard, Trigger bouncing ahead and returning often to thrust a big, wet nose in Matt's hand.

"Some guard dog you are," Matt said. But he remembered the way the dog had risen wary and silent at his approach, and scratched its neck.

Limping across the street, he staggered back with a twenty-pound sack of dog food on his shoulders. Clare might boot him out of her bed, he thought wryly, but she wouldn't starve his dog. The idea had some potential. He could move in on her slowly, accustom her gradually to his presence in her house and her life. Unreasonably, his spirits lifted.

He'd start with the dog dishes.

He fed Trigger in the kitchen. Dinner gulped, the dog bounded after him into the living room and eyed the couch hopefully, tail wagging, big toothy grin stretching his face like a dolphin's.

"Don't get any ideas," Matt warned. "We're not exactly welcome here."

Trigger barked. Matt swore. Had they woken Clare?

Gliding to the hall, he listened at the foot of the stairs. The empty darkness echoed with the click of canine toenails on the wooden floor and the rush of air in and out of his lungs. And something else.

The hair on his nape rose in warning. He stilled his breath.

Not the water in the pipes or the wind in the chinks or the cat two doors down... Soft and intermittent and ugly, he heard the choked sound of Clare's sorrow.

He gripped the bannister until the hard knob bruised his palm. She was crying. He'd made her cry. The thought ripped at his gut.

His cop's brain sprang into defensive action. God knew, Clare had plenty of other reasons for grief. It wasn't every day she saw one of her best friends shot. It wasn't every evening she relived her own loss sitting vigil with the wounded man's wife.

A raw sound escaped into the hall. Matt's knuckles turned white as his mental list went on. It was almost certainly the first time she'd been screwed by an edgy, insensitive cop with rotten timing and worse control. Or had her life threatened in a drive-by shooting. It was just her tough luck her new lover reacted to her danger by throwing her husband's murder in her face and yelling at her.

The kindest thing the jerk could do now, Matt considered, was keep the hell away.

Of course he didn't. Calling himself three kinds of fool, he dragged his sorry carcass up the stairs. He was trained to respond to people in crisis. He would go in and comfort her. It was a simple professional obligation.

Sure it was.

As discreetly as a cracksman, he stole down the short corridor and tapped at her door. All sound within stopped. Well, what did he expect? She wouldn't want a repeat of tonight's performance. Any of it, he thought, wincing.

"Clare?"

More silence. Trigger whined from the foot of the stairs. Matt knew just how the dog felt.

He knocked again. "Are you okay?"

The door opened inward. He hadn't heard her approach

from the other side. She stood just inside the narrow gap, blocking the entrance with her body. Silhouetted against the faint light from her window, he couldn't make out her expression, but her voice was truculent.

"What next? Are you going to yell 'Police! Open up!'?"

Relief relaxed his muscles. He leaned one hand on the door frame. He had a feeling he was grinning foolishly, but maybe in the dark she couldn't see.

"I will if you want," he offered.

"No. Thank you," she added politely.

She didn't budge. Didn't invite him in to dry her tears or hold her close or rumple her neat, white bed.

He sought for a subject to excuse his flagrant violation of her privacy. "I took a look around outside. Everything's quiet."

"One o'clock and all is well?" He imagined her eyebrows raised.

"Yeah. I mean, is it?"

The shadow of her shoulders lifted, as if she shrugged or hugged her elbows tighter. "I'm fine. Do you need a blanket?"

"No. I—no."

"Good night, then." She turned to lay her hand on the door.

Just as quickly, he reached to prevent her. Because, as the pale light behind her touched her profile, he'd seen the glistening track of tears on her cheek.

"What are you doing?" she demanded as he muscled his way in.

"Tucking you in," he answered peaceably, his heart beating fast. Would she allow that? "Haven't you ever been tucked in before?"

"Not recently, no." Her tone was dry, but she didn't object as he threw back the disordered covers.

"Well, then, it's time you were." He snapped the bottom sheet tight. "Fortunately for you, I've had experience."

"Really?" She moved to the foot of the bed. He was very

conscious of her watching him as he lined up the blankets with military precision. "Do you have references?"

"Not that much experience," he said hastily.

Her watery chuckle entranced him.

Fishing a pillow from the floor, he plumped it up, smoothed it down, and stepped back to view the results. She didn't offer an opinion, so he prompted her.

"Almost perfect," he said.

"Almost?"

"Yeah. It's missing something." He snapped his fingers. "A hot water bottle!"

"I don't have a hot water bottle."

"No?" He scraped his jaw with his thumb, pretending to consider. "I can't really tuck you in without a hot water bottle. Unless, of course, I'm prepared to offer my body for the cause."

Against the pale rectangle of light, her shoulders stiffened. "I don't think…"

"Oh, it's okay," he assured her. "As an officer of the peace, I'm trained in making sacrifices."

Her defensive posture tore at his heart.

"It's okay," he said again, gently.

He folded down a corner of the neatly aligned blankets. Turning his back, he skimmed out of his T-shirt. He lay down on the other side of the bed, on top of the covers.

Extending one arm cautiously along her pillow, he waited.

She shivered in front of the partially opened window, wavering like the curtains in the breeze. Finally, propelled by practicality or need or cold, she crawled in beside him. Under the covers. Flat on her back, staring straight up, stiff as a corpse in the morgue.

It was a start, Matt told himself.

He flexed his outstretched arm, bringing her against him with calculated care. They lay down together on the soft, narrow bed, and her lashes were wet against his throat.

She relaxed by degrees. First her hand on his chest, then her shoulders, then her neck. Her fine, smooth hair tickled his jaw. Without turning his head, he could inhale the fresh scent of it and the darker perfume of her skin. His headache ebbed, in spite of the tension making itself felt elsewhere in his body.

She sighed, a small, confiding whisper of air that stirred the hair on his chest and other things, lower down.

To distract himself, he asked hoarsely, "Tough day?"

Her breath caught, a soft sound suspended between a laugh and a sob. "I've had better."

It was important that he say the words, so he did, staring over her head into the darkness. "I'm sorry, Clare."

Her fingers curled, as if she tested the resilience of his muscle. "Thank you," she said gravely.

"For what?"

She hesitated. "For making me feel better."

His heart fissured. "Yeah, I'm real good at that."

Clare lifted her head from his chest. "What is it, Matt?"

She was so precious, so perfect and precious in his arms. He'd hurt her. He'd let her down. Maybe he would always let her down, but at least he could try to match her honesty. He wasn't used to sharing himself with anyone but his partner. And Will, thank God, had never required words. But after the way Matt had snapped at her tonight, he figured he owed them to Clare.

"I'm just not much good in the hand-holding department, that's all. Never have been."

"And just whose hand have you tried holding?"

Too many, he thought, expelling his breath. "This is stupid."

"You got a girl on the side, cowboy?"

He was genuinely appalled. "Hell, no. Sugar, I can't handle more than you."

He felt her waiting. When he didn't speak, she took a shot into the darkness, hitting her target with devastating accuracy. "Who got to be the man of the house when your dad was out playing cops and robbers?"

He was silent.

"Who was there for your mother when your father was gone?"

"I was the oldest," he said defensively. "I was supposed to help."

Her fingers touched his jaw. "That's a lot to ask of a child."

"I'm no good at it," he muttered.

She laid her cheek against his arm, and he felt the knot in his chest ease. "You do all right. You were there for me today. I'm grateful."

Her words were like ointment on a wound, healing and stinging at the same time. He'd never had a woman content with his rough comfort. And he didn't deserve Clare's gratitude now. He tightened his arm around her. "Sure. You can count on me. Supercop to the Rescue. After you've been shot at, yelled at, and generally screwed."

She was quiet for so long after that he thought maybe she'd fallen asleep. That was okay. Her being unconscious made it easy to keep his hand from straying down her back and his mind from drifting into trouble. Easier, anyway. Sunk in her sheets, surrounded by her fragrance, it was hard to dismiss the memories of their lovemaking.

In spite of his stupid self-confession and various physical complaints, the twinge in his thigh, the throb between his legs, Matt felt curiously peaceful. Something about the feel and the fit of Clare in his arms satisfied some soul-deep ache inside him.

Her cheek moved against his shoulder. So, she was awake after all.

"Actually," she said softly, "I liked the screwed part."

His heart pounded under her hand. Maybe she'd forgiven him, but that didn't mean she was going to give him the chance to hurt her again. Hell, he didn't want another chance. She deserved a secure relationship and an unclouded future, and he was the last man to promise her those things.

Her light touch drifted down his belly, and his muscles contracted. "Sugar, this isn't going to solve anything."

"I know," she whispered.

The gentle movement of her hand ceased. He clenched his molars on his frustration. He bore the long, aching moments, willing his earlier satisfaction to return, struggling to recapture the easy contentment he'd felt just holding her close. Only now there was no peace, only pressure and tension. He was too conscious she was awake and wanting him back. Her naked feet rubbed restlessly together. Every little breath she took pressed her puckered nipples into his side.

"Of course," he rasped at last, "I did offer to sacrifice my body for the cause."

Clare felt the temptation flood her veins like sap rising in the spring. She ought to resist it, she knew. Matt was right. Their making love would solve nothing. She needed to reestablish the distance between them before he got hurt, before she got hurt.

Yet even as her mind argued, her body acquiesced to the hundred tiny sensual pulls of his: his scent stealing into her lungs, his strength pillowing her head, the implicit promise of that mobile mouth.

He lifted his head and kissed her, nuzzling her lips. Without thinking, she parted to admit him. His tongue explored the tender inner surface of her lower lip before he caught it between his teeth. When she gasped, he followed her indrawn breath with his tongue.

His hand made gentle circles on her back, urging her closer. The light cover that separated their bodies slid away as she wriggled against him. His muscular chest received her weight. His jeans abraded her smooth bare thighs.

It wasn't enough.

She reached for the button at his waistband, but Matt had other ideas. Threading his fingers with hers, he brought her hand to his mouth and pressed soft kisses in her palm, warm kisses on the point of her chin, damp kisses down her throat to where her breasts peaked against her cotton nightshirt.

She arched her back to give him better access. Her heart soaked up his tenderness like thirsty ground absorbs the rain. Earlier, his unbridled passion had swept her away. His leisurely seduction now devastated her. Now he knew where to touch, and how. His fingers sought and stroked, fluid, coaxing. He lifted her nightgown up and away. The prickling caress of his beard-roughened jaw against her throat, the taunting brush of his body hair on the sensitive tips of her breasts, made her quiver like lake water.

His hands shaped her body, washing every rounded surface, seeking every crevice. His exquisite care made her feel feminine, safe, cherished, loved. Even if it was an illusion, it was a sweet and powerful one. She floated, lapped by sensation, too heavy with pleasure to do more than stroke his thick, soft hair and murmur in response.

"Sugar," he breathed against her mouth. "Sweet. So sweet."

He lifted her to lie on top of him. Body to body, she moved and he flowed with her, never stopping his slow, drugging kisses or the unhurried kneading of his hands. He shucked his jeans, making her moan and sigh as he arched off the mattress. Mindlessly, she rotated her pelvis, seeking more of the delicious pressure. Grasping her hips, he squeezed her buttocks and filled her with his strength.

With one long, slow thrust, he entered and completed her. Warmth radiated outward from her center where they joined along the connecting rivers of blood and nerve until every part of her was replete with him. Delight tingled in her fingertips, bubbled in her veins, spilled with her breath. And with the rising tide of pleasure came the slow, deep welling of emotion, surging from a secret place in her heart like an underground spring.

Love.

The realization shattered her. Crying out, in revelation, in protest, in delight, she convulsed around him. His hands hardened. Twice more he lifted her and plunged. And then he let her collapse, spent, onto his broad, damp chest, his touch soothing on her neck and shoulders, his deep voice encouraging in her ear.

Clare didn't hear the soft, comforting words. Her body still trembled. Her mind still spun.

She was in love with Detective Sergeant Matt Dunn. With Supercop, an inarticulate hero whose job put him in constant danger. And she didn't know what in the world to do about it.

Chapter 13

Something was bothering Clare, Matt thought.

She would have made a lousy undercover. Everything she felt was in her face to read. Her soft mouth was closed on a secret and her eyes were worried and wide. Concern for her rode him like an itch.

With jerky movements, she rinsed and refilled the coffeepot. In spite of the amount of coffee the two of them were putting away lately, he didn't think caffeine had caused her agitation. He wanted to believe she was rethinking the wisdom of staying in the neighborhood. More likely, she was regretting last night. Regretting him.

Damn. He didn't know what he could say that wouldn't make the situation worse. He'd never been good with words. According to Marcia—or was it Kimberly?—he was an inarticulate macho block with the sensitivity of an iceberg. So, he hooked his thumbs into his belt loops and leaned against the kitchen counter and watched Clare count scoops into a brown paper filter. Just like last night.

Grounds spilled over the countertop. Her breath hissed.

"You all right?"

"Yes." She didn't look at him. "I lost count."

"Uh-huh." He didn't even try to hide his disbelief. When she swung past him on her way to the refrigerator, he caught her elbow and pulled her close. "What's wrong?"

Her gold-tipped lashes shielded her eyes. "What makes you think anything's wrong?"

"My highly honed powers of observation?"

That one brought her head up, swift humor lighting her face. She was so beautiful his heart stuttered. Violet shadows bruised the thin skin under her eyes.

"If you're having second thoughts about getting away—" he said.

Her surprise appeared genuine. "No. It's not that."

Doggedly, he continued. "I could help. If it's the cost of a hotel that's stopping you, you could stay with my parents."

Now where the hell had that come from? Matt thought, panicked.

She must have wondered the same thing, because her eyes brightened wickedly. "Inviting me home to meet the family, cowboy?"

"No. I just figured—"

She shook her head. "It doesn't matter. That's not it, and I wouldn't leave the project anyway."

"What, then?"

Her gaze fell. He watched, fascinated, as a wild blush climbed from the delicate points of her collarbone to the roots of her red-gold hair. "Don't take this the wrong way, okay?" she asked. "I don't expect you to do anything about it."

She wanted him to leave. "I'm not going," he said, his voice harsh.

She laughed shakily. "Maybe you should. But I'm not asking you to go."

He waited, his body braced for a blow.

"I didn't plan on this, but..." Her eyes raised to his, and what he'd thought before was true. Everything she felt was reflected on her face. "I'm afraid I might be falling in love with you."

Her declaration reverberated between them like a shot.

When Matt had been hit in the holdup, it had taken a while for his body to register what had actually happened. Initially, he'd felt no pain, just the shock of impact and a spreading numbness and a seeping realization that things weren't ever going to be the same.

He felt like that now.

I love you. He'd heard the words before, and they some-times—no, always—signaled trouble. "But I love you," Su-san or Amy would wail, brandishing their demands, attacking his hours or his moods or his silence. As if their feelings jus-tified their claims on him.

But he'd never before heard the words from Clare.

She lifted her chin. "I said I don't expect you to do any-thing about it."

And he'd never before heard them offered with no expec-tation of return. Last night had been her choice, he reminded himself. She was a grown woman.

A vulnerable woman, his conscience replied strictly. Had he taken advantage of her?

"Clare—" Responsibility strangled him. His tongue felt thick. His heart swelled. Clearing his throat, he tried again. "You're wonderful. Last night was…"

"Wonderful," she volunteered.

Dammit, did she look amused?

He frowned. Didn't she understand the enormity of what she'd just said? "Yeah. But I'm guessing it's the first time in a long time you… Your first experience of—"

"Sex."

His teeth hurt. He was clenching them too hard. He was trying to safeguard her emotions, and she was running con-versational rings around him. He'd rather be cross-examined by an aggressive defense attorney than face another of her cheerful prompts.

Manfully, he continued. "Anyway, under the circumstances, it's only natural for you to feel—"

"Horny?"

"Confused!" He took a deep breath. "You know, it's easy, when things are as good as they are for us, to mistake your feelings."

Strangely, as his own confidence slid away, hers seemed to return. She arched her red eyebrows.

"You think I'm romanticizing sex with you, cowboy?"

He didn't know what to think. Carefully, he said, "I think it's possible."

She shrugged her slim shoulders, her expression suddenly cool and irritatingly kind. "Think what you want. I know you don't plan on sticking around. I just thought I'd better alert you to the possibilities. Well." Her smile flickered. "I've got to go thin spinach."

As easily as that, she walked away. No pretenses, no pleas, no games. She was as honest in her emotions as in all her other dealings. He was convinced he could never live up to her, terrified he would hurt her.

Wait, he almost called. *We need to talk.*

But he didn't have a clue what he would say. He had to fight the urge to grab her, the compulsion to spill his heart and guts and babble promises. Downing the dregs of his coffee, he stumped outside after her.

Matt was planted in Clare's garden like unwanted statuary, a distracting focal point. He'd pulled his disreputable lawn chair into a thin slice of shade, his elbows resting on his knees and his gun was in plain sight on his hip. In spite of his civilian clothes—jeans and a navy T-shirt—and relaxed posture, he looked like business and smelled like trouble. He wasn't even pretending to read the morning paper she'd provided.

The man might make her senses swim and her heart sing, but right now he was driving her crazy.

Clare yanked at a handful of seedlings. They came up easily, their thin roots showering dirt. Swell. She was distracted, she was scared, she was tumbling in love, and now she had dirt in her socks.

She'd thought she'd made things easy for Matt this morning by qualifying her declaration, letting him know where things stood with her without crowding his Lone Ranger routine. She'd failed to consider that Matt Dunn was a bottom line kind of guy. She'd said, "I'm afraid I might be falling in love," and he'd heard, "Marry me."

Well, the hell with him. She wasn't any more ready for that kind of commitment than he was.

Approaching Matt at the end of her row, Clare set her hands on her hips. "Don't you have anything better to do?"

"Like what?"

Work slowed on the nearest rows as George and Benny paused to listen to their exchange. Clare sighed.

"I don't know," she said, frustrated. "Walk your beat. Chase some bad guys. Arrest somebody."

His face tightened. "One, I've got a bad leg, so walking the beat is out. Ditto for chasing bad guys. At least my playing guard dog here frees an able-bodied detective to look for Boothe."

Clare squelched her immediate sympathetic response to his obvious frustration. Sympathy was the last thing her wounded hero needed. "You look fine to me. Your leg obviously hasn't kept you from...well, from..."

Images ignited: slick bodies sliding, warm bodies clinging in a tangle of limbs and sheets. Matt's eyes were alight with temper and memory. Her own body heated as if she'd been dipped in a scalding pot.

She was a target, Clare reminded herself, the thought like a douse of cold water. And as long as Matt's stubborn sense of duty kept him close, he could get hurt just being near her.

Worry sharpened her voice. "Anyway, you're making my crew nervous. Didn't they teach you how to be inconspicuous in police academy or detective school or whatever?"

Matt leaned back in his chair. "I told you I was no good at undercover. And I'm not trying to be inconspicuous."

She bit her lip. Of course he wasn't. He was determined to either scare her assailants off or draw their fire. If he got shot protecting her, she didn't know how she would cope with the guilt.

"Well, I'm going in," she announced. "I've got to change for an appointment at two."

His dark brows snapped together. "What appointment?"

"Bob Collins, City Parks and Recreation? You introduced us Saturday night. I'm negotiating for those empty fields in White Oaks." She sighed at his thunderous face. "I was pretty sure you weren't going to like this."

"You knew darn well I was going to hate it. Clare, the Vipers mean business. You move on taking more turf away from them, and they'll come after you."

"They're after me anyway, aren't they? Besides, the gunman said he was only firing to frighten me."

"Uh-huh. And if he'd said he was the Easter Bunny, would you have believed that, too? Don't provoke them, sugar."

"I'm not trying to provoke anyone." Especially not Matt, she thought. "I'm just trying to keep the project going."

"Fine. But your timing on this expansion stinks. Wait until they've picked up Boothe and at least established a connection so they can hold him."

"The way they established a connection in Paul's case?" Clare asked bitterly. "No. If I can get those four acres in the park, I can get another whole crop of tomatoes in by the end of the month."

"You can't risk your life for tomatoes, Clare."

"The expansion will give me the basis for at least one new hire."

He stood, looming over her, the warmth and breadth of his body at once a bulwark and a threat to her carefully achieved composure. "And that couldn't wait another month?"

It could. Of course, it could. If she didn't plant tomatoes, she could plant corn or squash. Once she had the land and the projected profits, she could hire new workers any time. There was something else at stake here, more important than profits or schedules. The Vipers had struck at the heart of who she was, of what she had made of herself after they'd murdered her husband.

"I can't let him frighten me away," she admitted at last. "I won't let him win. Eddie Boothe took my husband away from me. Well, I'm taking his turf away from him. Every child I hire away from the Vipers helps me live with the loss of the children Paul and I might have had together."

If anyone could understand, she thought with a stirring of hope, it would be this man with his battered body and his warrior's heart. If only he could accept that inside her unimpressive body she was a fighter, too.

"I made my life over," she added. "Don't ask me to give it up."

Silence stretched between them. Her pulse hummed. She waited.

And then his dark, level gaze met hers like a salute, and her heart stilled at the look in his eyes. Acceptance. Acknowledgement. Respect.

"Go get changed, then," he said. "I'll go with you."

Matt had changed his clothes, too, Clare saw when she came down the stairs twenty minutes later, noting his white shirt and gray slacks with approval.

His attitude could have used a similar adjustment. He frowned suspiciously at her linen jacket and flowered skirt. Tension rode his shoulders.

"For heavens sake, smile," she commanded lightly. "I feel like I'm going out with my bodyguard."

Humor gleamed in his face, but he didn't shift his protective posture at the bottom of the stairs. "Smart woman."

Rolling her eyes, she started to brush past him. But after last night, her senses were too finely attuned to him to ignore the lure of his deep muscled chest under that fresh cotton shirt. With a sense of shock, she accepted she wanted him naked.

She wanted him sweaty. She wanted to thread her fingers through the short curling hair on his neck and draw him close for her kiss.

Unable to stop herself, she touched him on the pretext of adjusting his collar, smoothing the nylon of his navy windbreaker along his broad shoulders. She didn't meet his eyes.

"I don't think you need a jacket," she said. "I'm just wearing one because I want to be professional."

"Yeah. Me, too."

Puzzled, she looked up. And then she felt under her exploring fingers the hard outline of his shoulder holster.

He wore the jacket to hide his gun.

Her hands dropped. His gaze met hers, aware and rueful. Clare tilted her chin. She didn't want him to see how frightened she was at this reminder of her danger or the risks he would run to protect her. If she wanted to partner this man, the least she could do was try to match his courage.

"Very effective," she commented, keeping her voice steady.

"Let's hope so."

He opened the door for her, making her wait while he looked up and down the street before gesturing for her to precede him. She wished she could protest his precautions. She wished she could laugh. But he was clearly deadly serious.

She glanced toward the lot where erratic progress was being made on the straggling rows of spinach. Isaac was taking a break in the shade, bending down, rubbing the top of Trigger's head. Clare headed for the project's flatbed, her neat, flat shoes crunching the gravel on the drive.

"My truck," Matt said behind her.

"Should you be driving?"

"You can drive. But we take my wheels."

Shrugging, she started toward his Chevy parked on the street. If he wanted to be macho about it, that was okay with her. Isaac's voice stopped her before she reached the curb.

"Hey, Clare!"

She turned as Isaac approached from the lot. Matt was still

halfway up the drive. He'd dropped to his haunches and was running his hand up under the cab of her truck.

"What does he think he's doing?" she wondered out loud.

Isaac, coming up to her, swiveled to look. "Checking for car bombs?"

"Car bombs?"

Her voice reached Matt. Straightening, he pulled a handkerchief from his pants pocket.

"Hasn't been tampered with, but we'll stay on the safe side. Get in the truck." He looked at Isaac. "How's it going?"

"Quiet. We had a couple guys didn't show for work this morning."

"That's not that unusual," Clare remarked.

The crew chief pulled off his hat and rolled it in his hands. "Yeah, well, I was coming to tell you it might be best if I took off for a while, too."

"Isaac, why?"

Over her head, he spoke to Matt. "Word is, Eddie Boothe is none too happy about Kenny getting arrested. Word is, he's looking to tell me so."

Comprehension jolted Clare. She appealed to Matt. "Can't the police do something?"

He looked almost angry. "What?" he demanded. "The department's stretched thin enough as it is. And no federal witness relocation program is going to help Isaac."

Responsibility for getting Isaac involved, for encouraging him to speak, made her stubborn. "But you—couldn't you...?"

A muscle worked in Matt's jaw. "No," he said flatly. "I couldn't."

She heard what he would not say. He couldn't keep a twenty-four hour watch on both of them.

"I got cousins in Garner," Isaac volunteered. "Figured I'd visit them 'til things cool down some. I just was hoping maybe you could pay me today for last week instead of waiting for Friday."

"Of course," Clare assured him. "I'll write you a check."

She struggled against an unfair sense of grievance as she hurried to the house. In spite of Matt's reputation in the press, she didn't really expect him to be Supercop, single-handedly taking on the forces of evil. Why should he come to the defense of a former gang member like Isaac? But still, Clare admitted, she wished he would do something, or at least want to do something, for her crew chief.

The computer was set to print checks every two weeks. Pulling out the ledger she used for miscellaneous expenses, Clare wrote out Isaac's paycheck, adding as big a bonus as the project could afford. Danger money. Conscience money. Whatever she called it, he would need something to support himself in Garner until he could either come back or find other work.

Folding the check, she left the house. As she locked the front door and turned, she saw Matt and Isaac shaking hands. Isaac's hand came away with something in it.

He shoved it in his pocket. "Thanks, man. I'll pay you back."

Matt shrugged as Clare came toward them. "Call it a payment from the department. We owe you."

He saw her over Isaac's shoulder and, as usual when she caught him at his compassionate best, his face went carefully blank. She smiled at him anyway.

She gave Isaac the check and hugged him. When she stepped back, her eyes were wet.

"Now don't get mushy on me, boss. I'm coming back."

"You'd better. I can't run this place without you."

Clare waited until they were in the truck, her purse and skirts arranged on the hard bench seat, before she turned to Matt.

"'Payment from the department?'" she repeated. "Did you get a receipt for reimbursement?"

He smiled some, even as his tanned cheeks reddened slightly. "Pushy, pushy."

Reaching out, she laid her hand on his thigh. "Thank you," she said quietly.

His big, warm palm covered her hand. "No big deal."

But it was, Clare thought. Every decent, honorable gesture he made toppled her deeper in love with him. The thought should have terrified her. She *was* apprehensive. And yet how could she deny the rightness of what she felt for this man? Maybe for this one day, for this moment, she could let herself ride the warm swell of feeling that engulfed her. She wrapped her arms tightly across her chest and held on.

Matt would be gone soon enough. As he was so careful to remind her, his assignment here was only temporary. She would enjoy what they shared while it lasted, until the press of his job and the danger of her situation recalled her to lonely reality.

Matt watched Clare's fists ball in her lap as Bob Collins treated her to a first-class city hall brush-off. She was in no danger, Matt reminded himself. But as the parks and recreation director continued to hem and haw, he felt his own muscles stiffen and his blood pressure rise.

"It's a security issue," the large, pale bureaucrat was explaining for the third or fourth time. "I understand your project's having trouble with the Vipers. And some of your employees have criminal records."

Clare lifted her eyebrows. "I would still think you'd prefer hardworking men and kids growing vegetables in the park to drug dealers around empty picnic tables."

Go get him, sugar, Matt thought.

But Collins was not impressed. "I'm sorry, Miz Harmon. Your dedication does you credit. But my department can't possibly accept the security risk."

Matt had had enough. He leaned forward across the teak veneer desk.

"You can leave security to my department, Bob. I've already recommended to Mayor Hunt that we move a new ministation into that neighborhood."

Beside him, Clare started. He didn't dare glance her way.

"You'll find the new community policing program fully supports the park garden initiative."

Collins waffled. "Well, in that case... If Robert is in favor of the scheme, of course...."

Clare swirled to her feet, smiling with false brightness. "I can get the proposal on your desk by the end of the week, Mr. Collins. Thank you so much for your time."

As they left the office, her neat, flat shoes slapped the linoleum floors. Matt stumped along after her. When he drew level, she gave him one of those sideways looks of hers and inquired, "The new community policing program—that would be you, right?"

Was she steamed at him? Matt wondered. He hadn't meant to interfere. He knew she was used to defending her own turf. He jammed his thumbs in his belt loops. "Yeah."

"And the park garden initiative—that's me?"

He nodded.

"It sounds very official," she observed, primming up her mouth. But her eyes were shrewd and amused. "Thank you for your support."

Cautiously, he smiled. "Don't mention it."

Allowing him to open the outside door for her, she preceded him down the brick-and-cement steps. "Speaking of not mentioning things..."

Here it comes, he thought, anticipation tightening his gut. He'd wondered how she'd react to that little bomb he'd dropped in there. He figured he'd earned her lecture. It made him uneasy, the way he felt for her, and yet there didn't seem to be a damn thing he could do about it. More and more, he didn't even want to do anything about it.

She put back her head to look down her nose at him. "Exactly when were you planning on telling me about the neighborhood ministation? Or were you going to let me read about it in the paper?"

Her tone flicked him on the raw. He'd been holding out on her, and he knew it. "No. But I sure didn't plan on discussing it on the steps of the municipal building with you, sugar."

Her smile twisted. "Worried I'd object to a police presence practically across the street?"

"No." He opened the door on the driver's side for her. "Worried you'd ask me who the mayor had pegged to command the new ministation."

Slamming the cab door on her exclamation of surprise, he hitched around to the passenger seat and levered himself in beside her. "That's right. He asked me." When she just stared at him, still silent, he added, "There's a promotion in it."

"But you don't want it."

He looked away, uncomfortable under the weight of that calm, intelligent gaze, unwilling to disappoint her. "I don't know."

"Why not?"

The words dumped out of his mouth before he could catch them. "Clare, I'm a cop. I serve the community. I can't be part of it." He tried to explain. "Depersonalization is one of the first things you learn as a recruit. One of the things you can never forget. You've got to accept that when other people look at you, they don't see you. They see the uniform. You are the uniform. You've got to be objective, you've got to be impartial, you've got to uphold the law no matter what your personal feelings are."

"And can't you do that working as a community policeman?"

"Maybe. I've got a couple of weeks to decide. But you've got to know, I like being a detective. There's no confusion. No pretense. Somebody commits a crime, I collect the evidence and arrest him. It's Us versus Them. It's easier to hold myself separate."

Quietly, she asked, "Hold yourself separate from them? Or from me?"

He clenched his jaw, unwilling, unable to answer her.

She touched his face. Her fingers trembled. "Why," she whispered, "do you need to hold yourself separate from me?"

Her voice evoked old memories, old arguments, half understood from his childhood. He had a sudden picture of his father coming home tense and tired in the middle of a grueling investigation. He remembered him sitting cross and uncommunicative at the kitchen table after a gory crime scene and his mother, hovering, her "brave face on things" gradually growing cold and strained. And yet his parents had, by many standards, a good marriage.

"I have to," he said. "I'm a cop."

Clare's hand returned to her lap. She stared out the windshield. He would have died rather than hurt her. God. He'd hurt her already.

"Clare."

Her chin raised in acknowledgment, but she didn't turn.

"This love business...I don't know."

She waited. Her silence drew on his emotions, pulled the words from him.

"You say you love me."

She hesitated. Nodded.

He rubbed the back of his neck where the muscles were tight as wet rope and his pulse pounded. "You shouldn't. I'm a lousy risk, you know that."

"I'll try to remember." Her voice was dry.

And it was that, that note of tough humor even as her hands clenched the soft folds of her flowered skirt, that allowed him to continue. "I can't be what you need," he said roughly. "Even if I wanted to, even if I tried, this job would tear you apart. Could you deal with me coming home preoccupied and edgy? Or late? Or not at all? Could you live with it if I got shot again?"

"I don't know," she said, giving his own words back to him. "But how can I find out unless you give me a chance?"

Her eyes were steady, her face, pale. She was, quite simply, the bravest and most beautiful sight of his life, and she went to his heart like a knife.

Abruptly, he reached for her. Sliding along the bench seat, she went into his arms as if she belonged there. Her head rested on his shoulder. He stroked her hair, the smooth, shiny strands clinging to his fingers, and spoke into the silence above her head.

"When my dad was working on a real bad case…" He stopped. The scent of her hair and the strength of her arms surrounded him, supported him. He didn't like talking. But it was the silence, more than the fights, that had echoed late at night in the kitchen of his parents' house. And this was Clare, who could be trusted not to quiver under the weight of confession.

Matt cleared his throat. "Anyway, my mom used to try to make these special dinners. Most of the time Dad would get home late, and dinner would be ruined." He remembered the smell of scorching food, the bad taste in his mouth and the churning in his stomach that he'd never been able to attribute wholly to the meal. "Dad would apologize, of course, and she would say it was okay. But in the kitchen, cleaning up, I could see her face, and it wasn't okay. It was never okay."

Clare's hands tightened briefly on his back. He didn't want her pity. But he needed her understanding.

"I'm not going to lie to you, Clare, and I can't kid myself. There have been women in my past. Nice women I've cared about. And sooner or later, every one of them got tired of putting burned meals on the table."

"You're forgetting something, cowboy." He lifted his chin from her hair to peer into her face. She smiled wryly. "I can't cook. I expect to burn dinner. All I need from you is the sense that, if you could, you'd be there to eat with me." She took a deep breath. "And some conversation over coffee, when you do get home."

There was nowhere he'd rather be than with Clare. Still, he raised an eyebrow. "Tough little cookie, aren't you?"

Her gaze was steady. "I've had to be."

Tough enough to survive loss, Matt thought. Gutsy enough to challenge his preconceptions. Maybe even strong enough to change them. Matt bent his head and, parked right there in front of the Buchanan municipal building, he kissed her.

Chapter 14

It was still light out when Clare pulled Matt's truck into the drive. The sun slanted through the greening trees, its heat lingering in the ground, releasing the scent of fertile soil. Stepping out onto the gravel, Clare felt the same warmth suffuse her soul.

Last night's rain had coaxed a thin edge of color along the closed buds of her azaleas. The pansies she'd planted in autumn rioted in abundant bloom beside the front door. Overnight, it seemed, the sticks of hosta had unfurled brave green flags. Only a month ago her garden had appeared dry and brown and desiccated. Dead. And all along it had only been sleeping, gaining strength in the cold earth, waiting for the right season and the right touch to waken it.

Waiting, just like her.

The passenger door slammed as Matt got out. Stiff-legged, cautious, he prowled around the front of the truck, his hands motionless at his sides and his eyes busy. On the other side of the chain-link fence, Trigger lurched to all fours, tail wagging in anxious greeting.

Matt ignored the dog. "Where's your day care contingent? Shouldn't they still be around?"

Pure affection filled Clare at his rapid return to professional watchfulness. "No. Alma's at the hospital with Reverend Ray. The kids and their teachers stayed at the school today."

He nodded. "Where's the crew?"

Patiently, she answered. "They finished at two. Isaac's gone, remember?"

"So you're alone?"

She grinned at him. "Not exactly. I've got this big, bad police sergeant staying with me."

"Very funny. Wait here."

After checking the lock, he eased the front door open, glancing back over his shoulder. In spite of his caution, Clare didn't really believe he would find intruders in her home. She propped against the cab of the truck, crossing her arms.

"I'm all right," she called teasingly. "Your dog will protect me."

Trigger whined as Matt melted inside. He reappeared a minute later, his hand slipping out from under his jacket.

Returning his gun, Clare thought with a jolt, to its holster.

The grim reminder of who he was and what he did shivered through her. She hugged her elbows tighter. The same qualities that made him a cop also made him the man she had chosen to love. Her alternatives were painfully plain.

Can you deal with it? Could you live with it if I got shot again?

He limped down the steps toward her, the sun gleaming on his dark, soft hair, and all her expectations for a safe, comfortable life lodged like a lump in her throat.

"All clear. You want me to start dinner while you change?"

She swallowed. "Thanks. That would be nice. There's soup in the pantry, I think."

He hesitated, as if he could see her turmoil on her face. But apparently he decided not to push it, because after a moment he nodded and proceeded up the walk.

"Soup it is."

"*Matt*," she said suddenly, urgently.

He turned back, hands in his pockets. "Yeah?"

"I— Nothing."

With swift, uneven strides, he returned, swooping to press a brief, hard kiss on her mouth. His breath was warm and scented with coffee. Her fingers curled into his jacket.

"It'll be all right," he promised. "I'll take care of you."

He thought she was afraid. She was, but not for the reasons he imagined. "Just take care of yourself, cowboy."

He gave her a look, dark and unreadable.

And Clare realized then that she'd asked him for the one assurance he could not give her.

From the tantalizing aroma that drifted up the stairs, Clare concluded Matt had found the soup. Beef vegetable, she guessed. If her nose was any judge, he was grilling cheese sandwiches to go with it. She smiled as she kicked her shoes into the closet. It was nice to rely on someone else's cooking for a change. It was nice to live with a man again.

Oh, no, she thought, carefully hanging up her linen jacket. She was not living with Matt. She was…sleeping with him, possibly? In love with him, probably.

In trouble, for sure.

She jerked a clean T-shirt out of the drawer and over her head. The cloth caught on something. Blindly, she turned. Her hip banged the open drawer, and Paul's picture clattered on the dresser top and fell to the floor.

With a soft cry, she dropped the shirt and reached for the pewter frame. Stooping, she ran her fingers over the glass, checking for damage.

The door burst open. Clare yelped and straightened hastily. Matt stood just outside the frame, gun drawn and shoulder level.

Embarrassment and fright held her rigid. "What the hell are you doing?"

"I heard you scream."

"I did not—" She stopped, remembering her exclamation of distress. "Oh."

"I thought somebody got in the house."

"No." She restored Paul's picture to its place on the bureau. "I dropped something, that's all."

Matt strolled forward, smoothly holstering his gun. "That your husband?"

"Paul. Yes."

He started to take it and then drew back. "Can I see?"

She put the picture into his hand, as nervous as if she were introducing them in real life. Matt studied the photo through the glass. She looked from the image of thin, witty, eloquent Paul to the reality of tough, terse, pragmatic Matt. Alike in their sense of honor and their basic decency, no two men could appear more different.

But then, she was different, too, Clare reflected, from the girl who had married Paul. Older, stronger and more resilient. She hoped.

"Looks like a nice guy," Matt said at last.

Something eased inside her. "He was."

"He the attorney that prosecuted Eddie Boothe?"

She nodded. "Paul thought he could change the neighborhood by defeating drug dealers like Eddie."

"And you figure you can defeat Eddie by changing his neighborhood."

His perception startled her. "Yes."

"Why, Clare?"

"I told you. I was frustrated when the police couldn't tie the shooting to the Vipers. Boothe wasn't even charged. Someone had to do something to strike back."

"But why you?"

"Why not me?" she demanded.

"You're hardly trained in juvenile crime."

"I worked with teens. I was a teacher at Douglas Middle School."

"Douglas, huh?" His thumb scratched his jaw. She heard what he did not say. There was a big difference between wealthy, suburban Douglas and the southeast side. "Nice school. Why give that up to come down here?"

She looked away, ashamed. But her innate honesty demanded the truth. "Guilt, I suppose."

"Guilt? You think you could have stopped your husband from going after Eddie?"

She'd asked herself the same question a thousand times. "Maybe not. But I should at least have known the risks he was running. I could have urged him to be more careful."

"Sugar, all the warnings in the world can't stop a man from doing his job."

Their eyes met. "Or keep him safe?" Clare asked bleakly.

Awareness darkened his eyes. "Or keep him safe," Matt agreed steadily.

"I think I would have felt better if I'd been prepared somehow," Clare confessed over the thrumming of her heart. "Paul didn't like to discuss his work."

"Yeah? How old were you when you got married?"

"Young. Twenty."

"God." She'd startled him. "I thought girls like you waited."

So, did he need to make her sound like some convent-bred virgin abstaining from sex? She lifted her brows. "Waited for what?"

He waved his hand. "To finish college. Start a career. Travel to Europe. Twenty's a little young to take on a husband and tackle the world, sugar."

His words lightened the burden on her heart, but she refused to accept his absolution. "Age is no excuse. I should have insisted that he talk to me."

Matt moved his shoulders uncomfortably. "Maybe he didn't feel he had the right to lay all that on you."

"Of course he had the right. He was my husband."

"So, maybe he felt he should take care of you. How old was he?"

Confused, she asked, "When we married? Twenty-eight."

"Eight years is a big spread between partners. I've had rookies assigned to me that were closer in age than that. He probably figured he was protecting you, keeping quiet."

"That's not what I want," Clare said firmly. She tilted her head, regarding him. "So, what's your excuse? How old are you, cowboy?"

"Thirty-two."

Clare grinned at his defensive tone. "Slow starter?"

He put back his head and laughed. "No. Maybe I was just waiting for you."

The sweetness of his words washed over her. She didn't know if they were true. But they filled a place in her heart that had been empty a very long time.

Their eyes locked. Setting down the frame, Matt reached for her. Willingly, Clare went into his arms. Her shirt lay discarded at her feet. With one hand, Matt tugged open his own shirt, pulling her closer, bringing her breasts into contact with his warm, muscled chest.

Clare had never figured her plain white cotton bra could be erotic. But when Matt held her upper arms, brushing against her, she had to close her eyes at the exquisite sensations he created. Her hips gravitated naturally against his, feeding her arousal, feeling his.

She might pride herself on her practical underwear, her self-reliance and sense, but body to body with Matt she felt small and soft and completely feminine. His torso was broad and hard. She liked the heat of his skin, the tickle of his body hair against the skin of her chest and belly, the scents of soap and sweat and man.

His afternoon beard brushed the side of her face. His lips followed, smooth and slick. He rubbed them over her mouth, and she welcomed him inside.

The assurances they could not give each other in words,

they bestowed in gentle, generous caresses. Kiss followed kiss. Her skirt sighed to the floor. His large hands roamed, kneading her back and buttocks.

"The soup?" she managed to ask, tugging at his buckle.

"I turned off the stove," he answered, stringing a line of little bites along her collarbone.

She shuddered, tilting her neck to grant him better access. "That's one nice thing about being involved with a cop."

He lifted his head. "What?"

She pressed her open mouth against his throat and felt his groan. "You're very—" it was her turn to sigh as he shifted her, handily dispensing with the front closure on her bra to stroke the hardened tip of her breast "—thorough."

"Yeah. They train us not to…" his hand toyed and teased until he was rewarded with her moan "…miss anything."

The sun poured through the window, painting them in amber light, veiling them in warmth. He dipped his head to suckle her breast, and the muscles of her womb contracted. His skin was smooth under her hands, his body hair excitingly rough. Her lips parted as her breath quickened.

He murmured encouragement. "Sweet baby. Pretty Clare. You make me hot, you know it?"

She knew. She gloried in the knowledge. Together, they ached and moved and trembled. Right before her knees buckled, Matt nudged her to the narrow white bed and followed her down. The soft mattress sank beneath their combined weight. She rolled a little into him. He took delicious advantage, turning on his side, tugging her thigh up and over his so that he pressed firmly against her.

She gasped.

"Sore?"

"No."

"Sure?"

"No-o."

He chuckled.

He was gentle with her. They were tender with each other.

She admired him with her fingertips, so solid, so male, intricately and marvelously made. Unbelievable that a bullet could stop the strong heart that beat under her palm, the pulse that raced under her lips. Unthinkable.

And yet after they'd made love, after the slowly built heat melted and consumed her and light splintered the darkness behind her closed lids, she did think about it. The notion terrified her.

Bodies warm, relaxed, replete, they lay as close, or nearly as close, as two people could get. Her arm sprawled across his chest. His shoulder pillowed her head. Her damp thigh still covered one of his.

Into the comfort and closeness, her worries crowded like weeds in a flower bed.

She'd been married before, and widowed, Clare reminded herself. She'd not only experienced love, she knew what it was to lose and feel lost. In the painful weeks and months after Paul's death, she'd drifted in grief. She'd seized on her vendetta against Boothe, clinging to her project like a spar.

But it had changed her. As she'd discovered and pursued a new purpose in her life, she'd become a different person, with correspondingly deeper feelings. What she felt now with Matt was so intense it frightened her. They were joined in some fundamental way. He was her equal, her other half. If she lost him, she would feel her own flesh tear away.

She wasn't sure she could survive loving and losing Matt.

The phone's shrill summons was both a premonition of danger and an uncomfortable reminder of the night before.

"You want to get that?" Matt rumbled.

"Not really," Clare answered frankly. She reached across his hard, bare chest for the receiver. "Hello."

"Clare, this is Letitia Johnson?"

Relief flooded through Clare as she recognized the voice of Richie's grandmother. A lifetime of slights and small humiliations had stamped the older woman's speech, so that most of her sentences came out as questions, with an interrogative lift at the end. "Mrs. Johnson, hi. How are you?"

"Well, not too well. I was hoping you maybe could tell me where my Richie is?"

Clare sat up in bed, tucking the receiver tight against her ear. "Excuse me?"

Matt observed her face. He didn't trust that tone of voice. He didn't like the twin lines of worry that formed between her brows or the set of her mouth. Oh, she got her voice under control soon enough, making soft, encouraging noises into the phone, but her face gave her away. Trouble, he thought.

She hung up, running her fingers through her hair.

"What?" he asked.

She reached for the soft blanket crumpled at the foot of the bed. With regret, Matt watched her cover herself, her slim, pale body disappearing under blue folds.

"It's Richie. He's missing. He never showed for his court counselor appointment at three, and he didn't come home for dinner."

Uneasiness stirred his gut. He attempted to ignore it, for Clare's sake. "He'll be okay. He's probably at a friend's."

"He would have called," she insisted, wrapping the blanket more tightly around her.

Hell, Matt thought. Right now his first concern was protecting Clare. Between her stubborn disregard for her own safety and the warm, confused tangle of his own feelings, the job was tough enough. His prized objectivity had flown out the window. He'd never been this way with a woman before. He'd never felt this way for a woman before.

But Richie... Matt rubbed his jaw. He was fond of the kid. The kid was important to Clare. And since his walks with the dog had been curtailed, Richie had seemed eager to prove his reliability. He wouldn't have broken the conditions of his probation without good reason.

"Miz Johnson...has she notified the police?" he asked.

"No. She told the court counselor he was sick." Clare made

a face, acknowledging his unspoken criticism. "I know. But she's scared, Matt."

"She'd rather see him in trouble with the Vipers than the police?"

"She just doesn't want to see him arrested again."

"I guess I could give Joe Stewart a call."

"Won't that mean telling him Richie violated probation?"

She was too softhearted for her own good. "He *has* violated probation," Matt felt compelled to remind her.

Clare just looked at him expectantly. He could no more resist her than he could fly to the moon, and that worried him more than Richie's situation.

"What do you want me to do?" Matt asked carefully.

"Go find him."

Right. He drew in his breath at the confidence shining in her eyes. "Clare, he could be anywhere."

"Not really. He's not at school, he's not at home, and he's not here."

"Exactly," Matt said grimly. "Anywhere. I'm not leaving you alone while I search half the city for an eleven-year-old kid who's probably snuck into some movie theater."

"I'll go with you."

"No."

"Why not?"

Because I love you. He almost said it. The words burst so loudly in his brain he was afraid for a moment he'd spoken them out loud. *Because the thought of taking you out on the streets with me, of exposing you to some thug with a gun, is more than I can stand.*

He expelled a lungful of air. He wasn't ready to say those things to her yet. He wasn't prepared to deal with the risk to his own professional detachment or the danger to Clare's carefully achieved peace. But there were other, more tangible threats he could protect her from.

"It's too dangerous, that's all."

She made a dismissive sound. "We wouldn't have to go far. Just around the neighborhood."

She was in her Joan of Arc mode again, he saw, and smiled even as he shook his head.

"Come on," she coaxed. "You've got to walk the dog anyway. We'll just keep our eyes open."

"You're pushing it, sugar."

"You know it, cowboy."

God, she was stubborn. And brave and concerned and determined to do the right thing. There might have been some man somewhere who could refuse her, with her eyes like a saint's and that blue blanket falling off her shoulders, but it sure as hell wasn't him.

"Once around the block," he stipulated. "And back before dark."

Her smile broke over him like sunshine.

Nearly home, Matt thought with relief, watching the shadows between the buildings, counting his steps. And never stopped to ask himself when Clare's house had become *home.*

They'd seen no sign of Richie, although when they stopped at the convenience store one of the corner regulars thought he remembered seeing the boy go by with Tyler Boothe.

"Appreciate it," Matt said as they turned away.

"No problem." The man hesitated, blowing out smoke from a cigarette. "My wife says you got the electricity turned back on in our building last week."

Matt remembered. He'd met the woman on patrol. "Yeah?"

The regular shrugged. "It's not so bad, having a cop live down the street."

Quiet satisfaction stole through him. "Thanks."

Trigger strained against the leash. Matt allowed the dog to pull him along the sidewalk, conscious of Clare's bright look beside him.

"Well, that was lucky," she remarked.

"Not lucky. He knew me, so he could talk to me. That's the purpose behind putting police into the neighborhood."

She raised her eyebrows, but there was no real challenge in her face, only warm approbation. "Becoming an advocate for the program, Matt?"

"Yeah," he said slowly, surprising himself. "I guess I am."

She tucked her arm in his. "So, what do we do now?"

Matt frowned. "Let's check on Tyler's whereabouts, since the boys were seen together. Though I'm warning you, Clare, if we don't catch up with Richie soon, we've got to call his probation officer."

She nodded, accepting that. "I have a home number. I can call Tyler's dad."

"Fine. And check again with Miz Johnson, see if—" Matt froze.

Foreboding flooded Clare. "What is it?"

"Stay here."

Thrusting the leash at her, Matt took off across the darkening street in long, loping strides that favored his stiff right leg. Trigger barked and lunged after him. Jerked half off her feet, Clare temporarily lost sight of Matt.

"Darn it, dog!" She stumbled, yanking at the leash.

Trigger subsided, doggy face anxious and confused. Clare could sympathize. Gripping the strap tighter, she looked across the street for Matt.

In the alley along a squat row of brick town houses, beside a brown spray-painted Dumpster, Matt loomed over his target. Clare recognized the death's head T-shirt and razor-shaved blond head of the teen slouching against the wall. Tyler Boothe.

Shortening the leash, she hurried across the road.

"…don't need to tell you nothing, man," Tyler was saying.

Matt crowded a step closer, still not touching the boy. "But maybe you want to," he suggested.

Tyler responded in a spate of ugly words.

"Tyler Boothe!" Clare planted her hands on her hips.

The strap bit into her wrist as Trigger jumped for the teen's legs. Clare relaxed the leash, satisfied when Tyler dropped his defiant posture under the dog's enthusiastic onslaught, petting and pushing its head away as the thin tail whipped back and forth.

Beside her, she felt a degree of tension leave Matt's big body.

"We've been looking all over for you," she scolded. "Where's Richie?"

"Don't know."

"Sure you do," Matt said.

Tyler shot him a baleful look.

Gently, Clare intervened. "We've been worried about you. Richie missed an appointment this afternoon. Is he in trouble?"

Tyler shuffled. "Don't know."

Her heart squeezed. "Meaning, maybe?"

He was silent.

"Where'd you leave him?" Matt asked.

Tyler looked down. Away. Anywhere but at the two grown-ups questioning him.

Clare bit her lip in frustration, worry knotting her chest.

"We know you were with him," Matt said calmly. "Somebody saw you. So, where did you take him? Willard's?"

"It weren't my fault. He wanted to come."

Clare could believe it. Tyler was older, dangerous, glamorous. A visit to the abandoned drugstore where the Vipers hung out would have seemed a sign of acceptance, an incredibly cool adventure. Eleven-year-old Richie probably begged to go along. And had no idea how to handle things when he got there.

"So, he's still there," she said, carefully making it a statement, not a question Tyler would feel forced to deny.

The teen shrugged. *Yes.*

She turned to Matt in appeal. It felt so natural to turn to

him for support she barely registered her growing dependence.
"We need to go."

"No."

"Matt—"

"You're not going anywhere."

"But Richie—"

"Richie should have known he was walking into trouble."
Matt turned back to Tyler, slumped against the dirty brick
wall. "Who else is there?"

He looked away. "Nobody."

"Then why did Richie stay?"

No answer.

"I'll call Stewart," Matt told Clare. "He can check it out."

"No." She gripped his arm. "I want to go."

"You're going home."

"You have no right...." She met his eyes, black, level,
demanding, and sighed. Some rights, it appeared, she'd sur-
rendered with her heart. She couldn't deliberately place herself
in unnecessary danger, knowing what her carelessness could
cost Matt. But she wouldn't abandon Richie, either.

"All right," she conceded. "But you go. Richie knows
you."

"He knows Stewart, too."

"Officer Stewart *arrested* him. Please, Matt."

Tyler shifted along the wall. Matt stopped him with a look.
"I'm not leaving you unprotected," he said, turning back to
Clare.

"I've got the dog," she offered with a tentative smile.

Trigger sat at Tyler's feet, tongue lolling happily.

"Some protection," Matt said. He rubbed the back of his
neck. Clare waited, willing him to see things her way.

"Okay," he said at last. "You go home. I'll call for backup.
We wait for Stewart. He sticks with you, and I'll go after
Richie and haul his sorry little butt home."

Clare wiped her palms along the thighs of her jeans.

"Shouldn't Officer Stewart go with you? In case there's trouble."

"It won't be anything I can't handle. Besides, according to Tyler, here, we don't have any particular reason to think Richie's in a fix. We know you are."

Clare shook her head impatiently. "I'm fine. I'm more worried about Richie."

And you, she added silently. But she couldn't tell Matt that. He didn't want the burden of her concern.

Chapter 15

"Coffee?" Clare offered, turning from the kitchen counter.

Officer Stewart hitched up his belt and sat down. "Yes, ma'am. Thank you."

The patrolman had arrived within minutes of Matt's call. Clare watched in quiet appreciation as the two policemen conferred, determining without any show or fuss what needed to be done. Matt took off moments later.

Strangely, Tyler lingered. He'd even volunteered to feed the dog and hook him to the lead by the shed. After the teenager had trailed the dog outside, Officer Stewart looked to Clare with an inquiring frown.

"He works for me," she explained defensively, but Tyler's unexpected cooperation bewildered her, too.

Stewart took a sip of coffee, brown eyes concerned. "Isn't he the one got your other boy in a scrape?"

Clare sighed. "Yes. Twice. But I think he's sorry this time, or he would have left."

"Boothe, isn't it? Tyler Boothe?"

"That's right." Clare perched in the chair opposite, irresistibly reminded of Matt sitting at this same kitchen table, drinking coffee, turning the orange mug in his large, capable hands. Matt, looking up with his wicked grin and dark, knowing eyes. Matt, whose terse style and tough physique couldn't disguise his moral strength and generous heart.

"Sure be interesting to hear what his cousin has to say about all this."

Memory fled as cold slithered down Clare's spine to coil in her stomach like a snake. "His cousin? Eddie Boothe? Do you think he's involved?"

"Matt does. He even suggested we question him regarding the attack on Reverend Carter, but Boothe's been real hard to find today." Stewart smiled. "So, if Matt doesn't pick Eddie up at Willard's, we ought to be able to get him for parole violation, at least."

Oh, lordy, Clare thought helplessly, and then amended it to more formal prayer. Please, God. Knowing Matt was headed to the Vipers' hangout was bad enough. She didn't want to think of him walking into a confrontation with Eddie Boothe. What if her husband's killer was at Willard's? What if Richie wasn't?

"Here," Stewart said suddenly. "Don't you worry. The sergeant can take care of himself."

Clare smiled ruefully. "It shows, huh?"

"Some. My wife bakes."

She blinked. "Excuse me?"

"When Millie's worried, she bakes to fill the time 'til I get home—cookies, brownies, pies." Stewart patted the slight bulge above his belt. "Biggest danger I'm in is from overeating."

Despite her worry, Clare was grateful for the officer's attempt at comfort. "I'm not used to waiting. I'm not sure I've got what it takes to cope."

"Now, why would you say that?"

Even to Matt's friend and fellow officer, Clare could not

unburden her fear. Lightly, she said, "Well, for one thing, I can't cook."

Stewart patted her hand. "You'll do. You're a brave lady. And there's nothing going to happen to Sergeant Dunn."

The streetlight over Willard's was out. Matt swore. He was getting too old for this crap. Let some young and hungry rookie spend his Sunday nights on patrol. Matt wanted to be home.

He sat in the truck, considering. Could be the lightbulb had burned out. The strapped city government tended to ignore maintenance on the southeast side. Or, it could be that someone who wanted the cover of darkness had shot out the light again.

The plywood over the drugstore windows wore the spray-painted legends of Buchanan's turf wars: the Vipers, the Dog Pound, the Eastie Boys. Less than a generation ago, Matt reflected, they'd fought one another with fists and sticks and bottles. Now it was knives and guns, and Willard's was indisputably Vipers' territory. Better armed and organized than the other gangs, the Vipers were responsible for much of the violence and most of the drug traffic in town.

He had no real hope of finding Boothe. Stewart had assured him they'd canvassed the place twice for the Vipers' leader. But Tyler had brought Richie here. Matt got out of the truck, wishing Will were along.

The front door was locked. Matt shrugged. Sometimes the simplest approach worked the best. He knocked.

No answer. He stood back, looking for light around the edges of the boarded-up windows. Nothing.

Unzipping his jacket, he moved silently down the dark alley to the back of the building. A low black silhouette scuttled across the gravel near the Dumpster. Rats. Matt's gorge rose. The animal paused to peer at him, and he recognized the swaying hips and banded tail of a raccoon.

Hell. He was jumpier than he thought.

Behind the buildings, the cinder strip was empty of everything except garbage and a few parked cars. He shone his flashlight into the vehicles. Empty. A few upstairs windows on either side of the deserted building were lit, but no faces appeared in the yellow squares, no voices challenged his presence. The stairwell leading to the back entrance was very dark.

Cautiously, Matt felt his way down the steps, giving momentary thanks that Willard, whoever he was, was no longer in the picture. Abandoned property required no search warrant. Quietly, he tried the door handle. It was unlocked.

Turning the knob, he pushed at the cold metal door. Nothing squeaked. He held his breath, listening to the roar of blood in his ears.

And a television, with the volume set low, coming from the front of the store. Adrenaline pumped through his veins. Grinning, Matt flicked off his flashlight and followed the sound of canned laughter down a dark and narrow hall.

His boots sticking to the linoleum, he passed a tiny, open kitchen. Smells—waste and refuse—drifted from a washroom on the right. Two other doors were locked, one with the key still in the knob. Storerooms, he guessed, or broom closets.

The blue glow of a television tube penetrated the last few feet of hallway. Matt paused, letting his eyes adjust.

Richie was nowhere in sight. But the room wasn't empty. Gaze fixed on a tiny, flickering screen, a young man in baggy clothes lolled on a dirty mattress someone had dragged before the counter. His legs stretched out before him. A fast-food bag lay beside him. He turned his head to suck on a king-size soft drink, and his earring danced in the light.

Matt recognized the writhing gold snake. He recognized the man. Scowling, he stepped forward into the room.

"Hello, Eddie," he said quietly.

Clare watched Tyler with concern and growing exasperation. He drummed on the table. He tipped back his chair. He jumped up to stride between the refrigerator and the pantry and sat down again without getting anything to eat. He was clearly uneasy and yet he wouldn't go home.

He must, she decided, have something he wanted to talk to her about. She knew better than to badger him. Teens talked in their own good time. Obviously, Tyler wasn't ready to confide in her yet. Maybe if Officer Stewart left the room...?

But when Joe Stewart, in response to her signal, left them alone for a few minutes, Tyler wouldn't even make eye contact. Bending double to tie his shoes, he buried himself under the kitchen table.

Clare waited. When he didn't resurface, she decided to take the plunge herself. "Tyler, what's up? Is something bothering you?"

"No." He tugged at his laces.

When Stewart returned a few minutes later, eyebrows raised in question, she shook her head in defeat. The policeman shrugged and turned back to the newspaper.

Sighing, Clare got up to make another pot of coffee.

"You can't touch me, man," Eddie said, uncrossing his legs as he lounged on the filthy mattress. "I'm not breaking any laws."

Matt strolled forward to turn down the volume knob on the old TV. "No? How about loitering? How about unauthorized occupation of a building? How about assault with a deadly weapon?"

Eddie widened his eyes. "Assault? You mean somebody got hurt?"

Matt wanted to swipe the mock innocence right off that smirking face. With an effort, he kept his tone even. "The minister at Grace Church, Reverend Carter, is in the hospital tonight. Was that a mistake, Eddie?"

"I wouldn't know. Besides, I heard you already picked up the shooter for that one. Violence, you know, that's not my way."

A slow rage ignited in Matt's gut. "Yeah? What about Paul Harmon, Eddie?"

Eddie tipped back his head against the wall, watching Matt with bright malice. "The lawyer? Can't nobody prove I did that guy. I was in jail."

"But you ordered the hit."

"I could have mentioned, like to a brother or a business associate, that it wouldn't bother me none if this lawyer went down. That doesn't make me responsible."

"And the threats against Mrs. Harmon?" Matt asked through his teeth. "I suppose you're not responsible for those, either."

Eddie held up his palms. "Hey, man, I got nothing against the little garden lady."

"I warned you to stay away from her."

"And I heard you. Of course, I can't control what my friends might get up to. But you can count on me—not to be responsible."

Matt's blood ran cold at the threat and then hot with fury. He was seized with a violent, primitive need to protect his own, to defend his woman, to pummel this low-life bastard to a whimpering lump who could never threaten anyone again.

But he couldn't. He was sworn to uphold the law. Clare's danger made him more aware than ever before of the restrictions of his job. And more scared for her sake than he'd ever been in his life. Frustration ballooned inside him.

"Why don't you come down to the station house with me, Eddie, and you can explain in detail how it is you're not responsible."

"You can't arrest me. You got no probable cause."

"This isn't an arrest. I'm inviting you in to show everybody what a good citizen you are."

"What if I—"

A muffled thump behind Matt made him jump back, half turning so he could watch the hallway and still keep Boothe in his line of sight. Boothe coiled his legs under him.

"Don't move," Matt ordered.

Another thump. Matt braced for an attack, reaching under his windbreaker for his gun. But no one appeared in the dark doorway, and Boothe was looking definitely uneasy.

A third thump was followed by a crash. As Matt whirled, Boothe hurled his cup at Matt's head. The limp container struck his forearm, showering ice and liquid over his face and jacket and onto the floor.

Matt cursed as Boothe sprinted for the front door. He leveled his gun, shouting the command to stop, but he couldn't fire with water dripping into his eyes, didn't want to squeeze off a shot in the dark. He took a step and slid on wet linoleum.

The front door slammed.

"Hell," Matt said.

He considered pursuit, but his throbbing thigh would slow him down. Running wounded, he was no match for the younger man. Better to call in from the truck. *After* he investigated the noise that had prompted Boothe's flight. He still had to find Richie.

Limping back the way he'd come, he fumbled for and found a row of switches by the corridor. He hit the lights and waited. Nothing.

"Police!"

No answer. He edged around the corner. Pale light fizzled from the ceiling, revealing graffiti-sprayed walls, peeling metal doors and another scummy floor. He tried the nearest door, the one with the key still in the lock. The knob turned. Cautiously, he pushed, standing back from the widening black rectangle, until the door met with resistance from something on the floor.

Matt looked down.

A metal folding chair lay on its side just inside, a boy's body bound to it with what looked like clothesline. Matt's heart stilled and then pounded with renewed energy. He dropped to his knees by the fallen figure, heedless of the tearing pain in his thigh, and reached for the pulse just under the jaw. Found it and turned the face toward the dim light from the hall.

A small face, a scared face, eyes wide above the duct tape that sealed his mouth.

Richie.

Outside, the dog barked twice in warning, and then repeatedly in a rising scale of excitement.

Joe Stewart stirred in his chair. "He do that a lot?"

Clare listened to the crescendo from across the drive. "Not really. Trigger's actually pretty tolerant. We have kids and crew on and off the lot all day. Of course, if someone approaches the house..." Her words trailed off as she realized what she'd implied. "Or it could be a neighbor walking their dog," she added.

The patrolman pushed back from the table. "I better go check it out."

Framed in the kitchen door, he paused. "Lock up behind me."

Clare nodded, her mouth dry.

Tyler got up and shuffled over to the door. He leaned his forehead against the glass. "You think there's really somebody out there?"

Collecting Joe Stewart's empty mug, Clare carried it to the sink, trying to disguise her own uneasiness for the teenager's sake. "Probably not."

"If there was, what would you do?"

He sounded serious. Too serious.

"Hide under the bed?" she joked.

He shook his head, coming closer, speaking earnestly. "No, really. What if somebody was out there, and he had a gun, and he wanted you to leave? Would you?"

Clare turned from the tap, drying her hands on a dish towel, buying time. For some reason her answer was important to Tyler. Maybe, with his cousin out of jail, he was facing new temptations and hard decisions. She didn't deceive herself that a project paycheck would be enough to keep him from the streets. She understood, a little, the pressures of his world, the edge he balanced on between law and belonging. It wasn't all that different, she thought, from the line Matt walked between duty and compassion, or her own tightrope between loving and the fear of loss. She framed her reply carefully, choosing words that might have meaning to the teen.

"It's a matter of respect. I couldn't respect myself, or ask anyone here to respect me, if I gave up on something I believed in because I was afraid."

Which was why, she realized suddenly, her stubborn heart refused to give up on Matt.

"But what if nobody knew?" Tyler persisted. "Or what if they saw you, like, had to do it, you didn't have no choice?"

"You always have a choice. You have to do what you believe is right."

Whatever he would have replied was cut off by a bang from outside, half-familiar and frightening. Tyler's head jerked up. She looked past him to the door. The knob rattled, and then the door flung open.

Clare's first impression was that Joe Stewart had come back; her second, that the officer had been hurt, and the young man in baggy pants who burst into her kitchen was seeking help.

With a sense of shock, she registered the snub, black muzzle of a gun in the young man's hand.

Everything in the corners of her vision splintered and all the elements of her safe, cozy kitchen re-formed like a crazy kaleidoscope image around the black barrel of the gun. *Danger.* Without thought or hesitation, she stepped in front of Tyler to shield him, only to have her perceptions shattered again when the intruder spoke.

"Hold her arms. I'll deal with you later."

Richie was crying, scrunching his neck to wipe his face on his shoulder.

"Man oh man oh man..."

Matt ignored the anger churning his gut, keeping his touch light and his voice easy. "It's okay, kid. You're going to be all right."

He disposed of the clothesline binding the boy's arms and moved along to his feet, working quickly, trying not to imagine the pain of returning circulation. There would be time for sympathy later. He had his probable cause now, he realized with a sense of triumph. He'd call in, and a patrol could pick up Boothe.

"Oh, man," Richie moaned.

"Give it a minute. You'll be fine."

"Not me." A sob burst from the boy. "Oh, God. We gotta go."

He wasn't making sense. "Sure," Matt soothed. "In a minute. We'll go to the hospital, get you checked out."

The boy struggled to sit up, clutching at Matt's jacket. "No. We gotta go now. Clare's."

A cold, queer pressure formed in Matt's chest like a fist around his heart. "Why to Clare's?"

Richie gulped manfully. "That's where he's going. Tyler."

The fist squeezed. "Why?"

"To scare her, Eddie said. To shoot her. I don't think he wanted to. That's why Eddie took me...tied me...because I knew. I heard. And he said Tyler better do it or he..." The explanation was too much for the boy. He began to sob again, clinging to Matt.

Terror yawned inside Matt, threatening to swallow him up. He forced himself to think like a cop, to react like a cop. Terror wouldn't help Clare. He seized the boy's shoulders and gave them a single, hard shake.

"Richie, listen! Tyler went to Clare's on *Eddie's* orders?"

Woebegone, Richie nodded.

"Is he armed? Does he have a gun?"

Another nod.

Matt swore. He'd left Tyler at Clare's house. And Eddie Boothe was out there somewhere, maybe armed and certainly dangerous. He needed to call Joe Stewart. He had to warn Clare. "Okay. We've got to get you out to my truck. Can you walk?"

"Oh, man…"

"Can you walk?" Matt growled through his teeth.

Richie sniffled. "Yeah."

He couldn't, not really. Matt half carried the boy to the truck and supported him on the bench seat while he called on the cell phone to put out a radio bulletin on Boothe and request backup.

"See if you can raise Joe Stewart," he said into the receiver as he shifted the truck into drive. "Yeah. I'll meet you there."

Richie huddled on the seat, looking small and scared. "Is it okay? Is Clare okay?"

Matt punched in another set of numbers on the phone. "I don't know. I hope so."

He waited through two clicks and an interminable silence for the connection, while he drove with one hand and two feet and his heart in his throat.

Click. Ring.

"Come on, sugar, answer the phone," he murmured, staring past the windshield into darkness. "Dammit, Clare, *pick up.*"

The phone shrilled again. Clare winced as Tyler jumped, jerking her arms. Eddie, pacing the kitchen, twitched.

"You might as well let me get that," Clare said, making an effort to speak reasonably around the dread that choked her.

"Shut up, bitch," Eddie said.

She put up her chin, refusing to be intimidated. "They'll only call back until you do."

"Yeah, well, you won't be around to be bothered by it. Tyler, I told you to take care of her."

Behind Clare, Tyler shifted and squirmed. "The cop was here."

"Well, he isn't here now, is he?"

Oh, no, Clare thought. Oh, dear Lord, please. "Where is Officer Stewart?"

"I shot him. Like Tyler's supposed to shoot you."

Clare closed her eyes, her own deep fear momentarily displaced by the memory of Joe Stewart joking and patting his waistline. "Is he dead?" she whispered.

"By now, maybe. He's not getting up to help you, anyway."

She opened her eyes to glare at him. He grinned, fingering his earring, and took a few steps closer. She could smell his excitement. She could see it in his face, the dilated pupils, the euphoric high of violence. Nausea stirred her stomach. She swallowed it, determined to deprive him of the pleasure of her reaction.

He peered into her face, seeking whatever thrill he got from his victims. Clare held herself straight, grateful for Tyler's unwitting support at her back, and forced herself to stare evenly back.

"Bitch."

The word hit her face like spit. Eddie swung away. "We're wasting time. Do her, Tyler. You want to be part of the family, you got to be a man."

The hands gripping her arms tightened. Tyler's voice protested in her ear. "You said I only had to scare her."

Eddie turned back, facing them. "And does she look scared to you? Does she?"

"No, but... Eddie, come on, man. She's all right. She's been nice to me."

"Is that so?" Eddie swaggered closer. He trailed the barrel of the gun insinuatingly down Clare's cheek and thrust it under her jaw. She swallowed. "You been good to him, garden lady? You want to be good to me, too? I bet you know how to be real nice."

Clare couldn't speak. She felt her pulse pound against the gun mouth, her life about to be spilled. She bit her inner lip until it bled, forcing herself to meet his eyes. Her attention was so focused on the cold steel prodding her jaw, the leering face filling her vision, that she barely registered Tyler's hands loosening and falling away.

"Eddie, don't." The teenager's voice was pleading.

Eddie pushed the gun, forcing her head up, and then shrugged and moved away. "Okay. If we're not going to poke her, you're going to have to shoot her. Go ahead. Do it."

Clare felt the younger man's nervous breath expand his chest. "I don't want to."

Eddie's face hardened. "I'm giving you a chance here, Tyler. Your last chance. Do her."

"No."

Clare wanted to applaud the bravery of his choice. She wanted to scream in protest and in fear. She wanted, desperately, to live. Oh, Matt, she thought. I'm so sorry.

Eddie sighed. "Fine. I'll do it." He raised his gun.

And Tyler stepped in front of her.

The wicked black hole never wavered. "Get out of the way."

"No." The word shook.

"I'll shoot through you if I have to."

From behind Tyler, Clare watched him flinch, as if he'd already taken the bullet. Her heart hammered. Her mind spun. She had to do something. But what? She was short and skinny, inadequate and unarmed.

Unarmed. But Tyler had a gun. He must, if his cousin expected him to shoot her. She had a sudden vision of Matt, reaching behind him to tuck his gun into the waistband of his jeans, and her gaze darted to the loose T-shirt billowing over the back of Tyler's pants.

Ducking, she made a grab for it. He yelped. Her cold hands fumbled under his shirt, scrabbling for the hard butt of the gun. She reached it and withdrew, trying to stand clear, trying to hold it firm in her shaking grip and fix it on the threatening figure of Eddie Boothe.

"Drop it."

"Aw, jeez." The gang leader looked disgusted.

"Drop your gun. Or I'll shoot." She tightened her hold, fear and indecision clenching her stomach.

Tyler stood to one side, dumbfounded and still. She barely noticed him.

Eddie faced her, shaking his head, almost absurdly regretful. "No, you won't. You can't shoot me. You don't have it in you."

Clare blinked. Her palms were sweaty. She could do it, she thought fiercely, staring into his wide, dark eyes. She would shoot him if she had to. But standing there, shaking, the imagined impact on flesh and bone, the red blossoming of blood on Eddie's shirt as another life leaked away, kept her finger from squeezing the trigger. Oh Lord. Maybe she didn't have it in her.

The back door opened.

"Don't worry, sugar," Matt said grimly. "I do. Get your hands up, Boothe."

Relief poured through her in a rich flood.

Eddie froze. Slowly, he started to turn, his arms creeping above his head, a disarming grin stretching his mouth. "Well, lookee, lookee, it's Supercop. I thought I'd seen the last—"

Quick as a coiled snake, he whirled, bringing his arms down, and fired. Two reports echoed through the kitchen. Clare screamed as Tyler dropped to the linoleum, arms shielding his head. The acrid scent of gunpowder blistered the air. Eddie fell back into the table. It screeched against the floor as he slumped, the gun dropping from his lax grip. Matt leapt forward to catch it.

Alive.

Her hands reached for him, eager to confirm her sight. He ignored her touch, already crawling on his knees to the victim, patting him down, bracing him up, wadding tea towels to staunch the flow of blood from his midsection.

He snapped on cuffs. Eddie groaned. "Call an ambulance,"

Matt ordered tersely. "Tell them we've got an officer down and a suspect casualty."

Nodding, Clare pushed to her feet and ran for the phone. But before she even reached for the receiver, she could hear the rising wail of sirens converging on her house like banshees announcing a death.

Clare's kitchen boiled with activity like a broken ant hill. EMS personnel in white rubber soles rushed through with gurneys and medical bags. Police officers in flat black shoes swarmed with guns and notebooks and questions. Lots of questions. The telephone rang constantly.

Clare tried to manage the traffic flow, but she was only a civilian. Swept to one side of the torrent, she answered the politely repeated inquiries of a female officer with short, curly brown hair and cynical eyes. It was a sign of Clare's own shock and distress, she supposed, that when she tried to recall the scene later she retained a very good memory of the police woman's appearance and forgot most of her questions.

Matt, in professional mode again, was talking to another detective across the room. Clare tried not to resent his easy immersion in the operational whirl that had invaded her home. Every so often he'd look up and catch her eye, and a little warmth would steal into her veins.

A tearful Letitia Johnson came to collect her grandson, to cry on Clare's shoulder and embrace Matt. With boyish awkwardness, Richie shared the tears and echoed the thanks. As he led his grandmother away, however, Clare noticed Letitia supported herself on his young arm. He bent his neck to talk to her. Clare's own eyes misted.

Eddie Boothe was the next to go, flat on his back on a high, wheeled stretcher, arrested for first degree kidnapping, attempted murder, conspiracy to commit murder, four counts of assault with a deadly and dangerous weapon and unlawful possession of a firearm.

"That should be good for life," one officer remarked.

"If he lives," the curly-haired police woman said with fierce satisfaction.

Hugging her elbows tight, Clare retreated to the living room with Tyler.

"Are they gonna arrest me?" he asked, huddling on the couch beside her.

"I don't know," she answered honestly.

"No," Matt replied, looming over them. "I've talked to the investigating officer. On the strength of Clare's statement, you're free to go. You have an appointment with your court counselor tomorrow."

Tyler stood, his face slack with relief. Clare hugged him before he left.

"I'm so proud of him," she said.

"I'm proud of you," Matt replied, his dark eyes meeting hers. "If you hadn't trusted in him, if you hadn't given him a chance, things could have gone the other way tonight."

His regard, his words, warmed her. She felt her cheeks heat with pleasure and looked away.

"It was Tyler's choice," she said. "He really tried to protect me."

"I believe you. I had a word with Shirley Dickson. They won't bring charges." His brows flicked together, and his professional face returned. "Use your phone?" he asked.

Clare nodded, her hungry eyes searching for assurance that he was truly all right. Matt dropped to the couch beside her, cautiously stretching out his right leg. Fatigue marked his face and slowed his movements. Sweat darkened his hair. But he was whole, and with her, and she was content with that for now.

She listened as he made the call to Joe Stewart's wife, Millie. Yes, Joe was alive. Yes, he was hurt, but the paramedics were optimistic. A complete recovery, Matt quoted one of them as saying. He murmured more reassurances and promised to send a police car to drive Millie to the hospital. The gentleness in his voice made Clare want to cry. His bleak expression as he hung up the phone broke her heart.

"I hate this part of the job," he muttered.

"That's because you know what it's like to be on the other end of the phone," Clare offered.

And so did she, Matt thought. Damn. Tonight's violence must have been a painful reminder of her loss, a potent warning of the risks of getting involved with a cop. With him. Concern and regret filled him.

"You do, too." He shifted to look at her. "How are you doing?"

She smiled bravely. "I'm okay."

"Clare...I'm sorry. I had to go."

"I wanted you to go," she reminded him, laying her small, neat hand on his. "I was glad for you to go. I was grateful you were a policeman, Matt, and knew what to do. Thank you for rescuing Richie."

"Richie was okay. Scared, more than anything. I should never have left you alone."

Her eyebrows raised. "I don't remember that I gave you much choice. Besides, you didn't leave me alone. You got Joe Stewart to baby-sit."

"I got Joe Stewart shot."

Her grip tightened. "Matt, stop it. You can't assume responsibility for everyone else. Joe chose to come over, he chose to go outside. He made the decision, he made the commitment to his job. You have to accept that."

God, she was good for him. An antidote for his overdose of detective ego. But her words only underlined his deeper disquiet.

"What about you?" he questioned, hating his need to ask, helpless in his need to know. "Can you accept it?"

Her gaze fell to their hands, linked on his thigh. And then she raised his hand in both of hers and kissed his knuckles.

Embarrassed, delighted, he protested. "Hey! What's that for?" But he left his hand in hers, ignoring the speculative looks from his fellow officers and a big grin from Detective Shirley Dickson.

"Does 'thank you for saving my life' sound too melodramatic?"

Matt winced.

Clare nodded. "I thought so, too. But how else do I say it? The dangers you face are part of the job you do. The job you do is part of the man you are. And I was never so glad to see any man in all my life as I was to see you burst in that back door tonight."

He didn't want her gratitude to his uniform. "Any cop would have done the same."

She nodded. "I know. But I'm not in love with just any cop. I'm in love with you."

Her gift humbled him. Her trust scared him. "I don't want to see you get hurt."

Steadily, she met his gaze. "What we have is worth the hurt. We each choose our risks, Matt. If you can choose the risk of your job, I can choose the risk of loving again." Her smile flickered. "Maybe this time I'll get lucky."

His chest swelled. He cleared his throat. "Clare. Clare, listen."

He turned that dark, intense gaze on her, and Clare's heart caught in her throat. The activity in the rest of the room just faded away like a black-and-white television set with the volume turned down.

"You really scared me today," he said.

Clare sighed and shifted on the overstuffed cushions. She'd hoped her declaration this time would break through his stubborn determination to protect her. She should have known better. "I know. But—"

He held up his large hand. "I was scared for you. Richie said Tyler was gunning for you, and I knew Eddie Boothe was out there, too, and I was afraid I couldn't get to you in time. But what I'm trying to say is..." he drew a deep breath "...I trusted you. I knew you would do everything you could to get out of that situation alive. Because in addition to this Joan of Arc complex you've got—''

"This *what?*" she asked, diverted.

"Let me finish. In addition to being calm and smart and gutsy, I trusted you to do what you needed to to keep yourself safe, because you love me."

He took both her hands. She couldn't have looked away now, or interrupted him, if her life had depended on it.

"You've got to trust me like that, sugar," he said in his brown velvet voice. "I can't control the circumstances of my job. I can't promise it will never be dangerous. But I swear to you, I'll do whatever is in my power to get the job done and get back to you. Because I love you like that."

And he leaned forward and kissed her.

When he finally raised his head, most of the police officers in the room were openly watching. Two applauded. Matt swore and stood, pulling Clare with him.

"So, now what?" she asked him, her heart high and light as a lark in the morning.

"Pushy, pushy," he complained, but the dents at the corners of his mouth deepened, as if he held in a smile.

He dragged her through the front door, down the steps and out into the yard. The slender branches of the maple tree were black against the moon. Crab apple, hawthorn and forsythia scented the air.

Matt wrapped warm arms around her. She rested her head on his chest. His heartbeat thudded, strong and sure. "If I'd thought about doing this…"

"Which you haven't," she prompted, smiling.

"Hell, no. If I thought this out I probably wouldn't have the guts to go through with it. Anyway…I'd have figured you deserved it done right. In the garden. Moonlight and roses, you know?"

She touched his cheek, where the beard lurked under the smooth skin. "No roses. Not for another couple of weeks at least."

"Thanks for the update. So, we don't have roses. And here I was thinking I could offer you everything all safe and tidy and perfect."

Love for him tightened her throat. "I don't need safe."

His dark eyes searched hers. "No?"

"No," she assured him. "Or tidy. I like Richie and Trigger tracking dirt into my kitchen. In fact, that would be my idea of perfect, dirt and dogs. And kids. I'd like children, Matt."

He sucked in his breath. "Sugar, I'd like nothing better than to try to give them to you." His arms tightened around her. "I want to give this perfect future of yours a shot. We've got the house and the dog and one kid already, kind of, with Richie living across the street. I can't promise you a white picket fence, but you've got the garden. I'll still be a cop, but I'll take the promotion and permanent assignment to the neighborhood. Hell, I'll even be home for lunch most days. What do you say?"

The roughness in his voice tumbled the last wall around her heart, and happiness flooded in like moonlight. Tenderness radiated in her chest like a star.

But she asked for the words anyway, wanting to hear them, knowing what it meant to him to say them. "Is this a marriage proposal, cowboy?"

He grinned. "Yeah. Are you up for it?"

"Are you promising me forever?"

Suddenly serious, he vowed, "I'm promising you all of my love for the rest of my life."

It was enough. All that she wanted and more than she'd dreamed.

"Partners?" she asked.

He laughed and kissed her. "Equal partners."

* * * * *

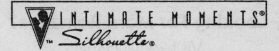

INTIMATE MOMENTS®
Silhouette®

invites you to go West to

Cameron, Utah

Margaret Watson's exhilarating new miniseries.

FOR THE CHILDREN...IM #886, October 1998:
Embittered agent Damien Kane was responsible for protecting beautiful Abby Markham and her twin nieces. But it was Abby who saved him as she showed him the redeeming power of home and family.

COWBOY WITH A BADGE...IM #904, January 1999:
Journalist Carly Fitzpatrick had come to Cameron determined to clear her dead brother's name. But it's the local sheriff—the son of the very man she believed was responsible—who ends up safeguarding her from the real murderer and giving her the family she's always wanted.

Available at your favorite retail outlet.

Silhouette®

Looking For More Romance?

Visit Romance.net

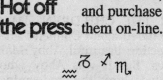

FOLLOW THAT BABY...

the fabulous cross-line series featuring the infamously wealthy Wentworth family...continues with:

THE SHERIFF AND THE IMPOSTOR BRIDE
by Elizabeth Bevarly
(Desire, 12/98)

When a Native American sheriff spies the runaway beauty in his small town, he soon realizes that his enchanting discovery is actually Sabrina Jensen's headstrong *identical* twin sister....

Available at your favorite retail outlet, only from

**Available September 1998
from Silhouette Books...**

That Mysterious Texas Brand Man
by Maggie Shayne

The World's Most Eligible Bachelor:
Man of mystery Marcus Brand, a
Texan with a wicked grin and a
troubled past.

Crime fighter Marcus Brand was
honor bound to protect a brave
beauty. He never dreamed that his
duty would bring him back to Texas, forcing him to
face the mystery of his past, and the true feelings in
his hardened heart.

Each month, Silhouette Books brings you a
brand-new story about an absolutely
irresistible bachelor. Find out how the sexiest,
most sought-after men are finally caught in...

World's Most
Eligible Bachelors

Available at your favorite retail outlet.

Silhouette ®

PSWMEB4

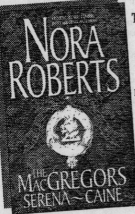

ＩＮＴＩＭＡＴＥ ＭＯＭＥＮＴＳ®

™ *Silhouette*®

COMING NEXT MONTH